Praise for Amy K.

Then Sings My Soul

"Flashing back between the present and [the] past, Sorrells stitches together a beautiful story of family and belief that illustrates the importance of closure and the peace derived from faith. Recommended for readers interested in realistic fiction in the style of Kate Breslin, Kristy Cambron, and Chris Bohjalian."

LIBRARY JOURNAL

"*Then Sings My Soul* is the most phenomenal and heartrending story I have ever read. This struck my heart and soul and will remain in my memory forever. The horrific treatment of the Jews during the Holocaust will never be forgotten. Amy K. Sorrells could not have described the events happening with more authenticity . . . than she did. If this story doesn't 'get' you, no others will."

FRESH FICTION

How Sweet the Sound

"This book will turn your emotions inside out and grip your heart with a clawed fist before pouring acid—and then balm—over the wounds. You have been warned. Now, by all means, go buy this unusually edgy and entirely moving inspirational novel and read it for yourself."

SERENA CHASE,
USA Today

"Debut inspirational novelist Sorrells opens her story powerfully . . . Sorrells will likely move many readers of faith, and she's worth watching."

PUBLISHERS WEEKLY

"You could read *How Sweet the Sound* because you love a well-told story, but Amy Sorrells delivers so much more. Here the depths of pain mankind can inflict meets the unfailing grace that waits to heal all who'll come."

SHELLIE RUSHING TOMLINSON,
Belle of All Things Southern, author of *Heart Wide Open*

"With poetic prose, lyrical descriptions, and sensory details that bring the reader deep into every scene, Amy K. Sorrells has delivered a lush, modern telling of the age-old story of Tamar. But that's not all. With a full cast of colorful characters and juxtaposed first-person narratives woven through, this story dives into the Gulf Coast culture of pecan orchards and debutante balls, exposing layers of family secrets and sins. In the end comes redemption, grace, forgiveness, and faith, but not without a few scars carried by those who manage to survive the wrath of hardened hearts. Bravo!"

JULIE CANTRELL,
New York Times bestselling author of *Into the Free* and *When Mountains Move*

"*How Sweet the Sound* is one of those books you want to savor slowly, like sips of sweet tea on a hot Southern day. Achingly beautiful prose married with honest, raw redemption makes this book a perfect selection for your next book club."

MARY DeMUTH,
author of *The Muir House*

"Meeting these characters and stepping into their worlds forever changed the contour of my heart. Sorrells's words effortlessly rise from the page with a cadence that is remarkably brave and wildly beautiful."

TONI BIRDSONG,
author of *More Than a Bucket List*

"Filled with brokenness and redemption, grit and grace, *How Sweet the Sound* is a heartrending coming-of-age debut about God's ability to heal the hurting and restore the damaged. Sorrells deftly reminds us that no matter how dark the night, hope is never lost. Not if we have eyes to see."

KATIE GANSHERT,
author of *Life After*

"A stirring tale of loss and redemption. Amy Sorrells will break your heart and piece it back twice its size."

BILLY COFFEY,
author of *When Mockingbirds Sing*

"A daring and enchanted story, Amy K. Sorrells's *How Sweet the Sound* beckons readers to a land of pecan groves, bay breezes, and graveyard secrets rising up like the dead on Judgment Day."

KAREN SPEARS ZACHARIAS,
author of *Mother of Rain*

Before I Saw You

AMY K. SORRELLS

Before
I Saw
You

Tyndale House Publishers, Inc.
Carol Stream, Illinois

Visit Tyndale online at www.tyndale.com.

Visit Amy K. Sorrells at www.amyksorrells.com.

TYNDALE and Tyndale's quill logo are registered trademarks of Tyndale House Publishers, Inc.

Before I Saw You

Designed by Libby Dykstra

Edited by Kathryn S. Olson

Published in association with the literary agency of WordServe Literary Group, www.wordserveliterary.com.

Unless otherwise indicated, all Scripture quotations are taken from the *Holy Bible*, New Living Translation, copyright © 1996, 2004, 2015 by Tyndale House Foundation. Used by permission of Tyndale House Publishers, Inc., Carol Stream, Illinois 60188. All rights reserved.

Psalm 103:17, quoted in chapter 28, is taken from the Holy Bible, *New International Version,*® *NIV.*® Copyright © 1973, 1978, 1984, 2011 by Biblica, Inc.® Used by permission. All rights reserved worldwide.

Before I Saw You is a work of fiction. Where real people, events, establishments, organizations, or locales appear, they are used fictitiously. All other elements of the novel are drawn from the author's imagination.

For information about special discounts for bulk purchases, please contact Tyndale House Publishers at csresponse@tyndale.com, or call 1-800-323-9400.

Library of Congress Cataloging-in-Publication Data
Names: Sorrells, Amy K., author.
Title: Before I saw you / Amy K. Sorrells.
Description: Carol Stream, Illinois : Tyndale House Publishers, Inc., [2018]
Identifiers: LCCN 2017053983| ISBN 9781496432797 (hardcover) | ISBN 9781496409560 (softcover)
Subjects: LCSH: Pregnant women--Fiction. | Single mothers--Fiction. | GSAFD: Christian fiction. | Love stories.
Classification: LCC PS3619.O79 B44 2018 | DDC 813/.6—dc23 LC record available at https://lccn.loc.gov/2017053983

Printed in the United States of America

24	23	22	21	20	19	18
7	6	5	4	3	2	1

To my sons, who continually bless me with the
undeserved gift of being called Mama.

The people in flight

from the terror behind—

strange things happen to them,

some bitterly cruel

and some so beautiful

that the faith is refired forever.

❧

JOHN STEINBECK
The Grapes of Wrath

1

Hope means everything when you've got nothing, and hope's all I have when I leave my brother, Jayden, to check on the baby rabbits.

It hadn't been hard to find their nest during the day. The swirl of grass and fur the mother had spun together around the shallow burrow gave it away when I'd nearly stepped on it a couple days prior. Though nearly midnight now, the August wind rustles hot through the leaves and creaking arms of the ash tree stretching over the moss-lined patch of brush I'd marked to remember where the nest is at night. When I see the red scraps of yarn haven't moved from where I put them over that morning, I know their mother isn't coming back. I use a twig to nudge the leaves, and I glimpse the rise and fall of the frail, downy chests, fluttering like there isn't enough air in the world to satisfy them.

I've been watching the mother rabbit for a while now in the mornings, my baby brother, Jayden, in my arms, taking his first bottle of the day as the horizon turns teal, then pale yellow like the cinquefoils while the western sky still glares black. If I'm still, she can't see me watching her through hazy sliding-glass doors. Isn't hard to tell her from other rabbits just passing through on their way to the meadow. As wild as she is, she has habits—the way she nibbles on the same patches of overgrown clover and sedge fruits, the way her nose and ears twitch, always looking out for predators. She is a good mama. That's why I suspected when I didn't see her three mornings in a row something was wrong.

"Fox got her, prob'ly," Sudie said yesterday.

Sudie's my neighbor, a wildlife rehabilitator—that is, when she's not taking care of the cemetery on the outskirts of town. I've been following her around ever since I can remember, learning that when it comes to wild creatures it's important to watch and wait. Plenty of folks come across a bunny nest thinking the babies are orphaned, but most of the time they're not. If those folks watched and waited, they'd see the mama come back at night, once, maybe twice, and just long enough to nurse them. Keeps predators from finding them as easy as if she was there all day long. If those folks knew to put crisscrossed strings on top of a nest like Sudie taught me, they could tell whether the bunnies—kits, as she likes to remind me—are truly orphaned like these.

I kneel and set the shoe box next to the nest, adding a handful of dew-damp grass to the clean, dry rags inside. The night smells thick and rich, like coffee grounds still warm from brewing. Nudging the leaves aside again, I see the kits can't be much more than a week old, their eyes still shut tight as if trying to keep the world out. They hardly look like bunnies except for their ears, long and laid back flat on their heads. I count a total of eight kits before I lift them one by one into the box. They squirm at my touch. Even so young, they recognize I am not their mother. The sides of their chests flutter against the palm of my hand, their heartbeats so quick they feel more like a tremble than a rhythm. It's a wonder something so small and helpless will be strong enough in just a handful of weeks to leap across meadows and fend for themselves.

I think about Jayden again, the glow in the window of our trailer across the field of high grass and milkweed reminding me I need to get back to him. I hated to leave him at all tonight, but Sudie's knee is acting up again—forty, sometimes fifty hours a week at the cemetery's a lot for a woman in her sixties. And the bunnies won't last another night without something in their bellies.

The last of the eight kits curls against the backs of the others as I lay it in the box. I cover them all with one of my clean hair bandannas and stand, the box weighty with the life inside. Overhead, the moon shines through the thick summer leaves, the white bark of the sycamores reflecting back like bones. Big brown bats dart overhead, chasing moths, mayflies. I hear laughter in the distance, then realize it's not laughter at all but barred owls carrying on like old ladies on a front porch complaining about the heat.

"The heavens proclaim the glory of God," Sudie likes to remind me when we're outside together. I can't hear all these sounds and feel all these creatures around me without sensing that's true.

Dew soaks through the canvas of my sneakers as I traipse toward her trailer, and I glance again toward our place. I'm out of earshot to hear if Jayden is crying. Mercy, I hope he's quiet. Before I came out here, I made sure he was settled in good in his crib that's in the room we share. I patted his tummy until the worry lines on his brow faded. I waited until the pacifier lolled out of his sleep-slackened mouth before leaving.

Lord, please let him be still.

He's been a hard baby to quiet since birth. Seems like every second of the day he requires swaddling or holding or both, and the cold and fever he's been fighting just adds to his fussing. Sudie says it's no wonder he's having such a time, *considering*, and I try to keep that in mind when the crying starts to feel like too much of a burden since Mama's no help. He's better than he was when he was a newborn, but the company Mama's keeping on this particular evening isn't the kind to put up with a screaming baby. That much they made clear.

Mice, maybe a snake, maybe a raccoon, scuttle away as I invade their spots in the quiet meadow. Ahead of me is Sudie's place, three down from ours, the last in a long line of mobile homes, rust stains running down the sides of most of them. Side by side they sit angled like white dominoes or tall, empty cartons of cream tipped over and forgotten, some on concrete, some still on wheels as if they held out hope of leaving someday.

Shady Acres is the name of our trailer park on the outskirts of Riverton, Indiana, tucked away tight in a curve of the Ohio River as if God himself is trying to hide us from the rest of the world. It's clear from the looks of the place none of us including Sudie have much besides hope, and not even that most days. Somehow she makes her poor-paying job at the cemetery, caring for herself and all the critters work. If something needs taking in, she takes it and finds free goat's milk from a farmer down the road, hunts for bugs and plants in the woods, even grows a few vegetables in her backyard next to the cages she keeps out there.

Sudie stands at the screen door waiting for me. June bugs, gnats, and mosquitoes swarm the struggling glimmer of her porch light. "Consider the lilies," she sighs, as she always does. The hinges creak open as she welcomes me and this next collection of needy critters. "If the good Lord feeds the birds, surely he'll feed me and these."

I don't know anybody besides Sudie—'cept maybe Reverend Payne—who takes the Lord's Word as flat-out truth and who doesn't worry about whether the food stamps or disability check will last the month, if the propane will last the winter, or if we'll lose another neighbor too young.

"I can't stay," I say, setting the shoe box on the counter, clean but stained from years of use. Next to the sink is an old green soda bottle, a couple of wild daisies stuck in the top of it. Along the opposite wall are wire cages and glass tanks of all kinds of sizes. Several brown bats hang, indifferent, from the screen lid of one cage. From another, the shiny, bead-like black eyes of a couple of adult squirrels follow my movements. And from another, a Cooper's hawk turns its head to one side to get a better look at me. I am not as familiar to them as Sudie.

"I know." Sudie nods in the direction of my place, her brow furrowing because she knows the reason for my worry. She turns her attention to the box and lifts up the bandanna. "How many kits?"

"Eight."

She turns the water on to let it warm, then brings out small syringes, paper towels, and powdered milk replacer to make up a batch of formula. There's a hand-painted scrap of wood hanging above the sink that reads, "In you alone do the orphans find mercy. Hosea 14:3." This is how she thinks of the critters. Her orphans.

"It's a wonder any make it at all," I say as Sudie lifts one out of the box.

The bony ribs and limbs look even more angled and weak in the light of her kitchen than they did in the woods. She takes a syringe of the formula and presses the tip of it against the side of the kit's mouth. The front and back legs push against Sudie's hand as if trying to get away, but I've learned they push against their mother when they nurse from her, too, nature's way of helping her release more milk. Still it always looks like they're struggling, awkward and blind to the fact someone is trying to save them.

"I'm sorry I can't stay." And I am. The first few hours of a new rescue are intense.

"It's all right. I'll settle them. You come by when you can," she says, using my bandanna to dab at drops of formula on the kit's nose, which is raised in protest to the hard plastic syringe.

Outside, the heat presses down on me, and I cough back the shock of the thick humidity. In the distance, an engine starts, then revs several times before squealing onto the main road. The blue flicker of a TV glows from one neighbor's window. The muffled sound of glass breaking against a wall echoes from another across the way.

I think about Jayden, alone with Mama and her company, and I run toward home.

2

I reach for the door handle, then stop.

I don't want to go in.

At least I don't hear Jayden crying, which is a relief. A gray tabby cat, one of several ferals that live under so many of the trailers, purrs and rubs itself against my shins. I nudge it away. I'll take any animal over cats any day.

Red paint gleams off the car from out of town that's been parked beside our trailer ever since the junkies got there late afternoon. For a second I was tempted to pull one of the handles up slow, easy, then let the door fall open . . . not long, just for a second, long enough to find out what a new, clean car smells like. But I figured it probably has an alarm.

I stand and listen on the front stoop, a redwood deck same as most of the others. Thick curtains pulled across our family-room window hide what's going on inside. A familiar male voice rises and falls, and my stomach clenches until I realize it's just the late-night weatherman on the TV. The only other noise is from katydids and the mess of frogs in the stagnant water of the meadow's low spots.

Things weren't always like they are now. When I was little, this place was my kingdom, the meadows my ballroom, the trees and the creatures my subjects. We didn't have much, since my daddy died before I was born. But we got by, at least until Mama hurt her back working at the nursing home when I was in the eighth grade. Found her sitting in the car when I came home from school—she'd been sitting there all day; she was hurting too bad to get out. Took me and more than a few neighbors to get her inside. Shawnie and Tim—they live next door—each of them took one of Mama's arms. Grover Sherman, who's since passed—he lent us the walker he'd used after his hip replacement.

Doctors tried to help, but the only thing that worked were the pain pills. She took them like they were Pez candy, one right after the other. She tried to keep her job, but eventually they let her go and she got on disability. After that, the doctors quit writing her prescriptions. That's when she found heroin. She didn't have to look far in Riverton to find it, either.

I close my eyes and pretend things are the way they were before all that, when I used to fall asleep to those katydids and frogs and Mama singing me to sleep.

Mama sang a lot in those days. "You are my sunshine," she sang as she got ready for work. "My only sunshine." I'd watch her put on her makeup. "You make me happy." First the foundation, then the powder that made her face look soft as velvet, then the way she held the black pencil so steady as she lined her eyes.

"Baby girl, do you know how much I love you?" she'd say as I stood on a step stool beside her. Same thing when I got big enough to sit and watch. She'd put her arms around me tight and look at our reflections in the mirror, studying the two of us as if we were a fancy picture, framed and hanging with a light shining on it in a museum.

I'd shake my head no, just to hear her say she loved me again. Her lips would brush against my ear, then my temple, as she whispered, and I'd carry that with me the rest of the day. When I got home from school, she'd watch me do homework or take me to the library, where we'd get big, thick books she'd read to me at night, and sometimes skinny ones full of poetry, and sometimes we tried to write our own.

Mama liked poetry then. She liked books. She liked life. Even our impossible life. But as I said, that was before she started liking heroin. Smack. Whatever you want to call it. I call it pure evil.

Now, if we do anything together, it's showing up at social services in town for food stamps and WIC money. The rest of the time she's chain-smoking or pacing the floor of our trailer, pausing every once in a while to peer out the window for junkies bringing her smack or money or both.

Most of them come and go without incident, sweat-shirt hoods pulled over their heads, more like shadows than humans. They think I can't see them, but I know who they are. They tell Mama their stories. One man buys it for his wife, who got hooked after taking pain pills for a C-section. Another's a mother whose name I see in the paper for her work with the PTO. Says she takes it for her headaches. Another is a manager at the factory, who hurt his back like Mama.

The ones who really make me mad are the kids not that much older than me, from the college, driving their parents' cars, wearing Greek letters on their sweatshirts when they come to the door. Or kids like Jack Lawson, who was on the front page of the *Riverton Journal-Times* for his full-ride football scholarship to the state university one week, and on the front page the next week for his funeral after over-dosing behind the stadium one Saturday night. Kids who have everything 'cept the sense to say no to smack.

The junkies who came here tonight are different, though. Two men and a woman. They didn't bother hiding their faces. Their eyes stare, shiny and black like the kestrel in the cage at Sudie's, as if I'm a finch or a vole. Runners, probably. They're bolder than plain old users. And they definitely don't care that there's a baby in the house. Mama doesn't either, these days.

I take a deep breath, turn the handle of the storm door, and step inside.

"Hey, Jaycee . . . ," Mama says, words slow and drawn out. Ragged.

The room smells faintly like vinegar, the smell of heroin cooking. A box of tinfoil, pieces of straws, and a couple of burned-out spoons litter the coffee table in front of the threadbare couch where the people are slumped, except for Mama, somehow still half-awake in her recliner. But none of that bothers me as much as the syringes lying there. I never get used to seeing those.

The three strangers are passed out, beady eyes hidden by sleep, tourniquets still tight around their arms, needles still in them. If they weren't snoring, I'd think they were dead. Their mouths hang open, slack, an improvement from the snide smirks when they first arrived.

"Hey, Mama." I try not to let my eyes fall to her chest, her T-shirt cut so low and tight it reveals every lump and bump and crease of her. She is thin, too thin, and the skeletal features of her face match those of the woman slumped on the couch, making them appear related in some macabre way.

Mama reaches for a cigarette smoldering on the table, and I head to the bedroom to avoid her exhale.

"Jayden," I whisper when I see him sleeping, legs tucked under him, his round bottom in the air like a roly-poly beetle. His crib is the nicest thing in the house, nearly brand-new thanks to Veda Spradlin from church, who knew of a family giving one away. Jayden's cheeks glow bright red, and when I put my hand on his back I can feel he's fevering again. A round stain of moisture spreads on the sheets around him.

"Let's get you changed, baby boy."

Sweat has dampened his blond hair, curling it around the

back of his neck and around his ears. He blinks once, twice, then sleepily reaches for an empty bottle on the bed—not one that I made him.

"At least they fed you, hmm?"

He's too thin, too. That's what the doctor said when I took him last week. I make sure to keep those well-child appointments whether Mama comes with us or not, because I know there's already a risk they'll take him from us . . . *considering*.

Mama promised me she was staying away from smack while she was pregnant. I wanted to believe her. I watched her take the methadone every morning, medicine they gave her at the clinic to help her stay off the drugs. She never used anything but that around me that I could tell, so I tried to push my doubts away even though the junkies never stopped coming around. "Helps us eat, don't it?" she'd say to me if I asked.

When she had him at the hospital, he wasn't early or anything. But it didn't take long for him to start jittering and fussing after he was born. I thought for sure the hospital tests would say he had heroin in him and they'd take him from us right then, but it turned out Mama was telling the truth. It's just that the methadone's near as hard on a baby as heroin. He spent almost a week withdrawing in the hospital, and weeks after that at home, too. Cried all the time, high-pitched and wailing like the coyotes at night.

He's better now. Almost nine months old. Still fusses more than other babies I see around, but he's calming down more every week. Doctor says all that fussing makes him burn more calories, which is why his weight isn't all that great. Not to mention the Mountain Dew Mama puts in his bottle when I'm away. I buy the food they tell me to with the WIC card, and I make the formula the way they show me, with an extra scoop. But I have no way of making sure Mama carries through with it while I'm at school.

I fasten his clean diaper, then lean down and kiss his cheeks, his hot forehead, and inhale the sweetness of his neck I bathed earlier. "I sure do hate leavin' you alone."

I hate a lot of things right now . . . Mama and those junkies and the pure evil they bring into our house, the stench of it hanging in the air even after they've gone home, along with the constant fear of getting shot if a deal goes bad. I hate having to work all the hours I can at the diner for measly paychecks to make up for the food stamps Mama trades for money to get cigarettes. I hate worrying all day long about Jayden when I'm at school, wondering if Mama will hear him cry or remember to feed him or make sure he's breathing or if a stranger will hurt him—or if I'll come home to find her dead.

Jayden coughs before settling into sleep again, a thick, junky cough that rattles deep in his chest. I hold him against me until I'm too tired to hold him anymore, his little heartbeat thumping twice as fast as mine, then set him back in his crib. He curls himself into a roly-poly again, and I rest my hand on his back to feel him breathe. If he's still hot in the morning, if that cough isn't better, I'll take him to the clinic first thing.

The night sounds press through the thin walls of the trailer, like static at first, then I can pick out the low hum of katydids and frogs. I want to go back out to the meadow where fireflies dance around my feet, my waist, and the fragrance of blue phlox replaces the sour sting of drugs in my nose.

When Jayden's old enough, I'll take him with me. We'll camp out on a blanket and I'll show him the Big Dipper and Venus. I'll show him how to spot bats chasing night bugs, and we'll fall asleep safe until the morning birds wake us up. I'll teach him how to tell a cottonwood from a sycamore, a maple from a hawthorn. I'll save and press leaves from an ash tree so that he can know what those are after the emerald ash borer has killed them all.

3

Something's very wrong with Jayden.

Daylight, yellow-tinged as it filters filmy through our smoke-stained trailer windows, illuminates Jayden's flushed cheeks. If his forehead was hot last night, it's on fire now. Heat rises off him like it does off asphalt in the middle of blistering summer days. Usually by this time he's fussing for his bottle, but he hardly stirs when I pick him up.

"Mama." I stick my head out the bedroom door, but she doesn't move in her recliner.

When I carry Jayden to the kitchen, the three strangers are still there and they don't move either. They're not snoring anymore and needles aren't hanging out of their arms, so that's an improvement.

"Mama," I say again, louder this time from the kitchen. "Jayden's sick. Please come help me."

His head lolls to the side and his eyes stay closed as I lay him on the counter and fumble with the fever medicine, then sift through the pile of dirty dishes to find a medicine dropper. A prescription bottle of Mama's methadone falls off the counter, the pills scattering all over the floor. There's no time to worry about that. I run the water till it's good and cold and wet a rag for his head, and I'm grateful he at least winces at that. But he won't wake up to take the medicine. I think about the baby bunnies, how they fussed and fought last night when Sudie fed them. If I force the medicine in Jayden when he's limp like this, he'll choke for sure. But he needs it. He needs something.

"Mama!" Angry tears prick my eyes. "Don't you worry, baby boy. Sissy's gonna help you." I lift Jayden's limp body from the counter and feel the fever blaze through my shirt. His breathing isn't right either. It's too fast. And his belly caves in under his ribs with every breath, the skin around his collar bones, too, like it's taking everything he has to suck in air.

He moans, but barely, as I hold him in one arm and rush to grab his bag and a couple of clean outfits. I can't think what else he might need—diapers? A bottle? Worry jumbles everything in my head. One last look around our room and the turquoise corner of his favorite blanket catches my eye. I grab it and start for the door.

"Mama!" I scream.

The woman stranger startles, her bony arms flying up in the air. She curses and settles back into the cushions.

"Mama! I'm taking Jayden to the hospital."

I know my words are in vain, but at least I said them. I yank the door open, not caring that the whole trailer shakes as the back of it hits the wall.

Jayden crumples into the curve of the car seat when I lay him in it. He opens his eyes halfway as I fasten the buckles, but they close just as fast.

"Dear Jesus, please help him. Help me."

The engine takes three tries before it starts. The nearest hospital is a half hour of rolling hills and curved, two-lane highway north of town.

Should I have called an ambulance?

I reach back and put my hand on Jayden's leg. Hot as ever. Mama.

Curse her. Curse the drugs. Curse our life.

Condensation builds on my windshield. The humidity didn't fall at all overnight. The rising sun flashes like a strobe light through the trees as I drive on the road that winds out of Riverton, past the curve where I used to help Mama put the white cross in the ground on the side of the road where my father died in the wreck that killed him before I was born. In the distant tree line, a hawk floats high and circles without any effort at all above the trees. And farther back, gulls from the river.

Gulls filled the shores in the pages of a book I found left in a booth at the diner, a typical romance set in a small town on the coast of North Carolina. The reader before me must've liked it as much as I did, judging from the worn pages, the softened spine. For a time, I imagined myself as the main character, a beautiful woman pursued by a handsome man. I imagined what it would be like to live among white picket fences instead of barbed wire, in a whitewashed cottage instead of a rust-stained trailer. Mostly I wondered what it would be like to live in a place where the sun rises new over the endless stretch of the sea.

How does God decide where someone is born? He could have put me and Jayden anywhere—the Horn of Africa, the edge of a rain forest in Brazil, a flat in London or France, that beach in North Carolina, five miles away in the same town to a wealthy professor at Riverton College and his wife. How did he decide to put us here?

Jayden whimpers, coughs, and I am relieved that at least he moves.

"It's okay, baby. We're getting closer. Hang on."

He was sick yesterday, cough and fever, but nothing he hasn't had before. Nothing like this. I don't understand how he got this bad so fast. Yesterday evening he was sitting in the bathtub splashing, laughing when we played peekaboo and I put the soapy wet washrag on my own face to hide. He helped turn the pages when we read *Goodnight Moon* and even found the little mouse on one. He fell asleep with his head on my chest while I sang him a hymn.

"He's such a good boy, Lord. *Please.* I'm sorry for whatever I did or didn't do to take care of him. Please help him."

I know the Lord can do miracles. I've seen the sickest animals get better when Sudie prays. Birds who fall out of their nests or break their wings flying into telephone wires, raccoons and opossums hit by cars, turtles with cracked shells, bunnies tinier than the ones I took to Sudie last night. I'm just not sure God will do a miracle for me.

A semitrailer rocks the car as it passes in the other direction, and I realize I've been worrying so much I have no idea how far I've gone, no recollection of the last ten minutes of driving.

The last thing I remember is passing the cemetery Sudie takes care of, same one my father is buried in, right next to the brick chapel on the way out of town. "A labor of love," she calls it, and it must be. She has one man, Shorty Smith, who digs the graves. If he has a proper first name no one in Riverton knows it since he's barely four foot nine and that's all folks would ever call him anyway. According to Sudie, Shorty can dig a grave in under two hours without help. Sometimes he brings a friend, or Sudie helps him, but most of the time he does it on his own. Sudie says the graves aren't really six feet deep like folks like to say. They're five feet deep and four feet wide. Still, that's a lot of digging for a small man and an old woman with a bum knee. And a lot of filling in, too. Takes her up to fifty hours a week to take care of it all, nearly fifteen hundred graves and eight and a half acres, some of the headstones dating back to the early 1800s when the first people settled Riverton.

I've been out there with her a couple of times to help

her plant flowers and such, but I don't like it much. I especially don't like the row of little white crosses with lambs and the names of children etched on them along the back fence line. Babies and children who died in the 1870s from the cholera epidemic.

I flip through the radio stations for something to help me focus on driving. Something to keep me from shaking. Nothing besides bad songs and static. I turn it off.

"You are my sunshine . . ."

I sing a few lines before my voice cracks.

"Please don't take my sunshine away."

In the rearview mirror I see Jayden, listless. I am glad when the road straightens some and the forest canopy opens up into stretches of corn and bean fields. Farmhouses with acreage start to appear, including one with a woman wearing an oversize straw hat on a riding mower, the stripes of green grass neat and straight. Eventually farms turn to an occasional trailer park like Shady Acres, or a single solitary trailer sitting all alone on a big, wide patch of land. Closer to town are rickety homes with stone front porches that must have been something a few decades ago. A man sits on the front stoop of one and tosses a cigarette toward a rusty metal rocking horse caught up in the weeds. Homes turn to strip malls, half of the stores boarded up, the other half dollar stores, liquor stores, and junk shops posing as antique dealers. Fast-food restaurants, a middle school, a high school. A car dealer. A funeral home.

A white sign with big red letters. *E-M-E-R-G-E-N-C-Y.*

If there's a place I'm supposed to park I don't see it, and I don't care to look for it either. I pull into the ambulance bay and don't bother to turn the car off, just put it in park and pull Jayden from his seat. His cheeks look too rosy. He collapses like a rag doll on my shoulder. The automatic doors fly open and a blast of cold air shocks my skin.

An older man in a uniform comes from the right. "Ma'am, you have to check in at triage—"

"I've got it." A woman in blue scrubs waves him off and reaches for Jayden. She takes him, holds her ear toward his mouth, his chest. She lifts his eyelids one at a time. Her brow knits and she fixes her eyes on me. "How long's he been like this?"

4

"Are you his mother?" asks another nurse when I get back inside from moving my car.

I might as well be. "No. I'm his sister."

"Well, where's y'all's mom?" she says, acting a little impatient. She turns to a third nurse and shakes her head. "She doesn't look older than twelve."

The third nurse rolls her eyes. Does she think I can't see her?

The second nurse goes back to putting white stickers on Jayden's chest.

A man in a different color of scrubs fastens a plastic mask over his face.

"He's very sick. And we need consent—" the second nurse says.

"She's sick," I say.

"Is there someone else? His father?"

My turn to roll my eyes. "Don't know who his father is."

"What about a grandparent?"

"There's no one else."

The nurse shifts her weight and crosses her arms, and the way she stops and starts a couple of times, I can tell she's working on choosing her words. "I'll have to call social work, then."

You go ahead, I want to say, but I don't waste my breath. The nurse has no doubt already come to the conclusion that I am stupid. Instead, I turn my attention to Jayden. He's connected to more wires and tubes than I can count, some on his chest, a clear tube running a watery fluid into his arm, another clear tube running pee out of him. His arms and legs aren't quite as pale as they were when they first laid him out on the gurney, and he looks cold. I'm afraid I'll mess everything up if I pull the blanket up or touch him.

He needs his blankie.

I pull it from the bag and tuck it under his chin, his arm. Nothing is connected to his head, so I smooth his hair to the side. I am ashamed of the smudges of dirt on his face, his neck, his hands and feet I didn't get clean in the bath last night. The bright light shows everything.

"It's all right, Jayden. You're gonna be all right."

A woman in a white lab coat pushes the curtain aside. "I'm Donna Howard. With social services."

She is a heavyset woman with soft brown eyes that remind me of the deer that peer at me from the edge of the meadow.

Ms. Howard straightens the lab coat across her generous bosom and pulls her pretty floral clipboard closer. "The doctor says to tell you they're waiting on some blood tests and hoping they can move Jayden to the pediatric unit. But if he doesn't improve in a few hours, we may have to transport him to the big children's hospital in Indianapolis."

"Indianapolis?"

She nods. "They're concerned about his breathing. If he needs more support, we can't provide that here. Have you gotten ahold of your mother?"

"No."

I try to text Mama again, but it's just one more in a long list of texts that aren't answered.

I try to call her, but she doesn't pick up.

Ms. Howard comes back later in the afternoon. She asks the usual battery of questions: where Jayden sleeps, what he eats. She asks a lot about his diet. The blood tests probably show he isn't getting enough of something, which is true since all Mama gives him is Mountain Dew when I'm not around—and which she waters down so it will last longer, even after I tell her the WIC gives us enough to use formula all the time. And Ms. Howard writes all of this down, balancing the clipboard against her arm, the words of Philippians 4:13 inscribed on the back of it: "I can do everything through Christ, who gives me strength."

When Ms. Howard asks what Mama does for work, I

mumble something about sales, knowing it's better to be vague than to lie outright. She will contact Child Protective Services, that's for certain. And once she does, there's a good chance they'll take Jayden away.

At least he'd have a chance if he lived somewhere else. I scold myself for thinking that, but I can't help it.

"We're going to move him up to our pediatric unit," two nurses say, and they organize his tubes and wires and set a miniature version of the monitor at the end of his bed.

The hallway on the way to the elevator is empty except for a janitor at the far end whistling and pushing a broom. When the elevator doors open, a girl from high school is on there, a girl I was friends with when we were younger. Mary Ashby. She startles, averts her eyes when she sees me, and hurries out, but not before I see she is wearing a shoulder sling and has a goose egg–sized bump and bruise on the side of her face.

The rest of the day is a blur. Jayden has a crib in this new unit, and cheerful paintings hang on the wall. There's a chair in the room so I can sit by the window and watch cars pull in and out of the gas station and fast-food drive-through next door. Cars pass by the hospital without slowing down at all, the drivers not knowing a thing about the sick people inside. Jayden's heart bleeps a steady rhythm on the monitor above his bed. Nurses come in to check his breathing, which seems faster by the minute, his tiny chest heaving with the effort. They change his mask out to a different one, something the nurse calls a CPAP, which hums and keeps time with his breaths. A doctor talks to other staff in the hall, using words like *transport* and *sepsis*, *intubate* and *blood gas* and *kidneys*.

Jayden fevers on, the hair around his face damp from the sweat of fighting the pneumonia. That's what the doctor says he has, but that's not what's making him so sleepy. They're still trying to figure that part out. A younger girl, about my age and wearing a badge that says *Volunteer*, puts a blanket with planets and rocket ships on the end of the bed, the fleece kind with ties along the edges. She looks at me and smiles and says we can keep it when we go home. Above the bed, a wavy line stretches across a monitor screen and Jayden's chest rises and falls to the rhythm. Spaces between all the bones of Jayden's chest tug and pull to inhale, exhale, inhale, exhale.

It shouldn't be that hard to breathe.

Under the breathing mask, Jayden's mouth moves rhythmically as if he's sucking on his pacifier in his dreams, and the sight of this causes tears to spill from my eyes. I stand beside the crib and take his limp hand, run my fingers across his dimpled knuckles, try to memorize the pale-blue cast of his eyelids. The bones of his shoulders and his hips stick out, too angled and harsh for a baby who should be chubby like the ones at church.

Maybe he's hungry. Could that make him sleepy? He hasn't eaten since . . . the bottle he had when I came back from Sudie's. The one that was empty last night.

A baby with pneumonia should be awake by now, the doctor said.

I didn't make that bottle last night. Mama did.

The methadone pills were beside the sink. Mama's not careful about much, but she's always careful to keep those pills in the bathroom.

The strangers didn't like his crying.

If he woke up when I was gone . . .

"Nurse?" I reach for the call button, but the nurse is already on her way into the room.

5

"Has the doctor told you about the transfer?" the nurse says.

"No." I shake my head. "But I think I know why he's so tired—"

The doctor rounds the corner and interrupts. His bright white coat is ironed stiff; his round, metal-rimmed glasses are shiny, clean. "What did you give him?"

Fear shoots down my chest and knots up tight in my belly. "I didn't give him anything."

The look on his face softens, as if he senses my terror. "It's okay, hon." He rests his hand on my shoulder. "I just want to help Jayden. Can you tell me, did he get into something?"

I think again about that empty bottle last night, the

methadone that was by the sink and fell all over the floor, about the coal-black eyes of the junkies, how angry they got when Jayden was crying until I got him to sleep. Before I left the house. If Jayden woke after I left . . .

"I—I didn't—it wasn't me. There were these people—"

"What people?" His blue eyes are not cold, but rather desperate, searching.

"I only left for a little while last night. He was asleep. He was fine when I left. When I came back, they'd given him a bottle, and Jayden—he drank it all. I didn't think it could be anything but formula, but this morning . . . " Why did I leave him?

"What happened this morning, hon?"

"I was looking for something to give him for his fever and there was this bottle . . . a bottle of Mama's methadone by the sink . . . the lid was loose. She always keeps it in her bathroom so no one gets at it . . ."

"Methadone." The doctor nods to the nurse, who pivots and hurries from the room. "That makes sense. You've helped your brother a lot by telling us this. Do you think your mom gave it to him?"

I shake my head. "She never has before. He was addicted to it when he was born 'cause she'd been taking it while she was pregnant . . . took a few weeks to wean him . . . Mama's done a lot of things, but she wouldn't hurt Jayden on purpose."

"Who else was there?"

"Junkies. Two men and a lady. I haven't seen them before.

They didn't like Jayden's crying, but I'd gotten him to hush and sleep. . . . I was only gone—"

"It's not your fault," he says, and turns to Jayden. "But you need to know . . . " He stops, then gently lifts each of Jayden's eyelids, shines a light in them.

"He's gonna be okay, right?" I step across the crib from the doctor and tuck the turquoise blanket closer to Jayden's face so he can know it's there and not be so afraid.

"We're doing everything we can," the kind, clean doctor says.

I realize as he walks away that he did not answer my question.

The nurse comes back in, pushing a metal cart and carrying vials of medicine. "We need to fly him up to the children's hospital in Indianapolis. He's getting too sick for us to keep taking care of him here."

"When?"

"Soon as we hear from them that they've got a bed. An hour or two. But we have to get an airway in him first."

"What's that mean?"

"We have to put a tube in his throat to help him breathe."

"But he is breathing," I say.

"He won't be much longer without it."

I don't understand. He is breathing.

The monitor above the bed starts flashing red and yellow, and the nurse hollers over her shoulder into the hallway. "I need some help in here."

Three nurses and the doctor come rushing, followed by a man in scrubs who rolls another machine into the room.

I can't feel my legs moving, but somehow I wind up in the corner of the room, the wall holding me up, and everything feels like it's not real, like I'm watching a movie. All I can see of Jayden is his little hand, palm up and open. Alarms ring and an overhead announcement blares something about a "code in Pediatrics," which I know from TV means something awful is happening. More nurses, more strangers in scrubs and white coats and suits fill the hall and stare like they're watching a basketball game or something.

More tubes.

Why did I leave him?

More wires.

I should never have left.

More alarms.

They were just rabbits. Rabbits have a whole slew of litters a year. Wouldn't matter at all if I had left them be.

More people hollering for things I can't understand.

The lines on the monitor are jagged, the numbers flashing.

Someone pushes on his chest.

Sudie did that once to a bird. Somebody brought her a sparrow that had flown into a window. She said it was probably bleeding all inside, but that she had to try to save it. I asked her why bother with a sparrow since there are too many anyway. "Not a one falls to the earth without the Lord knowing it," she said. "Not a one."

The kind doctor's eyes find me across the room.

I think about the cemetery by the brick chapel on the way out of Riverton and the row of little white crosses along the back fence line.

"We need to call it," he says.

The nurse stops pushing on Jayden's chest.

"We've done all we can do."

The sparrow didn't make it either.

All I can think of is how Shorty and Sudie'll be digging a new grave this week.

6

The clock on my dashboard says 7:50 a.m.

I knew I shouldn't have pressed the snooze that last time, but I'd been up late helping Sudie with an influx of big brown bats falling like Osage oranges onto the sidewalks, the sudden cold snap forcing them back into a hibernation they weren't expecting. Most are concussed, a few with wing tears Sudie repairs with superglue. They're too dazed to fuss much at the mealworms and crickets we offer them, so it still takes a while to feed them.

The stoplight takes its time to change to green as I tap the beat to the rock song on the radio onto the steering wheel.

Thick frost isn't budging from the windshield despite my defrost blasting on high. Too cold outside—or busted, more likely. One more thing to fix.

You at work? The text lights up my phone screen, my boyfriend Bryan's name above.

You'll have to wait a hot minute. Besides the fact that I'm driving, I'm tired of answering. If he isn't sure about where I am, he blows up my phone with texts until I answer him. I cringe at the thought of how mad he gets when I don't reply right away. Carla was right when she warned me about him. But we've been together too long now for me to admit it.

Finally the light changes and the late-model SUV in front of me moves.

I swerve to miss the huge chuckhole that seems to have appeared overnight with the crazy mix of freezes and thaws we've been having this spring. I swerve again, barely missing the raccoon waddling across the highway. It's March, the start of breeding season, and in the rearview mirror I can see its fat belly. Must be a female. Of course, the way they scavenge, it could just be a male who's been feasting on a lot of trash.

I'm glad when the winding county road widens into Main Street with large riverfront homes that look like they've been copied right out of the pages of a storybook—gabled roofs, window boxes stuffed with seasonal greenery or flowers, wrought-iron and picket fences around front yards where an occasional schnauzer or Westie barks. This section of town seems immune to the factory shutdowns, with Riverton College students helping keep the stores in business most of the year. This section of town is where children should be raised. If I ever have children, they'll have a house like one of these and they'll have a daddy, that's for sure. They'll have clean clothes that fit right and they won't have to rely on charity sacks of food to eat on the weekends, the kind I had to eat and that church folks hand out Friday afternoons as kids climb onto the bus. And they won't live where empty syringes hide in the yard and stick them on the side of the foot when they play hide-and-seek with friends.

My tires squeal as I turn too fast into the parking spot on the town square in front of the diner, condensation frozen around the edges of its wide, shiny windows. A bright-blue, newer-model Jeep I haven't seen around town before is parked out front. Reverend Payne, pastor of my church, comes out with his daily cup of coffee, which he orders with an inch of room left in the cup for all the cream he likes to add. He sees me and waves, and I nod back.

I grab the fresh mums for the centerpieces off the passenger seat and make sure my big sweater and my coat are covering everything they need to. I shut the car door and text Bryan back, making sure to add lots of heart and kiss emojis, as I walk toward the diner. I forget about the one annoying piece of sidewalk that's been jutting out for years, which the town is always promising to fix but never does. My shoe catches on the edge and I trip forward for what must be the hundredth time, bracing myself for another set of skinned knees.

Impact doesn't happen.

Someone grabs me under the arm.

"I'm so sorry," I say, my face burning with embarrassment. "Thanks for the save."

"No problem," the young man says. He eyes me as if making sure I'm steady before he leans over to pick up my phone and hands it to me. The crisp inflection of his voice lacks the typical drawl of folks native to Riverton. "Maybe we should put one of those bright-orange street cones on top of that."

"Right. Because *that* might make the town notice it and fix it."

He grins at my sarcasm. "I'm Gabe. Gabe Corwin," he says, extending his hand.

I flush again under the gaze of his kind brown eyes and the way his fingers grasp strong and firm around mine. "Jaycee Givens . . . I . . . you'll have to excuse me; I'm late for work."

"I think we're headed to the same place."

"The diner?"

"Yep. First day." He straightens and points both thumbs at his chest. "Meet your newest coworker." Then he points a key fob at the bright-blue Jeep and locks it.

"You don't have to do that here, you know."

He shrugs. "Habit."

Carla was right when she said the guy she'd just hired was good-looking. I'm the sort of person folks normally bump into without stopping to see what they hit, whether on a sidewalk or at Walmart or refilling cups of coffee. Besides that, the buzz of my phone with another text from Bryan, along with one of the frequent waves of nausea I'm trying to ignore, remind me I'm technically taken.

The smell of Carla's fresh-baked cinnamon rolls greets us as we walk into the diner.

"Morning, Carla," Gabe says cheerily, disappearing into the back.

"I see you've met Gabe." Carla winks at me from behind the counter, where three gentlemen sit sopping up egg yolk with sourdough toast, tufts of white hair sticking out from under the edges of their dark-blue Korean War Veteran hats. Joe, Harry, and Paul. The usual Tuesday morning crew. Behind her, Clyde Herschal, "Hersch," whose hair is as white and whose back is as bent as the old vets', is intent on scraping the grill surface clean.

"I didn't know he was starting *today*," I say.

"You didn't ask."

I try to ignore the gleam in Carla's eye. She's always working to set me up with somebody even though she knows I'm with Bryan. Says I deserve better. More and more I'm thinking she's right.

"Cute, isn't he?" Carla tops off Paul's coffee.

"Stop." I pull a clean apron off the hook beside the register, hang it over my head, and tie it loose behind my back. I fluff it out in front and try to blame the rise there on the oversize sweaters and sweatshirts I've been wearing. Seems to have worked so far.

"He's an EMT." She looks at me sidelong, one eyebrow

raised, as if I should be so lucky. "I'm glad to see the two of you getting acquainted."

"We're not 'getting acquainted.' I just ran into him. Literally. What's he doing in Riverton?" Maybe there was a time that people moved to Riverton—when the land was undeveloped, when the river wasn't lined by shut-down factories, when folks could make a living in a small town. But nobody comes here on purpose anymore.

Carla doesn't have time to answer before Gabe, struggling with his apron, emerges from the back.

"Jaycee, help our new employee tie his apron, would you?"

"Of course." I give Carla the stink eye as soon as I'm behind Gabe.

Gabe steps back and adjusts the apron, then takes the Cubs hat off his head and tousles his thick, wavy brown hair before putting the cap back on backward. He turns to Carla for approval. "Do I look okay?"

"I think so. As long as you wear that hat, you shouldn't need a hairnet." She nods toward Hersch, wearing a Reds hat, as he adds more bacon to Joe's plate. "Hersch here'll show you the ropes."

I start arranging mum stems in the green bottles and listen as the two men fall into easy conversation, or what passes for conversation for someone who talks as little as Hersch does, anyway. They start jawing at each other about baseball statistics and spring training, and I'm relieved for an excuse to get out from behind the counter and away from Carla's ribbing. The bells on the door ring and a family of six arrives and I show them to their table. They're not from around here, judging from the fact that every single one of them wears a Riverton College sweatshirt or hat or both. Locals aren't that big on team spirit.

I take their orders and fall into the familiar routine that has kept me upright in the years since Jayden died. Post the order. Fill the waters. Make sure the coffeepot doesn't run empty. Slice the lemons. Stock the servers. Straighten the chairs. Check the bathrooms. Wipe the counters. Shine the stainless. Fill the salt, pepper, and sugars. Roll the silver. And smile. Always smile. I can keep time to this cadence, lose myself in it, be without thinking, breathe without inhaling.

"Have you talked to your mama?" Carla asks halfway through the day. She knows Mama writes me regularly from the prison, and that I don't write her back.

I shake my head, conscious of Gabe a few feet away. "No."

I'm used to Carla making it her business to stick her nose in none of her business, and normally I do not mind her asking about things like Mama since she's one of the few people I talk to about that. She and Hersch both know my whole story, of course, but Gabe does not, and I'm not sure I want all that to be the first thing the new guy learns about me. He might not be used to the fact that most everybody around Riverton knows or is related to someone who's done heroin or been to jail or both, as in Mama's case. She's been in the state prison for months now, with no sign of getting out anytime soon.

Carla says I should forgive Mama, that maybe she was

doing the best she could with what she had, and considering it was the fault of the doctor who'd prescribed her the pain pills that she'd fallen into heroin. I don't buy that. I've had every chance to use heroin myself seeing as how it was in our house all the time. Could have sold it, too, so we'd have more money. But as tempting as that was, I didn't.

Sudie also says I should forgive Mama, adding that all things—including someone dying—work together for good if you love the Lord. But I say the only thing good that came out of Jayden dying was Mama finally going to prison.

The judge had no mercy for a user who'd let her baby be poisoned, and even less for one who'd been dealing on top of it. Said he sees too many dead babies these days, and I don't doubt that. Sudie says she's been digging graves for too many, and she includes the teenagers in with the babies.

Jayden was the third baby from Shady Acres alone who'd lost his life because of the heroin. One, Rosie Lee, wasn't even a month old before she died. Folks across town weren't immune to the epidemic, either. Jack Lawson lived in one of the new subdivisions and had real hope of getting out of Riverton on a football scholarship until he was found in his car with a needle still stuck in his arm. I don't hardly notice the ambulance sirens anymore, people calling to get the naloxone for their overdosing friends and family. Nobody's gonna notice until more popular kids like Jack Lawson die.

Forgiveness sounds like a good idea, but I bet it doesn't feel as good as the relief that came over me when the officers put handcuffs on Mama's wrists and led her out of the courtroom. By that time, after watching Shorty and Sudie lower my brother's casket into the black-earth hole with ropes because it was too small for the metal lowering machine, after court hearings and witness testimonies about the unimaginable things she'd been doing beyond what I'd even known, and after crying myself to sleep every night without feeling his heartbeat under my hand, I had nothing left to say to her. I don't have anything to say to her now, either, despite the fact that she sends me letters saying she's sorry and hasn't she lost enough without having to lose me too? I guess I just don't get the point of forgiveness after all that.

The other day I wrote her a letter. Tore it up when I was walking to the mailbox to send it. But I meant every word.

Dear Mama,

I got your letter, the one where you told me you're sorry again.

People keep telling me I ought to forgive you. That forgiving you is what the Lord would want. And that not forgiving you is only hurting myself.

But I guess I'm sorry too, because I can't forgive you. At least not right now. Maybe not ever.

Besides that, I'm having a hard time believing you. You had so many chances to get help or do things different, and you never did.

Do you know that every morning I get up and the first thing I think of—still—is what I need to do for Jayden that day? And every morning, I remember again that he's gone, and why he's gone. And then I remember that if it weren't for you and the drugs, he'd still be here.

Sometimes I go visit him out at the cemetery, next to Daddy.

Don't you realize you could have killed even more people besides Jayden with what you were doing? You probably did and just don't know it. Every time you sold the stuff, that person could have died taking it, or if they sold it to someone else, someone else could have died taking it. Half the fresh graves out here that died from an overdose could have been linked back to you somehow. Somebody's son or daughter. Somebody's husband or wife.

Didn't you ever think about that, Mama? You weren't just killing us. You were killing other people, too. People you didn't even know.

So if I don't write you back much, that's why. I don't know what to say to you anymore.

"Sorry" doesn't make up for all that.

And I can't figure out where forgiveness fits into any of it.

Jaycee

7

"So, what do you do for fun, Givens?" Gabe says to me. The place is empty of customers, and it's the first direct thing he has said to me all morning. The late-winter sun slants in the windows and catches on the clean, upside-down glasses waiting beside the soda fountain to be filled. He polishes the stainless-steel counter, the backsplash of the grill.

"I don't know."

"You don't know?" He stops what he's doing and looks at me with big gray eyes that glisten, then leans against the counter and crosses his arms as if he's preparing to study me.

I'm annoyed at myself for noticing his broad shoulders, the definition of the muscles in his upper arms, and for blushing at the way he looks at me. "I have fun. I just can't remember the last time someone asked me that."

"Maybe you need to have fun more often." The corner of his mouth turns up.

Stop blushing.

"Like I said, I have plenty of fun." I turn away so he can't see the red I feel rising to my face and focus on polishing my own section of stainless-steel counter.

I'm glad Gabe can't read my mind and see that "fun" for me, since Jayden died, has consisted of dating Bryan, which gets me out of the house and is an improvement from all the time I spent watching Mama and her friends shoot up. I guess I could call working with Sudie fun, seeing the creatures back to health, setting them free back where they came from. Working at the diner isn't so bad, either.

But I'm sure Gabe means the kind of fun small-town people have in TV shows or commercials—curling up on a porch swing and looking at the stars in the spring, ice cream and Fourth of July parades in the summer, pumpkin carving and apple bobbing and holding hands on hayrides in the fall, and a scene from a Currier & Ives print at Christmas. He doesn't know yet that while Riverton might look quaint, the architecture and brick streets and picket fences are more like memorials than a representation of what really goes on. Towns like Riverton aren't what they used to be. They aren't places to settle down and have fun. They're places to run from or die.

I go on taking and filling orders and try to get my mind

off Gabe, and the rhythm of regulars and folks just passing through Riverton helps. The Gilbert sisters are here in their polyester print dresses, Mary Jane pumps, and matching cardigans. Well past fifty and never married, Sue and Athena Gilbert come every Monday afternoon for sugar cream pie and coffee and to plan the lesson for the Wednesday morning women's study at church.

I find myself watching Gabe when he doesn't know I'm looking. He seems like a good worker. Looks for the work. Doesn't have to be told. By midafternoon, he's using some of the lingo Hersch and I use . . . a crowd of eggs and a belly warmer, a burger with horns on and run through the garden, a Reuben with legs on it, and dog soup—the way we say water.

Shorty brings a couple of guys from his tool company for pie as an excuse to flirt with me—this is according to Carla, who's been right about such things before. He comes into the diner all the time, and he's handsome in an elfish sort of way, soft wrinkles around his eyes and the hair around his temples graying, far from the appearance of someone who digs graves in his spare time. He makes me laugh. But even if I were older I couldn't date him. I could never date a guy I'd have to lean down to kiss.

Besides that, I already have a man. "Don't look now," Carla says, emerging from the storeroom, "but here comes Jaycee's fun."

"Be nice," I say, shooting Carla a warning look as the black, rebuilt Camaro pulls into the handicapped parking space in front of the diner, right next to the bright-blue Jeep, and Bryan gets out. He's picking me up to take me to the high school wrestling meet. His idea of fun, since he was a wrestler and his dad is the head coach.

Carla pretends to zip her lips shut, raises her eyebrows with amusement at me, then Gabe, then plants herself by the cash register and begins to pretend she's sorting receipts. I know she's really sitting there to listen to our every word.

On his way inside, Bryan takes one last draw from his cigarette and tosses it on the sidewalk without bothering to stamp it out. The bells on the door clang louder than usual when he yanks it open.

"Hey, baby."

I come around the counter to greet him. He pulls me close, a little too forcefully, so that I feel off balance. I startle when he puts his hand on my rear end. "Bryan. Stop."

"What's wrong, babe?"

"Not here," I say through my teeth. He knows I don't like it when he starts touching me in front of other people. He also knows Carla doesn't need more about him to dislike.

He steps back and puts his hands in the air in a mocking, exaggerated movement. "Just having a little fun, babe."

"I still have the floors and bathrooms to do."

Annoyance flashes across his face, so quick Carla and Gabe don't notice, but long enough that it's clear to me I should have paid more attention to the time.

"Take your time. Carla will give me a slice of that sugar

cream pie. Won't you, Carla? And he'll get me a cup of coffee. Won't you?" Bryan nods at Gabe and sidles up to the counter.

"If you're paying, I will," Carla says, her sweet voice edged with distaste.

I grab the mop bucket and wheel it into the dining area, glad for the chance to gather myself.

In Riverton, you're only known for one of two things: sports or trouble. Though I had plenty of reasons to be in the second category, I fell in with the rest of the nondescript residents who show up, do our work, and do our best to either leave Riverton or live the rest of our lives here and repeat the dead-end cycles of our families.

Bryan was like Jack Lawson and fell into both categories. He was a star wrestler in my high school class. His dad was the coach back then too. He was supposed to go to college on a full scholarship, but a run-in with the police for sexual assault charges killed that opportunity. The girl who'd made the charges was Mary Ashby, which—as I'd learned later—explained why she was all beat-up and wearing a sling at the hospital the day I brought Jayden in.

I'd been friends with Mary once, back in the third grade. Back before I learned the hard way how much being poor mattered. Mrs. Buchanan was our third-grade teacher, and she assigned me and Mary seats next to each other. We were best friends immediately, trading stuff from our lunches, playing together at recess. Clothes and shoes don't matter much in third grade, so I hadn't noticed that Mary wore things from a boutique, and Mary hadn't noticed that

I wore things from the thrift store. We drew pictures of horses and rivers, flowers and rainbows. And one Friday after school when I asked Mary to come over and play the next day, she said yes.

That morning I rubbed a round spot clean on my smoke-filmed window and saw the sun, which meant it wasn't raining and we could play on the swings that one well-off trailer owner had erected in the Shady Acres common area. I dressed in my best terry-cloth jumpsuit and sat on the concrete blocks under the ash tree, seeds from a nearby cottonwood falling all around like snow. Before long, I saw the white car and heard the slow crunch of its tires on the gravel road that wound through the trailer park.

"Mama!" I'd hollered. "She's here! Mary's here!"

Mama came outside, the screen door slamming as it closed behind her. She crossed her arms and took a long draw from her cigarette, then exhaled, "A Mercedes."

I could see the red leather and trim inside the car. I saw Mary's face pressed against the back window. I ran to greet her. I still remember the spring sun, warm on my face. The air smelled of trees beginning to bud and the ground beginning to warm and green things beginning to grow. Grasshoppers and chiggers threw themselves at my ankles and shins as if cheering Mary's arrival too.

But the car did not stop.

"You passed me! I'm right here!" I hollered, jumping up and down as if they'd not seen me. But I knew they had, because Mary was now staring at me through the rear window of the car.

Surely they'd turn around, I remember thinking.

But they didn't.

An hour later, the phone rang, reverberating against the thin aluminum walls of the trailer.

Mama hadn't said much, just listened to whoever was on the line. She placed the phone back on the receiver, and without turning around said, "Mary's sick. She won't be coming to play today. I'm guessing she won't be coming to play ever."

"But why?" I asked.

I'll never forget the look on Mama's face when she turned around. She had a funny sort of smile on her face, one I couldn't understand then, but I do now. "They're rich and we're poor. Best you not ask her to come over again."

After that, I noticed how most of the kids' mothers brought treats to school on their birthdays, that their shoes weren't worn through on the bottoms and their toes weren't pressed up against the ends, and that their pants were long enough to cover their ankles. I listened to classmates talk about having eggs or pancakes for breakfast and figured out most mothers were awake in the mornings to say good-bye. And I never again asked a girl who dressed better than me to come over and play.

But as well-off as Mary and her family were, she didn't have a chance against the lawyers the Blair family hired, or against the newspaper, which was known to print what it was paid to print. Bryan had wriggled out of jail time with the whole town behind him, but the prosecutor had made sure the university was notified, and they pulled his scholarship. Now he's stuck in Riverton with the rest of us.

I suppose that's how I ended up with him. There were few options for him, and even though I should've known better, being lonely makes a person do stupid things. When Bryan starting coming into the diner more often in the weeks after Jayden died, I didn't think anything of it, like the way I was being naive about Shorty. Carla kept telling me to watch out, that Bryan was sweet on me, but I didn't believe her. People like him didn't have anything to do with people like me. I got curious, though, and couldn't help the heat that flushed through me whenever he came around. He was something to look at. And for the first time I felt like something, too, when he looked at me. At least at first.

"What's your story?" Bryan says to Gabe.

Gabe goes on scraping the grill, even though I can see from where I'm standing that it's clean.

I keep my head down and focus on mopping the floor and listen.

"Hey. Big guy. I said, what's your story?"

Gabe turns, eyes Bryan's coffee mug, and grabs the pot to top it off. "Don't have one."

"Well, you're new around here, am I right?"

"Yeah."

"Then what's your story? People don't come to Riverton for kicks and giggles."

I don't like Bryan's tone, but I know better than to hush him when he's talking to somebody. Besides that, I've been wondering the same thing. I try to move the mop slow enough to hear Gabe's answer.

"I'm an EMT. Riverton Fire Department was advertising positions, and they didn't have any in my town. Came where I could get a job." He shrugs.

"Why you working here, then? At the diner?"

"The EMT job is only part-time. For now. A way to get my foot in the door for full-time."

Bryan is quiet for a moment, and I'm sure he's thinking up a wisecrack.

"An EMT, eh? Do you get to wear a badge or something for that?"

I can see, even without looking, the sneer on Bryan's face.

"No . . ."

"So if you catch me smoking pot or something, you can't arrest me, right?"

Hersch, usually focused to the point of oblivion to everything going on around him, turns his head ever so slightly and studies Bryan from the corner of his eye. Even from where I am across the dining room I can see that the natural downturn of his wrinkled mouth sags further.

"Here's your pie, Bryan. Why don't you work on it instead of interrogating our new employee?" Carla slides the slice across the counter at Bryan.

"Interrogating is way more fun, sweetheart." He takes a

bite of pie, making a point to chew with his mouth wide open and smiling at her.

When I finish the floors out front, I move on to the bathrooms, but not before catching Gabe's eye, the questions on his face plain as day: *Seriously? This is your boyfriend? How can you stand to be with this jerk?*

I liked a nice boy once. His name was Adam Montgomery, and he was the kind of boy who always had a seat on the stage at the end-of-the-year awards. Besides that, the way his jeans fit him drove me crazy. Liked him from junior high all the way until his family moved away in tenth grade.

I couldn't hardly look at him if we passed in the halls, I liked him so much. But he had a girlfriend. Her name was Angel, of all things, and she looked like one, too—perfect hair, the right label on her jeans, the way she walked like a dancer across a stage. All I could do was look at him, though, and imagine what it would be like to be Angel, to have Adam look at me the way he looked at her, to have him hold my hand, to have his arm wrapped around my waist as we walked to and from class.

I imagined doing with him the things I heard girls talking about in the bathroom between classes, how far they went with their boyfriends, and I thought that's what loving and being loved by somebody meant. Mama never told me otherwise, and I heard the sounds she and the men who came over made through the thin walls of our trailer.

So when Bryan was the first boy I ever kissed, I just let him do with me what I figured I was supposed to let him do. I took what he gave since I hadn't been used to receiving much of anything. For a good while, his giving made me feel alive, something I'd about given up on after losing Jayden. I might be a nobody, but apparently I'm pretty enough to hook up with when every other available girl our age is off to college. The things we do together fill a hole inside me—at least they did—a hole Mama and losing Jayden carved wide and long as the Ohio River Valley.

I'd pray as he peeled my clothes away, that the Lord would please let Bryan love me like Adam Montgomery loved Angel, and to please keep me from getting pregnant. I liked it all just fine, until the mean came, the kind of mean Mary Ashby must have known. And after that came the life growing inside my belly that I haven't told a single soul about.

I pour bleach in the toilet. The fumes rise up and sting the inside of my nose and throat, and I fight back a wave of nausea before scrubbing it clean and moving on to the sink and mirrors. The drops of blue glass-cleaner spray cling, then drip down my reflection. My brown eyes stare back at me as I wipe, so different from Mama's clear-blue ones. My hair is dark. Mama's is mousy gray-brown. Pictures are all I have of my father to know I look like him. I like to think I'm not like Mama at all, until I notice the bruises fading on my upper arms as I reach up to wipe the lights, bruises that never seem to go away before there are new ones, bruises like the ones Mama's boyfriends left on her, too.

I tuck a stray piece of black hair behind my ear and think

about Sudie, how she doesn't like Bryan either. Sudie says a good man does more than just the things me and Bryan have been doing, and that a good man doesn't ever hurt a girl. I've never told her, but somehow she can see thoughts and feelings on my face without me breathing a word. Sometimes I think she can see the bruises I'm careful to cover with clothes.

I would leave him.

I would.

But the nausea reminds me I need to stay.

8

Riverton won the wrestling meet, and the fresh air from Bryan's car window is a relief from the musty smell of sweat and mat dust. The pale gray of the country road whirs by as the sun drops below the horizon. A great horned owl dive-bombs from a distant tree, then drifts across the pale-orange edge of the sky before disappearing into another grove. Bryan turns the radio up and pretends the steering wheel is a guitar.

When we get to the Red Pepper, Riverton's pizza shop where all the high school teams go after a win, I see from the stickers on the car windows that most of the wrestling team is already there. Inside, I find a booth and sit alone until Nick and Gus, two quiet, acne-covered kids whose claim to fame is being the sole members of the highest weight class of the team, ask if they can sit with me. They aren't much company since they're glued to their phones, elbowing each other on occasion to check out random YouTube videos or lifting their eyes once in a while to look at my chest.

I roll my eyes and pull the zipper on my sweatshirt up as high as it will go without choking me. Bryan goes from table to table, sometimes sitting with the wrestlers, more often flirting with underage girls. He comes back to me when he needs another slice of pizza or a refill on his beer.

This is what I do for fun, Gabe.

I look up when a family of three comes in, and recognize Mary Ashby and her parents. I don't recall that I've seen her since our high school graduation. She went away to college, so she must be home for spring break. I duck my head and slump in the booth and hope she doesn't see me or that I'm here with Bryan. At the time of their scandal I felt bad for Mary, but I didn't believe what she said about Bryan. No one did. She acted hysterical. He acted like a jerk, but not a jerk capable of rape. But that was before I started dating him.

Across the dining room, Bryan doesn't notice the Ashbys. He's too busy looking into the eyes of a blonde who can't be older than a freshman.

I am wondering if the Ashbys will stay if they see Bryan is here, when Mrs. Ashby picks a booth two down from ours and sits with her back to everything. Mary slides in next to her. Mr. Ashby sits across from them, but he wouldn't know me from Eve. Besides that, the booths are high enough folks can't see over the tops of them.

I decide to join Nick and Gus and lose myself in my phone, playing through a couple of games, trying to ignore the fact that I have to use the bathroom. I don't want to get up and risk Mary seeing me, but I can't wait any longer. Feels like she and everyone else at the Red Pepper are looking at me as I head to the back.

I take my time in the bathroom, redo my hair, put on some lip gloss, and I'm washing my hands when Mary bursts through the door. Red anger splotches her cheeks and her face has completely lost the soft lines of adolescence. I wonder if I look that way too.

"It *is* you," Mary says.

"Hi, Mary." I try to fake surprise.

"Are you here with . . . *him*?" Her chin trembles, the last word of her question barely audible.

My face must give away my answer.

"Why? Did you believe his friends and the paper, too?" *Et tu, Brute?*

I hear the words of our high school English teacher reading *Julius Caesar* and telling us to underline that passage. I think of the white Mercedes with the red leather interior and third grade. We are not so different, Mary and I, the way life has forced us to assume false things about each other. And about ourselves.

"Well, it's true, Jaycee. All of it. He *did* rape me."

"I—"

She holds up her hand. "You saw me that day at the hospital. He beat me because I thought I was pregnant. Up until then he was fairly smart about it, always careful to hit me where no one would see the bruises. But I guess the possibility of a pregnancy pushed him over the edge. He broke my arm, punched me in the face, kicked me in the gut." Her hand moves over her belly. "Nothing would have survived that."

"Mary, I'm so sorry."

"Yeah?"

It is a question and an accusation. An admonishment and a warning. I want to crawl under the sink to get away from her hard stare.

"Yeah . . ." I nod. My voice sounds like a wheeze.

"My advice? Get away from him while you can." She flings the door open and I'm left alone again.

With one hand, I grab hold of the counter to steady my legs, which feel as if they will melt right out from under me. My other hand covers the growing curve of my own belly.

A couple months back, alone in the bathroom at the diner, I'd prayed, *Lord, please don't let me be pregnant. Please?* I prayed over and over as I unwrapped the white stick and studied the tiny window where the lines change color. My thighs burned when I crouched and struggled to stay balanced while holding the pregnancy test and trying not to let it fall into the toilet. I laid the stick on the counter on a couple of tissues and waited, acutely aware of every sound in the diner, from the whoosh and rattle of the kitchen worker pushing plates through the dishwasher, to the clanging of the doorbell as more people came in. I backtracked in my head for the thousandth time. . . . I'd had a lighter period in September and not at all in October. A site on the Internet said stress can cause missed periods, and goodness knows I was stressed. I'd clung to that possibility for a few weeks until my normally flat chest started overflowing my bras and I couldn't button my jeans.

Early on, I spent every second I could on the Riverton library computer, searching the Internet about pregnancy, trying to convince myself something else was making me late. And praying.

God had always protected me before. Mama'd brought home so many different guys, and I'd had too many late-night and hallway encounters with them to count. Strung out on drugs or alcohol, they'd stumble into my room—before and after Jayden was born—and I'd lie there, still as a rabbit cornered in a pile of brush, praying they wouldn't see me, or if they did, that they wouldn't touch me. The Lord had answered my prayers and kept me safe from all those junkies. Not one had laid a hand on me.

I convinced myself that since I lost my virginity with Bryan by choice I didn't deserve for God to hear me. In the bathroom at the diner I'd sat on that toilet and waited the three minutes. Then five minutes. Then a minute longer before I got brave enough to look at the results. My insides trembled same as they're trembling now in the bathroom at the pizza place. I'd folded myself into two then like I do now, trying to hide the roundness of my belly, the same place that'd made me twist with longing whenever Bryan had touched me.

There had been no mistaking the positive results.

I'd seen the same two lines on the test Mama'd bought when she'd discovered she was pregnant with Jayden. I remember how she'd gone out partying that night, trying to force a miscarriage. I thought about how it'd felt not having a daddy for the father-daughter events at school, no one to teach me how to ride a bike, no one to turn to when Mama wasn't there, no one to blame besides Mama for not having enough to eat or wear or for freezing in the winter because the propane ran out again. I can't blame Mama that my father died before I ever knew him. For a while we'd been all right, until she started making bad choice after bad choice and we ended up where we are now. Two family members in the ground, and not a lot of hope left for the living.

I'd looked at the mirror in the diner's bathroom same as I'm looking in the mirror now, thinking again about how there's no way I can bear raising a child in this mess.

9

Somehow I manage to leave the bathroom and see that the Ashbys have gone. A waitress stands bewildered, holding their pizza by their empty table.

"We'll take it if they've gone," Nick says to her.

She shakes her head and rolls her eyes, then brushes past me on the way back to the kitchen.

Bryan is still talking to the underage blonde. His back is to me, so I veer outside and get to the parking lot in time to see the taillights of the Ashbys' old white Mercedes blink once, then twice, before the car turns onto Main Street and disappears.

Nausea threatens when I think about Mary, and about

what could happen to me when Bryan finds out about this baby.

I start walking to the town square and the diner, where I left my car. I can be there in ten minutes, faster if I hurry.

Lord, please. Don't let him notice I've gone.

The wind has picked up. Haze surrounds the moon. Three-story buildings with arched windows and ornate trim line the street to my left. To my right are more shops interspersed with historical homes whose backyards slope down to the river, an inky ribbon this time of the night, dotted with an occasional light from a fishing boat or a barge. I like to imagine what the river looked like to the first settlers in the valley, before homes and then towns and then cities were built, before trees were cut and land cleared, before the wood rats and muskrats, the badgers and the mink, the kingfishers and the heron, the stocky little flycatchers and all the other animals were shoved aside and forgotten by people who didn't know how much they mattered. Chop and burn. Build and pave. Wildlife is adaptable, after all. Survival of the fittest.

Maybe that's why Jayden's in the ground.

Maybe that's why Mary's baby, if she really was pregnant, was beat to death before it took its first breath.

What kind of a chance does any child have around here anymore?

I am yards from the diner and can see the moon reflecting in the plate-glass front window when car lights cast my shadow long on the sidewalk. Bryan's car rolls to a stop in front of me. Exhaust chugs from the rumbling muffler and I veer to avoid inhaling it. The car jerks as Bryan puts it into park and gets out, the car door swinging from the force of his exit.

"What are you doin'?" he says through clenched teeth.

The flash of annoyance I am well acquainted with is replaced with fury. I've never challenged him like this before.

The street and sidewalks are empty. Stores are dark and closed. We are well past homes and the soft glow of porch lights and side-table lamps spilling onto front lawns.

"Always careful to hit me where no one would see the bruises," Mary said.

I cross my arms and step back. *Act like it's no big deal.* "I'm just tired. You were having fun," I say, trying my best to stand straight, assured. My voice sounds cheerier than I want it to. Fake.

"What did she say to you?"

"Who?" How could he have seen Mary talking to me? He was talking to the blonde.

"John said he saw them leaving. The Ashbys. And that he saw both of you come out of the bathroom." John is Bryan's best friend, and a better gossip than most of the girls in Riverton.

"I don't know what you're talking about." I take a step back again.

He takes three more steps toward me, his hands balled into fists at his sides. "I don't need my girlfriend standing me up. You hear?"

"Like I said, you were having fun. I didn't want to bother—"

His fingers wrap like a vise around my arm and I feel my head snap backward as he shoves me. His breath is hot, heavy against my face. "That's a lie."

A bit of courage rises in me, enough for what I need to do. "I didn't want to break up with you in the middle of the Red Pepper or in front of your friends."

He lets go of my arm and takes a step back. He chuckles. Then starts to laugh, a mocking cackle that scares me. "You don't mean that."

Help me, Lord. "Yes. I do."

For a split second his face looks like that of a little kid, one coming off the field after losing his first Little League game. But that only lasts a second.

"Girls don't break up with me. 'Specially girls like you. I'm the one who's breaking up here. You never were worth it anyway."

The smack against the side of my face that follows his words is hard and blinding. I'm glad I'm too shocked to absorb the names he's calling me. He grabs both my arms hard now. Feels like his fingers are squeezing against my very bones.

"Stop it, Bryan. You're hurting me." I think about Mary, how the kick I'm sure is coming next must have felt against her belly.

"There a problem here, Jaycee?"

Bryan's grip on my arms slackens, and he's as surprised as I am to see the man behind him.

Hersch stands there, back stretched straighter than I've ever seen it. He holds a push broom in one hand, and I can see the Marine POW tattoo on the thick curved forearm of his free hand. He's still wearing the white pants, white button-down shirt, and white apron he wears every day, though it's hours past closing. His brown eyes are kind, knowing, as he looks past Bryan and right at me.

"I was just coming for my car to go home," I say.

Hersch steps between Bryan and me before I know it. "Hear that, son? The lady's going home now."

Bryan glares at me, his hands still in fists, which open, close. Open, close. He raises one and points at me. "There's no going back on this, Jaycee. We're done. You hear me? Done."

I step behind Hersch and watch as Bryan climbs back into his car. Black lines of rubber steam from where he squeals off. My arms ache.

"How'd you know?" I say to Hersch.

Just like when he's cooking an egg or flipping a chopped steak at the grill, Hersch barely turns his head as he says over his shoulder, "Hersch just knows."

Hersch waits and watches until he is sure my car starts before turning and heading back to the diner and whatever business he has there. Maybe some late-night deep cleaning of the grill. Whatever he's been doing, I'm sure glad he was there.

10

Dear Jaycee,

I don't blame you for not answering most of my letters. Wouldn't blame you for hating me, either. I hate myself. Not much else to do here besides think over what I've done to get here, what I've done to you, to your brother.

A preacher was here on Sunday. He's here every Sunday, but I decided to go to the service this time. He and his people brought fresh donuts, and we don't have anything like that on the block. He talked about the same things Reverend Payne always talked about, but I don't think any of that is for me anymore. What kind

of God would want a woman who's done the things
I've done?
    But I'll keep telling you I'm sorry.
    I guess I'll keep telling Jesus I'm sorry too.
    I love you.

Mama

I don't have an answer for the question in Mama's letter, which I find on top of the stack of usual bills and mailers. 'Specially since I wonder the same thing myself lately.

I don't expect answers from him anymore. I'm not like Sudie, who says she hears God speaking to her in the wind when she's tending the graves or watching her critters heal and return feral as ever to the wild. But like Mama, that doesn't stop me from talking to him. I guess for some crazy reason I think maybe he'll get tired of me talking and say something back.

Walking across the matted-down path of grass to my home, the trailer looks especially small, fragile, and I shiver at the unusually cold spring night. The dried brush, all of the Joe Pye and ironweed, the asters and oxeye daisies are brown and withered from the long winter. If spring wasn't such a sure thing, I'd never believe they could be tall and green again. One snowflake, then two, land on my eyelashes, and I can see even more falling across the uncovered bulb that lights the front stoop. A barred owl yelps from a nearby tree: *whooh-whooh-whooh-woo-woo-woo-woo.*

I almost step on the plate wrapped in tinfoil on the top

step of my stoop. It's still warm, and I lift up a corner and see it's full of butterscotch cookies.

The note on top says,

Church at 8:30 tomorrow morning.

—Sudie

Inside, I flip the light on. The place is quiet except for the hum of the old refrigerator and the click of the furnace. I lock the door behind me, even though there's about as much inside to steal as there is outside.

Anymore, nobody leaves anything around they don't want stolen. Folks needing their drugs steal everything but the siding off trailers if they can turn it around for cash and a balloon full of smack. They stole the fake wooden wishing well from the front yard of Shawnie and Tim's place, the bald tires off another neighbor's car that was up on blocks for repair, and the clothes—including underwear— off Sudie's clothesline. The fact that Dewey and Virginia Johnson's couch hasn't been stolen from their side yard is a testimony to how gross it is.

For the longest time after Mama went to jail, I lay awake at night listening for the doorknob to rattle, seeing shadows— real and imagined—creeping by my window. Took several weeks of Mama being gone before word got out and they stopped coming around for their fix.

My stomach growls and I'm glad I remembered to buy fresh milk the day before so I can have it with Sudie's cookies. The first soft, buttery bite melts on my tongue, and the milk is cold and silky on my throat, still tight from Bryan's anger.

I intended to tell him about the baby. Really, I did. But after this, no way.

Hot tears come, tears I've been holding back since the sting of Bryan's hands squeezing my arms, and they keep coming as I go to my bedroom and pull out a pair of pajamas, pink flannel pants Sudie bought me for Christmas with a pattern that looks like they were made for a little girl, only I'm not a little girl anymore. Little girls don't sleep with their boyfriends. Little girls don't get pregnant.

I curl into bed and turn on my phone. I wrap myself around a spare pillow in the spot where Jayden used to lie, and I try not to acknowledge the shadowy thought in the back of my mind as I flip through the latest Internet and Twitter news. I didn't think it would ever be something I'd consider, but I didn't think I'd be pregnant like this either. Feels like two sides of my brain are arguing with each other.

It's just a clump of cells.

God's knitting him together.

Get rid of it.

He has a heartbeat.

Kill it. Get an abortion. It's legal. People do it all the time.

I count the months again since I last had a period.

October . . . November . . . December . . . January . . . February . . . March.

I'm at least six months along, maybe closer to seven.

My fingers feel like they have weights attached to them, clumsy as I type the word into the search bar: *A-B-O-R-T-I-O-N*.

I'm about to hit Enter, then add Cincinnati. The closest city.

There are almost five hundred thousand results, everything from a map with icons identifying surgical centers to information about the abortion pill. The closest clinics are about an hour's drive from Riverton.

I could easily get to and from Cincy in a day. Maybe even a half day and not be missed. I'll call in sick. Carla won't mind. And she won't have to know.

Other results include things like postabortion help, postabortion syndrome, and snippets of information like how the cost of the procedure increases after the first trimester.

I'm way too far along to even be looking at this.

I click on a button that reads, *Find Help,* and another that says, *One Girl's Story.* The girl's about to have the abortion and she sees the baby move like it's waving, its tiny legs kicking, its heart beating. I read about all the abortion doctor did to her, all he did to the baby with the forceps and severing limbs and the bleeding afterward and the shame and the regret.

Nausea threatens before I can finish reading everything.

What am I supposed to do, Lord? I can't kill this child. But how am I supposed to carry him? And what am I supposed to do once he's born?

Silence answers my questions and I shiver with loneliness.

The blue glow of my phone screen glares at me: images of girls who look like me; images of embryos and fetal development; images of shiny-faced couples seeking adoption; links to things like choices and life and rights and morning-after pills and abortion risks and parenting and child support; words like *safe* and *legal* and *options*.

I scroll to the clinic website and click through the pages about the procedure.

Ninety-nine percent effective.

Safe.

Legal.

Confidential.

Fast.

Common.

An abortion would make all of this a memory. An annoyance. I'd be free from Bryan, free from this one little mistake. After all, it was just a mistake. Everyone makes mistakes. I don't want to turn out like Mama.

But still.

It's a baby.

Inside me.

My *baby*.

After Mama turned, I never felt like I belonged to anyone, and now here I am with a baby growing inside me who not only belongs to me, but somehow, I feel like I belong to him.

It's just a line on a stick. It can't live any more than the kits born too soon whose mothers leave them. It happens in nature. Nobody knows. Nobody ever has to know.

And Bryan wouldn't have to know.

He'd be furious.

I think of Mary and imagine her crumpled from the blow to her gut.

Before tonight, I told myself I'd marry Bryan. Seems like forever ago when we first started dating, not long after Jayden died. Back then, when I was with Bryan the emptiness of losing Jayden disappeared. Wouldn't have been a perfect marriage, but I thought I could make it work. Thought I could tolerate him, his temper. Especially if I had a baby to focus on. I thought we could have a second, even a third. We'd be fine, like me and Mama were fine when I was little. And we'd have a roof over our heads, a real house on one of the streets in town.

I thought I could live with Bryan if I had all that. Anything to fill the heart-hole inside me. Now I know no man, no roof, and especially no baby can fill the empty. Bryan would beat any chance of joy, any chance of life, out of us for sure. Even now, being with Bryan means no more than things the feral cats do under the trailer or the coyotes I hear screaming in the meadow as they come together.

I'm far from the only unmarried girl who's been pregnant in Riverton. There'd been at least a dozen in my high school class alone. Terri Brown sat next to me in anatomy class and I saw how each passing week it became harder for her to fit into the all-in-one chair and desk. Eventually she'd started sitting at one of the lab tables in the back of the room because she got tired of sitting sideways. We were lab partners and spent hours dissecting a cat and a cow's eye, but Terri never spoke of her pregnancy, even though it was right there in front of us in plain view. And I never asked.

Terri ran with the rough crowd, the sort of kids who smoked in the bathrooms between classes and wore impossibly tight jeans, usually paired with a concert T-shirt of some kind. The sort of crowd who asked me if I sold smack since they knew Mama did. Pregnancy happened a lot in Riverton. It just didn't happen, at least as far as people knew, to people like Bryan Blair.

I click off my phone and put it facedown on the floor next to my bed. Getting rid of this child is not a solution. He can't help that he was created. The fact that I'm going to have to carry this baby and deliver him is getting more and more real. And I'm more and more scared.

Help me, Lord.

The wind blows through a crack in my trailer window, but it sure sounds like a voice says, *Trust me.*

As if on cue, I feel movement, gentle as a feather, pressing inside me, against the rise of my belly. It's the first time I've felt anything. But it's there. My baby. Inside me. Alive.

I curl my knees up tight against me, as if to protect the life inside me from my own dark thoughts, and slide under the sheets. I long for Jayden and the way he curled himself against me at night before I put him in his crib. He was so fragile—all velvet, wrinkled skin when he was first born. So perfect. So completely reliant on Mama—on me—to live.

I'd chosen rabbits over Jayden.

I might as well have been the one to put the methadone in his bottle.

How in the world could I raise a child of my own?

Help me, Lord.

Trust me.

That voice isn't the wind. And it's not my imagination.

It's the voice I've heard before, in the summer when the rain dies down, when the whole earth is swollen with deep green life, the whole world is coming into its own, and the first of the monarchs are returning to the milkweed. It's the voice I hear in the spring, when katydids are floating on top of the meadow grass, cardinals and sparrows are calling, rabbits are chasing each other and tumbling over themselves in a dance of courtship. It's the voice I heard when my toes sank bare into the sand along a quiet bend of the Ohio River, the day Sudie gave me the Bible that's on the table next to me.

Reverend Payne and the two deacons had looked a little silly standing waist-deep in the river, the big white gowns floating up all around them. A handful of adults and my eighth-grade confirmation class were dressed in the same white robes, waiting our turns to be baptized. Bryan Blair included. None of us knew how we'd turn out back then.

Behind us, Ida Lambert directed a little choir of about half a dozen in songs like "Take Me to the Water," "Shall We Gather at the River," and "Abide with Me."

Hawks hung in the air above the trees on the opposite side of the river, and a heron flew by, neck tucked in an S, while a few sandpipers played with each other along the shoreline. And Reverend Payne went on about how just like the river, things change up and down the shoreline of our lives, but the water running through them never changes course. It never stops and always runs the same direction downstream. Unchanging. Living water, just like the Lord himself.

One by one, folks waded in ahead of me, my stomach clenching at the thought of coming up wet in front of every-body or my nose plugging up or choking on the water. My feet sank into the soft river bottom and mud squished up all around my toes as I half walked, half swam out to Reverend Payne. His hands were strong but gentle to steady me, since I had to struggle to find my footing. When I turned back to the shore, Mama and Sudie were standing together, tears of pride running down both their faces.

Reverend Payne said something about the Father, Son, and Holy Spirit, and I remember looking for a dove to come down like it did for Jesus and John the Baptist, but none did. Still, I felt the old go and the new come as Reverend Payne and the deacons floated me back and under and brought me up out of the water, and I knew right then I was new and clean as I'd ever be.

The crowd along the riverbank clapped and cheered, Mama and Sudie loudest of all. After the last person had their turn, we all held hands in a big circle and sang a song before praying and then sang one last hymn before changing back into our Sunday clothes in the park's public restroom and joining up for a picnic in one of the shelters. I remember pulling on my old stained canvas shoes, the rubber edges split and cracked, my heart full from the very certain feeling that God was smiling down on me.

That's when Sudie gave me the Bible, the one that prom-ises that like the river, God doesn't change. The one that tells about Moses and David being murderers and Gideon and Peter being afraid, of Rahab being a prostitute and Jacob being a cheater, of Jonah running away from God. The one that says God never gives up on anyone despite the sinning and the running and the coming and going and the fearing and doubting people do.

I'm not much different than them, am I, Lord?

I love you, the voice says.

But I'm a mess, Lord.

I'm your strength.

But I don't know what to do, Lord.

Be still and know.

But I'm scared, Lord.

I am with you always.

Help me, Lord.

Trust me.

Before I turn off the light, I open the Bible and settle on Psalm 139, how God made me and he's making this baby, every little part he's knitting together. He watched as I grew in Mama's belly, and he's watching as this baby grows in mine. He saw me before I was born, and he sees this baby inside me. He recorded all my days, and he's recording my baby's days, too. There's no place I can go and no place this baby can go without God going there first.

And somehow, for now, that's enough.

11

In the morning I hear a baby wailing and for a moment my heart stops.

Jayden.

But then I remember. It's just a neighbor baby, across the way. The thin metal walls of the trailers allow sound to travel like kids playing telephone with a couple of cans.

I still reach for him when I wake up in the mornings like this. I miss his heartbeat. I miss him reaching for me. I even miss his fussing. Sometimes I keep my eyes closed on purpose and imagine nothing ever changed, because sometimes I don't know how to live without him, or without Mama if I'm honest. She was there, on the bank of the river, cheering for me once.

I fix my eyes on the ceiling, yellow in spots where the roof leaked and I patched it up with Sta-Kool for the hundredth time, something I learned about by watching the neighbors. My eyes adjust to daylight, my mind to the airy stillness until a breeze presses against the sides of the trailer, making it creak. I hear the wind rustling through the branches of the old ash, and I remember the snowflakes on my windshield last night.

Pushing the curtain back, I see frost settled hard on the world, along with about half an inch of snow, just enough to coat the trees, each blade of grass, the roofs of storage sheds, shimmering with a thick layer of icy white. I shiver and feel the soft rise of my belly.

Nausea rises when I think about what I was considering last night. Bryan or no Bryan, there's no way I can do away with the life inside me. It's bad enough that one beating heart stopped on account of me.

I shower, blow-dry my hair, and put on my makeup for church. Usual things feel unusual since last night. Next to a bong stain on the kitchen counter, my cell phone is still for the first time in a long while. I'm caught between feeling relieved and being angry that Bryan gave me up so easy. I take my time letting the oatmeal cook; watching the eggs turn from clear to soft, formed gold; and feeling the way they warm my insides on the way down. One thing's for sure: this child inside me wants me to eat.

Before heading to Sudie's, I fill the bird feeders. Outside, the new snow muffles the morning sounds of doors creaking open as folks fetch Sunday papers and traffic passes along the highway. The world smells clean, as if the snow has brought newness with it, and I imagine what it would be like if the brown wasn't underneath it all. A squirrel arcs along the ground, pauses, and rises on its haunches to stare at me before continuing on, circling up and around the ash tree.

I walk to Sudie's and stop at a tall, narrow cage outside her trailer.

"Hey there," I say to the kestrel perched on a peg. He doesn't seem to mind the light snow at all, and his beady black eyes follow every one of my movements.

Sudie calls this her elevator cage since the only direction a bird can fly when it's in there is up or down. Birds in rehab lose their wing strength, the muscles that move them being the most important part of flying. Once they've mastered that, they can move on to the flight cage, a long, tall structure behind her trailer that has a cover and shelf on one end and a trapeze that moves like a swinging branch in the wild to test their strength before they're released.

"If they can fly up, they can fly out," Sudie says.

The steps of Sudie's red-stained wooden stoop creak as I try the door and find it unlocked. She doesn't always pay attention when I tell her to lock her door at night. Maybe working at a cemetery takes all the fear right out of her.

"Morning," I announce. I hear her in the bedroom, so I check on the turtle, the only other critter she has at the moment, a leftover from last summer. The rest of the tanks and cages lining the shelves and tables and chairs around her cramped front room and kitchen are empty. Winter months are slow since so many animals hunker down or migrate. Now that spring is starting, things will start to happen. Breeding season.

"Did you feed the turtle yet, Sudie?" I call.

"No, I haven't—worms are in the fridge."

I find the Styrofoam container of worms between a half gallon of milk and a bottle of mustard in the door of Sudie's sparsely stocked refrigerator.

This box turtle has been with us so long it feels like he ought to have a name, but Sudie refuses to give names to any of the rescue animals. Says we're not supposed to be their friends. "Releasing them is hard enough without getting too attached." Says the hardest part about taking care of the cemetery is seeing the names that go with the babies who died.

The turtle's red eyes—which is how I know he's a male—turn up and down as he watches me pull a worm from the cold black dirt of the container. A clay-colored patch zigzags up and across his shell, Bondo we put on to seal the crack he had when he came to us. He was dazed from being hit by a car and knocked clear off the road like a tiddlywink, and I laughed when Sudie said we'd use Bondo to fix him. Sure enough it's working, though. She says we'll paint the Bondo to match his shell before we release him.

"Enjoy that worm," Sudie says to the turtle, emerging from her room. "'Fore long, you'll be hunting them yourself."

I watch as the worm disappears into the turtle's mouth one bite at a time, tail end twitching until the very last gulp.

"There's treasure in cracks," Sudie says.

"Mmm-hmm," I reply, since I know what she's gonna say next about the Lord being the potter and us being the clay.

"Second Corinthians," we say in unison.

"Land sakes, if I don't have some cracks in my old pot," she says.

"More space for the light to shine through."

"That's right." She wipes down the counters, then plods to the couch, where she sets herself down with a heavy sigh. She pulls on her thick-soled brown tie-up shoes, which she wears with everything, including her Sunday dresses. "Sounds mighty confusin', but that's how the Lord works. He makes sense out of things we can't understand. Uses the foolish—things folks who ain't lookin' can't see. Uses 'em so he gets all the glory. Try and find a perfect man or woman in the Bible," Sudie says as she gets up and pulls on her coat, her hat, her mittens. "You won't find a one, besides Jesus."

It's as if she knows everything I'd been praying last night.

Riverton Community Church occupies a high corner of a block just north and east of the town square. From its steps, four curves of the Ohio River are visible, the only place on earth that can boast such a thing.

Mama's done a lot of things wrong, but she always made sure I got to church.

"The Lord gave us his life," she'd say. "We owe him at least one hour a week."

And we were sure to give him that, until she started on the pills and then the smack and Jayden came and then he died.

I've never been so tired. But coming here, hearing a hymn, mouthing the words to the Apostle's Creed, keeping my eyes on the black-robed pastor speaking big words like *almighty* and *affliction*, *judgment* and *resurrection*, all while promising something vast and wonderful beyond woebegone Riverton, well, that's sure helped get me through the weeks. I know some folks don't believe the stories of men saved from fires and lions, of oceans parting and bushes bursting into flames, of rescued slaves and a baby born to a virgin, of cities crumbling to a trumpet blast, sticks turning into snakes and water turning into blood or wine, of manna from the sky and talking donkeys, of withered hands being healed and loaves and fishes and Jesus coming back to life. But if I can't believe in all that, there's not much left I can believe in.

The words from Mama's letter haunt me, though. *What kind of God would want a woman who's done the things I've done?*

Believing all that is one thing. Whether it still applies to me and the trouble I've gotten myself into, well, that's something else altogether.

Sudie parks on a side street and as we walk toward the church I fix my eyes on the sidewalk, concrete slabs jutting and slanting from the force of great tree roots growing thick beneath them. The gauzy blanket of snow is blinding under the early spring sun. Naked tree branches creak above us in the wind, and the sky is a deceiving blue, as if it is questioning the frigid cold of the morning. Will it ever be warm again?

Up ahead, a half-dozen hunched, white-haired congregants shuffle as children giggle and push by them. Spade-shaped leaves of crocuses and hyacinths poke up through the snow near the church entrance, and the square brick tower of the church's vestibule casts a long shadow on us.

"Every year, I think it's too early for the bulbs, but every year, they prove me wrong and do just fine." Sudie nods. The pearl necklace she wears every Sunday looks especially splendid in the sun. The pearls are the nicest thing she owns as far as I can tell, and she only brings them out to wear on the Lord's Day or for funerals.

"Sudie! There you are." Veda Spradlin hollers and waves from across the street. "There's a covered dish after service. Will you be comin'?" She and Trina Bishop and their covered-dish Sundays are something to behold.

"I'm headed to the cemetery today. Can't let this sunshine go to waste, or the frozen ground," Sudie says as the two ladies meet up with us. A couple weeks back when there was a warm streak and days of heavy rain, her mowing tractor got stuck in the low back section. By the time Shorty got it chained up and pulled free, they and their vehicles all looked like they'd been mud bogging at the county fair.

"Good mornin', Jaycee." Carla offers us a program as we enter the oak-laden sanctuary, fresh with the faint scent of lemon oil. She leans over and whispers in my ear. "Gabe's here. Sitting over there by himself."

"Stop," I say and roll my eyes. The last thing I need is her matchmaking. The last thing I need is a man. The last thing a guy like Gabe needs is a girl like me.

Thankfully Sudie heads the opposite direction and takes the spot in the back pew where we sit every week. Gabe's sitting in Shorty Smith's spot, and he'll figure that out soon as Shorty gets here. Everyone at Riverton Community has assigned seats, even if this is an unspoken rule. If a visitor happens to come and unknowingly sit in one of them, the whole morning is thrown off, the organist hitting sharps when she should've hit flats, the elder stumbling over the Scripture reading, even the Lord's Prayer off-kilter if the visitor doesn't know they are supposed to say *debts* instead of *trespasses*.

The wood pew feels cold through my stretch pants, which I insist on wearing despite the fact Sudie says I ought to wear a dress. I figure the Bible means what it says in James about folks all deserving the same seat, whether dressed fancy or not.

In front of us sits Mr. Crawford, a plump man whose lower lip is always shaped in a pout. I imagine this is because he is both the town lawyer and accountant. Ahead of him are Hersch and his wife. I'm glad Hersch is facing forward so I don't have to make eye contact after last night. In front of him are the usual families, little girls in frilly dresses and little boys with clip-on ties, teenage boys slouching in their seats and teenage girls staring and giggling into their smartphone screens.

One girl, her dark hair in long braids, peeks over the top of the pew and stares at me. I wave to her and giggle when her face turns bright red and her head disappears quick. After the children's message, the kids will all shuffle off to Sunday school to nibble on animal crackers and sip fruit punch and listen to the same stories I did when I was their age.

I squint to read the hymn numbers on the board above the pulpit and notice Bryan's mother, Elizabeth Blair, staring at me. I try my best to pretend not to notice and pray my cheeks don't turn red like the girl with the braids. Mrs. Blair likes to remind me as often as she can that I am not worthy to date her son. Well, she can stare at me all she wants now since we're through.

Except for the fact that I'm carrying her grandchild.

Ida Lambert, the organist, belts out the first chord of the call to worship so loud the windows rattle. Reverend Payne stands, and when Ida's playing quiets down, his voice booms across the sanctuary. "I will sing of your steadfast love, O Lord, forever."

"With my mouth I will proclaim your faithfulness to all generations." We follow along with the words in the program.

"I declare that your steadfast love is established forever."

"Your faithfulness is as firm as the heavens! Praise the Lord!"

Reverend Payne is a large man with shoulders so broad it looks like he's wearing football pads under his robe. Folks like to take bets on which is older, Reverend Payne or the church. There isn't a soul alive who can remember anyone who's preached here but him.

When peace like a river attendeth my way . . .

The first hymn's a favorite, but though I've sung the words a hundred times they stick out to me today, especially after thinking on my baptism. I think about all the times I've knelt along the edge of the Ohio River, the grit of the sandy shore stinging my bare knees, the smooth, cold feel of the currents against my hand, currents that can kill and have killed plenty of people who weren't careful in it. If my life were a river, it'd be full of waterfalls and toppled trees and muddy marshes where water snakes and leeches slither wild.

When sorrows like sea billows roll;
Whatever my lot, thou hast taught me to say,
It is well, it is well with my soul.

It is well.
With my soul.
Lord, let it be well with this baby inside me.

I was quiet on the drive here, and Sudie'd asked me more than once what was wrong. I didn't want to tell her about Bryan. Didn't feel like hearing an "I told you so." But here in the middle of church, with Ida ramping up for the offertory, seems as good a time as any since it'll be tough for her to lecture me over that and the sermon to follow.

I lean over and say, "Me and Bryan broke up last night," as Ida pounds out the chords.

Sudie's eyes widen and meet mine; her soft mouth and cheeks turn into an O.

Ida releases the keys and Reverend Payne bellows from the pulpit, "This is the day the Lord has made!"

"We will rejoice and be glad in it," the congregation replies in unison.

"Amen!" Sudie hollers, so loud everyone around us turns and stares. She grins and grins and I can't stop my cheeks from glowing since I know her witness is about the fact me and Bryan are through.

"Today's reading is from Exodus, chapters 5 and 6," Reverend Payne continues. "We've been studying the life of Moses, if you'll recall. And this week, we'll learn how the Israelites were so broken by their circumstances it was difficult for them to trust God."

That'd be me.

"But we'll see how when life gets hard, God remains faithful, even when we doubt him."

I rest my hands across my belly. The baby hasn't moved much during the service, but a fullness lingers there, a warmth. A presence. The children are excused and leave for their Sunday school classes, and Reverend Payne starts into his sermon. He talks about Moses and his mother, the woman who hid him and put him in the river.

"She loved that baby with all her heart," he says. "She gave him up not because she didn't love him. She gave him up because she *did* love him. She gave him up to protect him from the Egyptians, to save his life. Sometimes God shows his faithfulness not by what he brings to our life, but by what he takes out of it; not by what he gives us, but by the joy we receive from what we let go of and give to him. Like he says in Isaiah chapter 43, verse 16, 'I am the Lord, who opened a way through the waters.'"

Reverend Payne pauses, and the sanctuary is thick with quiet except for someone clearing their throat.

"What is the Lord asking you to give up today?" he says, looking left then right across all of us, before finally saying, "Let's pray."

I am glad to bow my head, to cross my arms over my belly, to close my eyes and hope he hears.

Dear Lord, this baby doesn't stand a chance with me. I want children someday. But I want to do it right. I want them to have a daddy and a roof over their head. I want to be able to buy them clothes that aren't used and toys that come new in a box. I want them to not have to go to sleep hearing ambulance sirens or the sound of babies crying from withdrawal in the next trailer over.

Maybe this baby is what I need to give up. He sure would be better off with someone else. It's just that . . . well, Lord . . . this baby's starting to feel like all I have.

I jump a mile high when, right in the middle of the prayer with my eyes closed and everything, Sudie rests her hand on my belly.

When I open one eye to look at her, she leaves her hand there and stares straight at me.

"You know?" I mouth, hot tears filling my eyes.

"Let's stand and sing together." Reverend Payne's voice booms across the sanctuary.

I've never been so glad for Ida's organ as when she sits and begins to play, the organ pipes heaving out heavy chords for "The Old Rugged Cross." When we stand, Sudie puts her arm around me and pulls me close. Her powdered cheek is soft against mine as she whispers, "Of course I know, child. I've known for weeks. Been a struggle not saying something 'til now."

"Why didn't you?" I whisper back.

"I was waiting."

"Waiting for what?"

"For the Lord. And for you to be ready. No sense talking about it if you ain't ready."

Of course she's known, just like she knew what I needed every time I ran to her place in the middle of the night without saying a thing. The worse things got with Mama, the more Sudie was ready with a batch of scotchie dough in the fridge waiting to be baked and a spot on her couch with a blanket and a pillow in a clean pillowcase.

My chin trembles from the relief of someone else knowing, like all I've been holding inside can't wait to get out. The service ends and folks start standing and gathering their things to leave the sanctuary. I turn so they can't see the tears running down my face.

When I do dare to meet Sudie's eyes, the blue of them

is clear as the sky, the creases and wrinkles around them offering kindness like the folds of a bird's wings over a nest. "What am I gonna do, Sudie?"

"Don't you worry, child. We'll figure this out together, and with the help of the Lord."

12

I wait until the sanctuary is mostly empty and I've collected myself before heading out to the gathering space where Sudie's talking and laughing with Walter Crawford about something that's evidently particularly funny, the way they're both carrying on. This surprises me, since he does not seem like the sort of man to find much of anything funny.

I manage to avoid Gabe, but avoiding others is impossible since going to church is like gathering with family in Riverton. Diner regulars and my former schoolteachers, Sunday school teachers and Mama's old friends, and what friends of mine haven't left town yet all want to say hello, and I can't just walk by them no matter how red my face and eyes must be. They brought meals to me after Jayden died and after Mama went to jail. They came to the funeral and took up a donation so we could give Jayden a proper burial. Bud and Larry, the handymen, still come by the trailer every now and then, tweaking the plumbing and finding whatever odd jobs they can insist on taking care of since they know I am alone, and even though I know how to fix most of it myself. Like Sudie's hand on my belly, the people of this church continue to find me when I don't even realize I am lost, even when I try to refuse them.

"Hey, Jaycee."

I turn around to see Gabe with Carla standing right behind him. She's beaming, of course.

I try to pretend I don't notice that. "Hey, Gabe. Did Carla make you get out of bed this morning and come to church?"

He furrows his brow. "Not at all. I've been looking for a church. Carla told me this one's pretty good."

I nod, annoyed at the butterflies starting up in my chest and the fact that I cannot think of a single thing to say to save my life.

"Reverend Payne gives a good sermon. I hadn't heard anyone talk about Moses like that before," Gabe offers.

"Mmm-hmm." I scan the room for Sudie. Surely she's about ready to go.

"Do you go to lunch after church?"

"No . . . I mean, sometimes. . . . I'm going to the cemetery—"

"Welcome to Riverton Community Church!" A woman's

arm reaches between us. "I'm Veda Spradlin. Noticed you're new. Did you sign up to get a pie?"

"I'm Gabe Corwin." He shakes her hand heartily. "Nice to meet you. And I am certain I did not sign up for a pie."

"Well, don't leave before I get you a visitor card. You can choose from Hoosier cream, apple, or derby on there, and when you turn it in, we'll drop it off."

"You sure know how to make a person feel welcome," he says. "Thank you, Ms. Spradlin."

"Oh, call me Veda." She is blushing. "Nobody who lives in Riverton calls anybody by their last name, unless they happen to be your teacher."

"Okay then, Veda. Thank you."

"He's my newest employee," Carla says.

"Is that right?"

"Line cook, busboy, whatever she needs," Gabe says, the same proud look on his face as the day I ran into him on the sidewalk.

"He's fantastic. And when he's not at the diner, he's an EMT."

"We like hard workers in Riverton. Welcome, welcome. Now if you'll excuse me, I've got to catch another new face I see over there." Veda nods, then skirts away.

"You ready, Jaycee?" Sudie says, approaching us. She turns to Gabe, looking him up and down. "You going to introduce me to your friend too?"

Between her and Carla stirring up romance, I don't have a chance.

"Sudie, meet Gabe. Gabe, meet Sudie."

"Nice to meet you, Gabe," Sudie says. "You still coming with me, Jaycee?"

"Yes."

"Where are you going?" Gabe asks.

"I help Sudie—she's my neighbor—I help her take care of a cemetery a few miles from here."

"You know I don't need that much help," Sudie says. She leans forward and I see a little glimmer in her eye. "Unless . . ."

"Unless what?" Gabe is wide-eyed.

"Unless I get there and find old Mrs. O'Reilly laid out next to her grave. Buried her Thursday. Had in her will instructions to be buried with all her jewelry. And I do mean all of it."

I see what she's doing and decide to play along. "All of it? That diamond wedding ring was huge." Sudie has managed to creep me out legitimately plenty of times. Says there's a man out there who wears bib overalls she sees out of the corner of her eye but who disappears whenever she tries to look at him full-on. A gypsy, too, in a twirling purple skirt. And a Civil War soldier who stands in the back next to the grave of the son he never met.

"Sapphire earrings. That big ugly fly brooch with the giant emerald eyes. All those gold chains." Sudie leans back and crosses her arms, just waiting for Gabe's astonishment.

And astonished he is. "You work out there all *alone*?"

"You look a little pale, Gabe," says Carla.

"The dead aren't anything to worry about. It's the living

who make my job a nightmare," Sudie explains. "Vandalism. Chasing off drunk kids from the college. Grave robbers."

"Grave robbers?" Gabe really does look pale.

"Sure, every once in a while. 'Specially if the wrong person catches wind about somebody like Mrs. O'Reilly getting buried in all her finery."

"You about ready?" I say to Sudie.

"I was actually wondering . . . ," Gabe says to me, shifting his weight, acting like he's still all nervous about Sudie's story. But it's not that he's worried about. "I mean, if you didn't have plans, I was thinking we could grab a bite to eat." He turns to Sudie. "But that's okay if you can't. Some other time—"

"You two go on and go to lunch," Sudie interrupts, then winks at me. "I'll be just fine."

I look from her, to Gabe, to Carla, back to Sudie again. What in the world is she thinking? She just gloried on about me breaking up with Bryan. Just revealed to me she knows about this baby I'm carrying. I sure don't need her trying to set me up with Gabe. There is something about him, something that has the potential to get complicated quick. He isn't like anyone around Riverton I've ever met. He doesn't have the same edge that in others means anger and fists hiding behind their wanting eyes. Baby or no baby, I don't want or need another man after Bryan. "I—"

"It's settled, then," Sudie blurts before I can protest. "Gabe, I'll be much obliged if you take her to lunch and then home for me. Pancake place on State Road 62—right on the way out to our place—has all-you-can-eat on Sundays."

❧

"Sorry about that," I say once Gabe and I are outside.

"Why are you sorry?"

"Sudie and Carla. They're just . . ." Maybe he didn't catch the fact that they were trying to match us up. I don't want to make this a bigger deal than it already is. ". . . funny, is all."

"Nice people, that's for sure. That one woman. . . they really give pies to everybody new?"

"Yeah, they do."

"Nice."

A flock of Canada geese flies over the street toward the river, squawking the whole way. The snow from the night before has already melted, and the sun feels warm on my face.

"Where's your car?"

"Near the park."

The Riverton city park is a couple of blocks from the church, and instead of getting in his car right away I head toward the river. "I like to take breaks from work out here when the weather's nice."

"I can see why," he says, following me.

On the river, a barge slides past so slow and wakeless it appears as if it's being pulled by some unseen force rather than motoring itself. A couple of families from church are taking advantage of the sun, their children clambering onto the swings.

"Stay away from the slide," one of the mothers calls. "It's too wet still."

A boy, about the same age as Jayden would be now, runs down to the riverbank and stops along the sandy edge. He waves at the barge, and I can hear him erupt with giggles as a sailor waves back.

My heart aches and I force back tears, but I am determined not to show emotion around Gabe. I guess I thought grieving for Jayden would lessen by now, but it hovers in my chest, like the hawks circling above the trees. I never know when it's going to come over me, things like this little boy, hearing someone in the church nursery singing "Jesus Loves Me" like I sang to him. Hormones from carrying this baby don't help.

I take a deep breath and settle myself on a massive old log, long smoothed by the river. The air smells clean and new as if the water washes the earth as it passes through. Grass tapers off to the riverbank, and I wonder what Jayden would've thought about the feel of it under his toes, if he would've liked the blue sky and bright sun and the chug of the big barge engine. I think about these things and how I'll never, ever know.

Just like I'll never know about my baby if I give him up.

The boy picks up rocks, one at a time, and throws them into the water.

Kerplunk.

Plunk.

Kerplunk.

Gabe picks one up and launches it, skipping it half a dozen times.

The boy turns to him in wonder, and Gabe skips another. Then another.

A gray squirrel scampers up the white bark of a nearby sycamore, and a blue heron flies low enough I can hear its wings pushing against the wind. The heron dives into the frigid water and comes up with a fish, juggling it in its long beak until at last he swallows it. Around the far bend of the river a smokestack chugs out steam so fluffy and white it resembles clouds. A bird of prey—maybe a peregrine, maybe a Cooper's, it's too high to tell—circles above several times before disappearing over another patch of trees. The world is quiet except for the occasional high-pitched screech of a ring-billed gull, the banter of the other children on the swings behind us, the *plunk-kerplunk* of Gabe's skipping stones.

The boy tosses one more stone, then turns and runs back to his mother. She opens her arms to gather him. I'll never know that feeling either if I give my baby up.

Gabe brushes his sandy hands off on the thighs of his jeans and moseys over. "Mind if I sit?"

I scoot down to make more room. "Sure. I mean, no. I mean—"

He laughs. "I'll take that as a yes." He looks around at the river, the paths, the trees. "It's nice out here."

"One of my favorite spots."

"You have others?"

"A few. You'd be surprised, all that's around here. Waterfalls, cliffs, hollers . . . "

"Hollers?"

"Yeah. Hollers. You call them somethin' different?"

"I don't know," he says, exaggerating what sounds like a TV anchorman's precise cadence. "A gorge, a valley. *Holler* is what I do if I'm angry."

"A holler's a holler. And nothin's wrong with my accent. Wasn't even an accent to anybody until you came to town."

"Maybe not. But it's cute. So's your dimples." He grins and nudges my side, too close to my growing belly, even if it is well hidden under my coat and oversize sweater.

I jump up. "You ready to go?"

"Sure," he says, bewilderment on his face at my sudden movement.

"Pancakes. All you can eat," I say, then start walking fast toward his car.

13

"You gonna tell me which way to go?" Gabe asks.

"That way." I nod right.

His hands grip the wheel loose, but in control. Doesn't take long before the road out of town opens up and we pass dilapidated farmhouses, patches of homes with mid-century architecture that were most certainly some family's pride until the factories started closing and they couldn't afford repairs. Trailers like the ones in Shady Acres sag, some in clumps, some alone on barren patches of land. Half the billboards advertise drug-treatment centers and the other half casinos and adult entertainment along the river.

"Is it really that bad down here?" He glances at me, then back to the road.

"What's that?"

"The drugs. Heroin."

His hair looks freshly cut, the brown layers precise but with enough styling product to make it look messy, like the celebrities on magazine covers. He wears a crisp, plaid button-down with a high-end logo on the chest, and a winter coat same style and logo as the students from Riverton College. No wonder he has a hard time believing the news about "down here."

"You have no idea."

"They've got us carrying Narcan in the ambulance. Guys in the department say they can hardly keep it stocked they use it so much. I only saw it used a couple of times when I was in training."

"You'll use it plenty here."

I'm not used to someone who doesn't know my story, someone who didn't read in the paper about Jayden's passing or Mama's court appearances. I wonder what it would be like to live in a place where the paper doesn't print the police reports.

"Has it always been like this?"

We pass a tractor turning over a frozen gray field, the dirt brown and rich behind it. I remember how long the summers seemed when I was little, when it didn't matter we were poor and Sudie wasn't telling us of all the graves she was having to call Shorty to dig. Running barefoot around the fields and hollers, catching butterflies by day and fireflies by night with the neighbor kids without being afraid of stepping on a used syringe, somebody renting a movie and shining it on the clean white side of somebody's trailer. We could count on each other, back then. Some of us still do, like me and Sudie, folks at church, the diner. But it's not the same. Not near the same.

"No. Not always."

I didn't tell him that it's hard to find anybody nowadays who hasn't lost a mama or a brother, a daughter or a sister. I didn't tell him that first it was the toothpaste factory, then the metal smelting factory, then the shipping facility, then the refrigerator factory, then the furniture factory that closed, wiping out jobs, then lives. The only reason I remember the story of Sherman marching from Atlanta to Savannah from history class is because it feels like something evil's been marching over our land burning everything down too. Same as those bugs killing all the ash trees. Can't see it outright, but the hurt's plain as day.

"You know anybody who's died from it?"

His question shoots panic fire straight through me. I like not being known for what's happened to me. "No . . . I mean . . ."

His eyes soften at my sudden unease. Never have been able to hide my emotions too well.

"I'm sorry," he says. "I didn't think—"

"I don't want to talk about it." I'm surprised at the way I snap at him, but at least I keep the tears down this time.

It's not his fault he doesn't have any idea about Mama and Jayden. Still, I snap like the opossums and grown coons do at Sudie when all she's trying to do is help.

A shadow crosses over the car.

"Watch out!" I cry.

Gabe sees the dark form about the same time as I do.

Thud!

It collides with the front of the car. Or we collide with it. Hard to tell which.

Gabe slams on the brakes and puts the car in park. The smell of burned tire rubber hangs in the air when we get out of the car.

"What is it?" Gabe asks when we see the brown speckled mound on the side of the road.

"Looks like a redtail."

"A red-tailed hawk? Is it alive?"

"I can't tell," I whisper, stepping slow and careful toward the rumpled feathers. When I'm close enough to peer over the top of it, the head rises slightly. A dark eye blinks and fixes on us. "He's still alive. Pretty dazed, though. Probably concussed."

"Birds can get concussions?"

I straighten and stare at Gabe. "You're an *EMT*."

"Oh. Yeah. Right," he says, then runs a hand through his hair.

He may be cute, but I don't think he's going to be much help.

One wing of the bird twitches, then falls limp. Though

his eyes follow me, the pupils are small, unchanging. Not a good sign, according to what I've heard Sudie say.

"Do you have a blanket in your car? A towel, maybe?" I crouch down beside the hawk. "And a box? A laundry basket? Something like that?"

"I think I might." He turns and hurries back to the car.

I inch closer to the hawk. He tilts his head, as if he wants to ask me a question, but he shows no signs of trying to get away. If he had his wits about him at all, he'd be claws out and fighting.

"Will this work?" Gabe hands me a cardboard box, empty except for a plaid wool blanket.

"Perfect."

"How are we going to catch him?" His brow is wrinkled with worry, and he has a funny look on his face.

"You scared of a bird?"

"No." He straightens, and his cheeks pink up.

"If you say so." I take the blanket from him, and he steps back. "I'm gonna toss this over the top of him, then secure his talons. It's best to have gloves, but this'll have to do. Once I've got the talons, he can't do a whole lot. That's how they fight, with their talons."

He glances at me, one eyebrow raised with concern, then back at the bird again. "Then what?"

"Then I'll put him in the box. Think you can handle holding it?"

"Absolutely," he says, but I think we both know he doesn't sound so sure.

I lean over the top of the hawk again, and it opens its beak a little.

"Do they bite?"

"Oh yes," I say as gravely as I can, and I try not to laugh. "It's the talons, not the beaks, you have to worry about with raptors."

Gabe runs a hand through his hair again and breathes out hard, like he's trying to muster up some courage.

"It's okay; you'll get through this," I tease. "Just hold the box still."

The hawk turns his head to one side and then the other to get a good look at me.

"What if he comes at you?" Gabe says, behind me.

"Then I'll swat him toward you."

"Oh . . ."

I grin and let Gabe think on that, then spread the blanket out wide.

Sudie says redtails are the smartest raptors around. Creamy white feathers on his chest and underbelly are speckled with brown and gray. His back and tail are a mixture of mahogany and rich browns, rusty red on the tail, and a stripe of dark brown along the edge of it.

"It's okay, baby. We're here to help ya. It's okay . . ." I keep assuring the bird as I move closer. "There's no blood, so hopefully nothing's broken. If his wing's broke, he'll have to be put down."

"Can't a vet fix a wing?"

"Hardly ever. Most of the time, even if they do they can't go back to the wild. They never heal right."

Overhead another hawk circles. Looks a lot bigger than this one.

"Wonder if that's his mate."

Gabe follows my gaze and watches the second hawk circle a couple more times before perching in a giant cottonwood tree and fixing its eyes on us.

"It's okay; I'm not gonna hurt you. If that's your bride, we'll fix you up and get you right back to her." I keep talking until I know I'm close enough to keep from missing, then throw the blanket over the top of the hawk.

He struggles underneath it.

"Oh, geesh . . . oh! Oh!" Gabe shrieks like a girl, and over my shoulder I see him ducking and cowering as if the bird's coming right at him.

"Will you *stop*?" I scold him while trying to find and hold on to the bird's talons through the blanket. "He can't get to you now. Bring the box over here. I'm gonna pick him up and stuff him in there. All right?"

Gabe's face is the same creamy color as the hawk's chest feathers.

"Who let you become a medic?" I smile as I say it so he knows I'm teasing.

"That's different," he says. "Humans are . . . well . . . they're more predictable."

"Right. I'd rather deal with animals any day."

He hasn't met the humans I've encountered. I crouch down and put my hand over the thick, round middle of the hawk's body. The darkness from the blanket cover helps to calm him. The thick, tough claws are pulsing, trying to fight, and I am careful to avoid the places where they taper to their sharp, hook-like ends. Once secured, I pick him up and start toward Gabe. He's holding the box as if it's already got something contaminated in it.

"Gabe. Honestly." His apprehension is getting a little old.

"All right. Okay. I got it."

I can tell he's working hard to stand still as I set the bird inside, then fold the flaps of the box over the top.

"What now?" Gabe looks at me like a little kid lost at the mall.

"Let's set him in the backseat. I'll stay back there with him, make sure he doesn't fly out or anything."

"That'd be good."

I grin. "We'll take him to Sudie's."

"Sudie?"

"The lady I was at church with. She's my neighbor. She rehabs birds and all kinds of wild animals. I help her when I can."

His eyes widen. "She doesn't have snakes, does she?"

The look on his face causes me to burst out laughing, and I can hardly stop.

"What's so funny?"

"I just had this impression of you is all." I wipe tears from my eyes.

He's not amused. "I don't like snakes."

"She doesn't have any snakes. Only reptile she's got is a turtle. You're not afraid of them, are you?"

"No." He sounds a little defensive, and gingerly helps settle me and the box with the hawk in the back seat of his car.

"I guess we're missing out on all-you-can-eat pancakes," I say when we pass the restaurant.

"I guess so."

Every so often I catch him looking at me in his rearview mirror. Whatever impression he had of me must be changing too. I'm reminded of Sudie's hand on my belly back at church. If Gabe's thinking he likes me, he won't once he learns I'm carrying a child, especially Bryan's child. If he can't handle a redtail with a bump on its head, ain't no way he could handle all that.

14

"Turn here."

I watch Gabe's eyes in the mirror to see if they change when he sees the Shady Acres sign, then the Johnsons' place with the furniture in the front yard, then the next neighbor with a sagging side porch and a faded plastic toy house tipped over on its side, then the next neighbor who used leftover bright-yellow road paint to brighten up the lattice around their redwood stoop, then the next one that used to be a white trailer before a thick layer of moss grew all over the side of it. Thanks to them, I learned moss grows on the north side of things.

He blinks without any visible change to his face.

"Follow this drive all the way to the end." The gravel crunches and pops under his tires.

"That's my place," I say as we pass my faded blue trailer. He brakes.

"You don't need to stop—keep on going to the end to Sudie's. There. On the right. That's hers."

He gets out and opens the door for me.

I start to get out while keeping hold of the box, but I gasp at a sharp tug along my lower side. *The baby.*

"You okay?"

I focus on breathing slow so I don't let on that it's something else entirely. "Hunger pain," I say.

"Sorry about the pancakes."

"It's all right." I force back a wince.

"Here, let me take it." He peers at the hawk, who isn't moving under the towel. "Is he okay?"

"We'll see. I'm not unwrapping him until he's in the cage." I use the car door to pull myself up and out, the pain dull but still very much there. I decide to fib so I can stall a little longer. "I think maybe I got a little carsick."

"Take a few deep breaths. That's what I used to tell my little sister, who got carsick driving on a straight road," he laughs. He sets the box on the hood, then looks around at Sudie's place, the neighbors'.

The image of a white Mercedes, red taillights, Mary's face in the back window flashes through my mind. Will he decide who I am based on this place too?

"Peaceful out here."

He seems to mean it. For now.

"It's all right," I offer, as if I need to assure him I'm okay with living here.

"What's that for?" He nods toward the cage where the kestrel is studying him.

"That's an elevator cage. Where the hawks and other birds in rehab go to get strong."

I take a few steps, breathing in the cool air, closing my eyes, and turning my face up to the sun to feel the warmth. "Stay here while I run inside and get a towel for him, for the cage we'll put him in. I'll be right back."

Sudie keeps old towels for the rescues under her kitchen sink. Away from Gabe, I rub at the pain in my side, but it doesn't help.

Lord, please don't let there be something wrong.

I know it'd serve me right for the times I've thought about how to get out of this mess.

I lean against the counter and take a few slow, deep breaths. That helps more than anything. Sunlight filters through the green soda bottle by the window next to me, creating a rainbow of light on the opposite wall.

"What's that for?" I asked Sudie about that bottle one day, years ago. She never moves it.

"Tears, child. It's to remind me that the Lord collects all our tears. Psalm 56."

I can't recall a time I've seen her cry, besides when we buried Jayden. But working at a cemetery, I'm sure she's had plenty of occasions.

The pain is nearly gone, so I crouch down carefully and grab a couple of towels. Back outside, I motion for Gabe to come with me. "The cage is back this way."

Sudie's built three bigger, open-air cages along the back of her place, screen and chicken-wire sides to protect them from foxes and coyotes and other predators. We head over to the smallest of these placed against the side of her trailer, which creates a bit of a shield against the wind. Winter and disuse have stiffened the latches and hinges, and the door creaks as I lower it. "Go ahead and set the box down."

He does, and surprises me by kneeling next to it.

"Feeling brave?"

"Trying to." He grins.

I kneel next to him and show him how the talons aren't hard to find under the blanket. When I'm sure I've got ahold of them, I lift the bundle out and place it in the cage.

Glassy-eyed and clearly still dazed, the bird hardly moves when I pull the blanket off of him everywhere except where I still hold his talons. "I think he looks worse."

Even when I turn him onto his belly his head hangs limp, enough so that I risk letting go of his talons so I can roll the towel into a tube. I arrange it in the shape of a donut around him like I've seen Sudie do, tucking it in around his sides and under his head to keep it up a bit. If a bird can be appreciative, he appears to be just that as I smooth his back feathers and rest my hand on him long enough to feel him breathe fast and shallow.

"Is he going to be okay?" Gabe asks, most of his skittish-ness seemingly worn off.

"I don't know. Sudie'll have a better idea."

I lift up the side door of the cage and we both reach for the same latch. His hand is warm and lingers on top of mine before I quick pull it away. "He'll be fine for now," I say and start walking back around to the front of the trailer before it gets any more awkward lingering there.

"Still up for pancakes?" he says, behind me.

"I don't know. Kinda lost my appetite."

"Oh. Right. Carsick."

I feel a twinge of guilt. He's just trying to be a friend. "I've got Coke at my place."

"Okay."

I point to my trailer. "You can park in that patch right next to the door. I'm gonna walk if you don't mind."

Inside my trailer, I click on the lights and see the place different. I can't remember the last time I've had a guest besides Sudie, much less a man over. Smells clean enough now, like the lemon and orange cleaners I used for weeks scrubbing every inch of smoke film and drug-making residue off everything. The refrigerator hums in the kitchen. A basket of clean, folded laundry is on the couch from when I went to the laundromat a couple days ago. The carpet's clean and the walls are white, two improvements I made with the help of Bud and Larry and the donations from the church after Jayden died. A real oil painting hangs on the wall over my TV, a painting of a creek, dappled with sunlight in the woods. I found it for a couple of dollars at the Goodwill. Reminds me of the creek behind Shady Acres where I'd hoped to one day teach Jayden how to catch frogs. I could teach my baby to catch them . . . if I keep him. . . .

"Have a seat," I nod toward the couch and move the basket to the floor.

Turning on the radio helps with the quiet, and the ice in the plastic cups cracks and pops as I pour Coke over them. He hasn't sat down yet. Instead, he's looking at the bookshelf, pulling out a book on North American wildlife, a castaside from the library book sale a couple years back. He sets that down and bends slightly to look at a framed picture of me and Jayden, one I printed off my phone at the Walmart shortly after he died.

He sets it down when he hears me crossing the room.

"Did you always want to be an EMT?" I say and hand him a cup. I still feel an ache low in my belly, and I'm glad to finally sit down again.

"Thanks." He takes a long sip, then sits next to me. "I did. Ever since I was in junior high. One of my friends, his dad was assistant coach of our soccer team. Big guy. Always cheering us on. One day in the middle of one of our games he just fell over. Heart attack. We were scared out of our wits. Somebody . . . someone's mom started CPR and I remember when the ambulance came. The paramedics jumped out, all their equipment, everything. They started working on him. Saved his life. I watched them bring him back and I knew right then that's what I wanted to do."

"Must be nice, being certain of what you want to do like that."

He nods. "What about you? What sort of dreams do you have?"

"You mean working at the diner and living in a trailer on the outskirts of Riverton isn't a dream come true?"

"I just meant—"

I laugh. He's cute when he's flustered. "It's all right. I suppose maybe I had dreams of being something more years ago. I don't know now, though."

"Really?"

A chunk of ice in my cup cracks and rises to the surface. "I don't really think about it."

"Everybody wants to be something when they're little."

I consider this and try to remember what I thought about, who I was, before, when the couch we're sitting on was new and didn't have black spots where strangers fell asleep holding cigarettes or joints, when my ears knew nothing about the sound of a baby screaming with the pain of withdrawal.

"You like animals," he says, more like an answer than a question.

"I do."

"Could you do Sudie's job?"

"Maybe someday. I'm fine right now with helping her. 'Sides that, I don't have the money or the setup to do it myself."

Gabe looks over his shoulder at the photograph. "Who's in that picture with you?"

I told him earlier I didn't want to talk about it. But now the truth is right here in front of us. "My little brother."

He looks around the room and I know what he's thinking. No car seat or playpen. No stray toys. No sign of a child at all. The awkward will only get worse if I don't tell him. If I do tell him . . . well, the worst that can happen is I'll have to watch his taillights leaving Shady Acres like Mary's did.

I take a deep breath. "He died a couple years ago."

More questions have to be forming in his head, the sort of questions everybody has when a baby dies. Babies don't just die, after all. I could tell him Jayden was poisoned, that it was an accident. But that's not what he's really wondering. I don't know how to answer for him what I don't have answers to myself.

"I'm so sorry," he says, finally.

"Yeah. Me too." Our glasses are empty, and I need a change of subject. "I'll get us more Coke." I start to get up but he grabs my hand.

"What happened to your brother, Jaycee? Where's your family? Do you live here all alone?"

I turn and face him. He puts his other hand on my arm, the warmth of his touch spreading up to my face. The kindness in his face overwhelms, confuses me. I close my eyes when I say, "You don't want to know."

He hangs his head, fiddles with his watch.

"I'm sorry. I just . . . ."

"You don't want to talk about it. You said that in the car. None of my business, really."

"It's not that. . . . Things . . . It's complicated."

He looks up at me and says simply, "Everybody's complicated, Jaycee."

"Maybe so." I head to the kitchen to refill our glasses. I can't imagine what could be complicated about his life. Probably grew up in a nice two-story house, had a backyard with a swing set, lemonade stands, and soccer games on the weekends. Clean new shoes.

He stands and goes over to the bookshelf again.

"Where'd you grow up?" I ask.

"Outside Columbus."

"Ohio?"

"Indiana."

"What could be complicated in Columbus, Indiana?" This comes out with a little more snark than I intended.

He shrugs. "I have good parents. Never wanted for anything. That much is true."

"Like I said, doesn't sound complicated."

"Maybe not. But that doesn't mean I can't understand something hard."

I glance at the picture of me and Jayden on the bookshelf. It was my fault he died. Could he understand that?

He crouches now beside the bookcase, running a finger along the book spines, including the romance set in North Carolina. "You got a lot of good books. You like to read?"

"When I have time." I set our refilled glasses on the coffee table. "You?"

"All the time. I get on author jags. Clive Cussler. Tom Clancy. Espionage. History's cool too. Civil War. World War Two." He pulls a book from the shelf. *Watership Down.* "I loved this one."

"Really?"

"My mom used to read it to me when I was little," he says.

"I read it in high school." I take it from him and flip through the pages, some still dog-eared, some full of pink and yellow highlighter stripes. I find my favorite passage and read it out loud:

"All the world will be your enemy, Prince with
a Thousand Enemies, and whenever they catch
you, they will kill you. But first they must catch
you, digger, listener, runner, prince with the swift
warning. Be cunning and full of tricks and your
people shall never be destroyed.

"I used to think what Frith said was true. That if I was cunning . . ." I don't want to talk about it, but there's something about him . . . I'm treading on stones I haven't stepped on before, ones where I'm not sure about my footing or how to steady myself. "All the world is an enemy. At least in this town."

"What makes you think it's better anywhere else? Columbus isn't exactly a utopia."

"I don't know. Too many reminders, I guess. Too many shadows."

"Of your brother?"

"I guess." Yeah, my brother. A father I never knew. Mama. The drugs. And this child growing inside me.

He pulls my hair back from my face and sets it gently on my back, and I can't help but take in the hardworking scent of him. For a second I feel like reaching to him, too, but that disappears quick as frozen breath on a winter morning.

"I'd like to know about him sometime . . . when you want to tell me," he says.

I take in his gray-blue eyes, his broad shoulders, the furrowed concern of his brow. A small place inside me trembles, and I wonder if this is how the redtail felt, eyes glassy with fear and pain and need as we scooped him up with our strange and human hands. I wonder if this is how the orphaned kits felt the night I saved them and not Jayden. They were so crazy from lack of milk, but kept fighting us as we tried to feed them one drop at a time.

"All right." I mean that. But I also mean what I say next. "But not now."

"Okay." He shifts his weight, lifts his hand toward me again, then drops it to his side. "I don't mean to pry. I just . . . I'd like to be able to get past cordial with you is all."

"I'm sorry," I say again, and cross my arms across my middle, hidden for now under my thick, oversize sweater. Maybe I just don't have much besides cordial to give.

He holds my gaze a moment longer, then steps toward the door. "All right. That's all right. Thank you for the Coke."

"You don't have to go," I blurt.

"I need to go."

I nod, then follow him as he walks out to his car. The neighborhood is quiet as it tends to be on Sunday afternoons, folks sleeping in or sleeping off the night before. The early spring grass gleams emerald under the bright afternoon sun.

Suddenly thumps and thuds break the stillness in the direction of the Johnsons' and I cringe.

"What in the world?" Gabe says.

"You're about to witness firsthand the wrath of Virginia Johnson."

Dewey Johnson flies booty first off their faded redwood stoop and lands with a muted thud a few feet shy of their long-abandoned, rusted-out grill. Virginia throws first one, then two, then three beer bottles out after him and slams the door shut.

Gabe looks astonished when he turns to me. "That happen often?"

"At least once a week. You haven't seen that in Columbus?"

He shakes his head and the two of us crumple into the kind of laughter that comes when nerves are tied up too long, all while Dewey Johnson stands and brushes himself off, and begins banging on the door of his own home.

Gabe's still laughing when he opens his car door, but he soon softens. "Thank you."

"For what?"

"For trusting me for lunch."

For trusting me, he says. "Okay . . . you're welcome."

"Let me know what happens with the hawk?"

"I will."

He shuts his door and the car engine turns, and my heart along with it. The taillights of his car blink as he drives away.

Lord have mercy, I think I like this boy.

Things are quiet again at the Johnsons' trailer, which I pass on the way to the community mailboxes after realizing I haven't checked mine since Friday. Like many in Shady Acres, they save everything, overflowing bags of aluminum cans, ancient televisions stacked on top of each other, and that horrific love seat, the floral pattern faded, gold foam stuffing sticking out of torn edges, and the constant smell of must hanging in the air. No wonder not even the junkies will steal their stuff. For some reason the Johnsons and others like them can't part with it, as if clinging to it will somehow keep the memories alive of when it was nice and new.

Sunlight reflects off the community stack of mailboxes clumped together and fixed to a couple of fence posts. I'm just about there when I see a familiar flash of orange and white where I'm about to step.

Another dirty syringe.

The cap is off, the needle bent and pointing up at the sky, where my foot would have landed.

Lord, have mercy.

Kids run around barefoot here all the time, doesn't matter the weather. I pick the filthy syringe up by the plunger and toss it into the nearby trash barrel like I've done with so many of the others I find.

At first I don't see anything but the usual Saturday mail in my mailbox: the phone bill, the electric bill, the water bill, a glossy mailer from the local ACE Hardware. I almost miss the letter from Mama stuck in the middle of the Dollar Tree mailer. Underneath the sheet of notebook paper is a form, along with a return envelope. *INDIANA DEPARTMENT OF CORRECTION: Application for Visiting Privileges.*

This is the tenth one she's sent me so far, and so far, I haven't filled a one of them out.

Dear Jaycee,

I've been going to hear the preacher every Sunday now, and I think I am starting to believe what he is saying is for someone like me. I wouldn't blame you for arguing against that. Not at all. But I had to write and tell you what he said.

He was talking about the woman at the well, the one who was there in the middle of the day, and how Jesus asks her for a drink. He talked about how that woman probably knew she wasn't worthy. She doesn't believe Jesus at first. But she's so thirsty and he promises she won't be thirsty anymore. When she's finally convinced and asks for the living water, he calls her out on all the men she's been with, all the terrible things she's done. He already knew all those things about her before he met her at the well.

I've heard Reverend Payne talk about that story many times. I remember learning it when I was a girl. But today it sounded different.

All of a sudden, in that room full of people and that preacher, I felt like I was the only one there, and I realized, the Lord knows all about me, too, and that if he saved that woman, I might have a chance at being saved, too.

I'm so thirsty, Jaycee. I figure taking a chance on the Lord won't do me no more harm than I've already done to myself.

It don't erase the things I've done. I think maybe it just means I don't have to hide.

I love you.

Mama

I want to believe her.

I'm so tired of running all the time, even when I'm sitting still. Running from Mama. Running from Jayden's death and the hole it left inside me. Running from Bryan. Even running from Gabe, when he's just trying to be a friend.

Against my better judgment, I fill out the visitor form.

I think I might be thirsty too.

15

I put the visitor form in the return envelope and put it in the mailbox before I can change my mind. The Mama who got sent to prison isn't the Mama who's writing these letters of late, and more and more, with this baby coming, I sure do need a mama. Maybe she hasn't changed at all, but maybe . . . if the Lord did all those big miracles, maybe he can help her get back to the old Mama. The one who took me for ice cream on summer Friday nights when I was little even though she couldn't afford it; the one who taught me constellations and the difference between an ash tree and a walnut tree; the one who took me to the library every Saturday morning; the one who sang "You Are My Sunshine" and rubbed my back at night until I fell asleep; the one I was proud to have help my grade-school class make valentines . . .

Despite everything, I was always good at school.

Things were looking up for me too, right about the time Mama got her addiction. I was making the highest grades in Mr. Shockley's impossible middle school science class, which got me a seat at the lunch table with the other book-smart girls in my grade. I'd been sitting with them going on three weeks and had just sat down with my tray of square pizza, runny applesauce, and tater tots when I saw Mama's familiar frame lurching down the main hall toward where we sat in the cafeteria.

"You gonna eat your tater tots, Jaycee?" my friend Lynlie asked.

I got up quick. There was no time to answer her. I headed toward the lunch line and made an excuse to buy an extra carton of milk so I could hide.

Please, Lord. Not now, I remember praying.

"Jay-CEE-eee!" Mama called. At first, no one seemed to notice, but then she hollered again. "Jaycee, you forgot your lunch. I brought it for you."

A hush fell over the cafeteria.

Mama stood in the middle of the lunchroom wearing a bathrobe over a tube top and a pair of pajama pants with the top rolled down so her belly showed. The bones on her face stuck out, highlighted by dark circles under her eyes, which were flitting back and forth in their sockets. Her face was pocked with scars, which fit in among all the kids with acne, but I knew hers were from where she tried to scratch at invisible bugs on her skin. The muscles in her bony arm twitched as she held up the plastic superstore bag.

I didn't have a choice about what to do. Every single eye in that cafeteria followed me as I walked toward her.

"Thanks," I said, taking the bag.

"Ms. Givens, you're so sweet to bring Jaycee her lunch." Someone had alerted Mr. Earl, the principal, and he directed a sorrowful look my way as he approached us.

I'd never been so glad to see the principal in my life.

"Next time, if you just bring it to the front office, we'll make sure she gets it," he said with an overly kind tone.

The suggestion was lost on Mama, who swayed slightly in front of the silent audience.

I leaned in as if to hug her, but really just to tell her what to do next. "Go on home now, Mama."

The look in her eyes was something between sorry and shame, but that only lingered a moment before she turned and stared blankly at Mr. Earl. He took Mama gently by the arm and spoke softly into her ear as he escorted her away.

I took the bag and my uneaten lunch tray straight to the conveyor belt and hightailed it out of the cafeteria. I ran down the nearest hallway, where shop classes were held, the sound of the saws and other woodworking machines covering the sound of my weeping, and I found one of the janitor closets unlocked.

That was the first time I met Hersch. He was a janitor at the middle school back then, along with Miss Helen, a wiry old woman we called Candy on account of her flaming copper-dyed hair, which was white at the roots, making it look like candy corn to us kids. That day, he found me in his little closet at the end of the shop hall, my arms and legs crisscrossed so I could fit in the space between the stacks of toilet paper and Dustbane Sweeping Compound—that nasty stuff sprinkled on vomit to soak it up. With Candy peering around the corner, Hersch reached up and pulled a clean rag off a shelf. He knelt down so his eyes were at my level, handed me the rag, and motioned for me to use it to dry my face.

"You can stay here anytime you're needing to feel better," he said, his voice gravelly, his eyes droopy with compassion.

I did use the space again. More than once. The smells of Pine-Sol and bleach-clean rags were a comfort when the schoolwork wasn't enough to keep my mind off the things happening at my home.

Good grades or not, after that I never did get asked to sit at Lynlie's table again. And after that, I took the high road with Mama, keeping my mind in another place, a safe place, so that even if we were in the same room together I was a world apart. She wasn't Mama anymore. I knew from health class and all the teaching the school'd been doing to try to educate us on the dangers of heroin that her mind had been chemically changed by the drug, so that the longer she took it, the more she'd need it, and the more she needed it, the less chance I had of the Mama who once cared about me ever coming back.

"What is the Lord asking you to give up today?" Reverend Payne's question rolls through my head again as I wait outside on my trailer stoop for Sudie to get home and check out the hawk. Clouds push across the sky above the bare and swaying arms of the ash tree, and I wonder if this is the summer I'll have to cut it down.

"Sudie!" I take off running toward her place when she finally drives by.

"Land sakes, what is it, child?" She heaves herself up out of her car.

"A redtail. Ran right into it out on the state road. Put him out back. He's pretty bad."

"Let's go have a look," she says, dirt on her face and under her nails from working at the cemetery.

The brown feathers are barely visible over the towel, and he is so still I am sure he has not survived. I tell her how it happened, that me and Gabe were on our way to the Pancake House when it swooped out of nowhere and flew right into the grille of Gabe's car. "I did like you taught, throwing a blanket over him and holding his talons. Made sure to put his head up on that towel there."

"Good. That's good," she says, unlatching the side of the cage.

A wing stretches out, wide and flat and filling the cage it's so enormous.

"I'd say that's a good sign," Sudie laughs. "Looks like a young one, too. Talons are still pretty smooth."

The bird rises and stands then, raising then stretching

both wings before folding them back in against itself. He hangs his head as if he's sorry to have startled us.

"Concussed, for sure. Seems to be favoring that left wing, too."

"Is it broken?"

"Hard to say. Let's give him a day. Let the shock wear off. We'll try to feed him tomorrow. See if he's moving it any better." She closes and latches the door.

"How was the cemetery?"

"Not as bad as I thought. Things are greening up so much, I'm gonna have to mow next time, though. Your brother's spot looks real nice. All filled in. Daffodils you planted last fall are already blooming."

I'd almost forgotten I planted those, pressing the brown, hard, papery bulbs deep into the soil, believing somehow they'd turn into long, soft green stems and leaves and bright-yellow blooms.

"Sudie . . . I'm scared."

"I know, child."

Everything I've been holding in about this baby comes pouring out, how I thought me and Bryan were being careful, how I kept making excuses for my cycle being late until it was too late to have an abortion, how I don't want to get an abortion anyway, how I thought Bryan and I could get married and work things out, how I thought he'd change once he found out I was carrying his child.

I tell her about Mary in the bathroom at the Red Pepper and the bruises Bryan was starting to leave on me, too, and how Hersch just happened to be finishing up at the diner last night. I tell her all this and she listens, just listens, neither angry nor sad, neither blaming nor disappointed.

Then I tell her I'm afraid—afraid of loving this child and afraid I won't. A child whose face I've never seen except in dreams, whose tiny limbs I've just begun to feel pressing against me, like butterflies stretching their wings in cocoons. A child whose certain birth reminds me of Jayden, who didn't ask to be born addicted or to have a mama who cared more about heroin than him but who hadn't had a choice.

"My baby doesn't have a choice either. I have nothing to give him. No way out of this place, this life."

She nods and turns her face toward the sun. "The Lord is gracious to us when we ask him for wisdom."

"How do you think he decides what kind of parents people will have? I mean, why didn't he give me a mama who's clean and a chance to know more about my father than just pictures and a grave?"

"How does he decide who's born at all, child? And after that, who survives? Why am I still around and over sixty and there are children . . ." Her voice trails off and for a moment it looks like she might be near tears. But then she turns from the sun and looks at me, as serious as I've ever seen her. She motions toward the side of her trailer where last summer's milkweed stands tall and gray and stiff. "I ever tell you about the monarchs?"

"You said this is where they lay their eggs." She always taught me to stay away from the milkweed in the early summer. Their tiny white egg sacs cling to the underside of the milkweed leaves until they hatch and grow into adults in time to migrate before the cold sets in.

She nods. "They're on their way back now. From Mexico. Lord only knows how they get all the way down there and all the way back here. Takes four generations of them, traveling on a hunch and the Lord's great mercy. Trusting whatever he's put inside them that makes them know which turn of the wind to follow, which ray of sun to aim for, from here to the mountain coast of Mexico and back again. Four generations. Can you imagine that?"

I shake my head.

"I'm not sure we're much different. Oh, we like to act like we are, planning for tomorrow when not a one of us knows what tomorrow will bring. But we know nothing, really. Only thing we can do is the best we can with what we've got. And trust him for the rest."

"But what have I got?"

She takes my hand. "You got a chance, child. You may not have had a choice in this, but you can give your baby a chance. It's up to you to decide what the best chance for him will be."

16

A chance hasn't crossed my mind. Maybe because I've never really had one.

Reverend Payne said Moses' mother gave him up not because she didn't love him. She gave him up because she did. She chose to set him in the river. She chose to give him a chance at life.

I feel the flutter of the baby against my belly and I imagine him stretching inside as if he knows what I am thinking, as if he already knows about this chance he could have to live without the burdens I carry, as if he can sense what it would be like to have a mama and a daddy, and to be wanted and loved by both. As if he knows, like those butterflies, which way I'm supposed to let him go.

The morning sun angles into the diner, catching on glasses of ice water so that they gleam like crystal. I smile at the customers and top off the coffee in the mugs of those sitting at the counter. Hersch fills plates with eggs and pancakes, and I catch myself resting the serving tray on the bump of my belly as I put the plates on it.

I can't hide this from everyone else much longer.

I push that thought from my mind and focus on the sound of conversation, full and buzzing at the start of the day. The *scrape-slice-flip, scrape-slice-flip* of Hersch's steel spatula on the grill top gives it rhythm. Old man Chester Flynn, who owns the hardware, complains to Joe, one of the veterans who is partially deaf, about the town council's decision to give a national big-box hardware chain a permit to build out by the interstate. Shorty Smith shuffles in and orders his usual English muffin, hold the butter, and three eggs over easy.

A middle-aged woman, complexion smooth as china, fine-gauge sweater over her shoulders, sits at a booth with a girl who appears to be her daughter. I'd put money on the chance they're here for a college visit, judging from the red and blue folder on their table with *Riverton College* in bold letters along with several photographs of smiling students.

The mother watches with scrutiny the girl's every bite, and when I stop by to ask if they'd like anything else, the mother declines for her. The girl looks at me and shrugs as I scribble down their final tab and set it facedown on the edge of the table. Somehow, her eyes remind me of my own.

It's almost eleven when I look at my watch. Gabe will be in soon, and my chest burns when I think about the way he pushed my hair back. The thick curve of his shoulders. The deep dimple on his left cheek.

"So, how were pancakes yesterday?" Carla asks, setting a tray of steaming-hot silverware, fresh from the dishwasher, on the counter. She sets a tall stack of white linen napkins next to it and tosses me a drying towel.

"Pancakes?" I always have liked rolling silver in the mid-morning lull, something about the folding, arranging, and wrapping up that helps pass the time.

"Yeah—you and Gabe were off to get pancakes yesterday . . . ?" she says, one eyebrow raised.

"Oh, pancakes. Right." I finish rolling another set of silverware and set it alongside the half-dozen Carla's already made. "By the way, thanks a lot for that subtle setup. Talk about awkward."

"Go ahead and roll your eyes now. You'll be glad I did that someday. So . . . how'd it go?"

"About as well as you could expect, considering he nearly killed a redtail."

"What?"

I tell her the whole story. "So we never actually had pancakes."

"Never a dull moment with you." She laughs. I don't.

"Carla, I don't want a boyfriend. Took all I had to break up with Bryan Saturday night."

"You did? About time!" She sobers. "I get that. I do."

"No, you don't," I snap, and am surprised by tears that well up in my eyes.

"Jaycee, are those tears? What on earth? I'm sorry, honey. I was just tryin' . . . Gabe's a nice young man. And *normal*. You know as well as I do we don't get *normal* around here very often."

"I know." I sniff and chuckle at that and use one of the napkins to wipe my eyes.

"You're not crying over Bryan, are you? We oughta be celebrating that."

"No, no. That was long overdue."

"Somethin' else bothering you then? I certainly didn't mean to upset you."

I shake my head and straighten, aware of the high-maintenance mother and daughter approaching the register.

The mother watches me punch the numbers into the register like she watched her daughter eat her breakfast. Her eyes settle on my middle. "So, when are you due?"

Her words are loud. Too loud. The gleam in her eye is the same one I've seen a thousand times from the college students who watched me pay for groceries with Mama's food stamps, shocked that the coupons actually exist and that folks use them, then a glance of pity, sometimes a smirk as Jayden slept, fastened in his car seat in the front of the cart. Feels the same as when a car full of them drives by, shouting "Townies!" and curse words, as if we're a different breed of people altogether than the ones in the cozy suburbs they came from.

I open my mouth knowing I'm supposed to give an answer to a customer's question, but nothing comes out.

"Well, spring babies are *wonderful.*" Her voice seems to boom across the diner as she slides a fifty-dollar bill across the counter. "My Anna Rose here is a late-spring baby."

I try to force a smile at Anna Rose, who looks panic-stricken, but tears spill from my eyes instead, so fresh on the surface from talking with Carla moments before.

"Go ahead and keep the change, sweetheart," the mother says, reaching across the counter to pat my hand.

Sorry, Anna Rose mouths to me as she follows her mother out the door.

I turn to the wall and the double coffeemaker behind me, my entire body hot with shame. I can't look at Carla or Hersch. I can't look across the dining room to see who else heard, even though I am sure every person in there did. I go through the motions of making a new batch of coffee for the one pot that's empty: replace the liner, scoop in the grounds, rinse what's left of the old coffee from the pot, set it on the burner, flip the switch.

Fake it. Just keep faking it. Fake that you're not pregnant. Fake that you're fine. Fake that you're asleep when one of Mama's one-night stands or a junkie finds their way to your bedroom in the middle of the night. Fake that you're fine when friends aren't allowed to play at your house because it's in a run-down trailer park. Fake that the bruises your boyfriend leaves don't hurt. Fake that you're fine when your boyfriend is sleeping around because at least he's still sleeping with you. Fake it all so the hurt doesn't have to be real.

A black stream of coffee slowly begins to steam into the pot.

Carla is next to me now, her hand on my arm. "Jaycee. Honey."

I shake my head, sure if I say a word or look at her I will fall completely apart.

"I don't know how I didn't see this," she says.

The doorbell rings.

A new customer.

I smooth my apron down and grab the other pot that's hot and full.

I turn toward the counter and run right into Gabe's chest.

Coffee sloshes and stings as I jump back, but I keep ahold of the pot. I can't drop it. It'll break. But the coffee is burning. Stinging.

The pot shatters on the ground and my hand is shaking now, pain shooting up my arm. The whole top of my hand glistens, and at first I think it's wet with coffee until I realize several layers of skin are scalded.

Hersch pulls the dish towel off the side of his pants and wraps it around my hand. The two men who'd just come in stand at the counter and gape as Carla shoos me into the back, Gabe following us and carrying a cardboard box.

When did he get here? Did he hear too?

One look in his eyes and I know he did.

I sit in the chair at Carla's desk and set my arm on the table we use for our breaks.

"Let's see the damage," she says, gently unwrapping Hersch's towel.

Gabe sets his box on the edge of the desk. "Here. Let me."

I bite the inside of my cheek to keep myself from yelping as Carla moves aside and he unwraps the rest. If I hadn't seen that the skin was gone already, I'd wonder if he was pulling my skin off with it.

"Lord, have mercy," Carla gasps.

Gabe inhales sharply.

The top of my hand looks like raw meat, the tissue where skin used to be white and pearly and streaked with blood.

"Second, maybe third degree." Gabe pulls a couple of packs of gauze and a first aid wrap out of the box. He doesn't look at me, won't look at me, as he runs his hand through his hair like he did when we were standing alongside the road staring at the redtail yesterday. "I brought these from the firehouse. Expired supplies. Thought you and your neighbor could use them."

"Good thing we have a resident paramedic here," says Carla. She forces a smile which does nothing to lighten the mood.

Gabe pulls a small bottle of liquid from the box, then kneels beside me. He lifts my arm from the table, arranges the towel, and sets my arm on it.

Heat rushes through me, as much from him as from the throbbing pain of the burn.

"I'm going to rinse it with this saline. It'll be cool, but it shouldn't hurt," he says, and finally we lock eyes. "At least not any more than it already does."

He's right. My whole arm is shaking from the pain. At first I jump at the shock of the sensation against the scalded wound, but then it feels okay. Cool. Welcome.

"This is antibiotic ointment." He pulls a small tube from the box. "You'll want to clean and slather it with this until it's scabbed over. These burns have a habit of getting infected quick."

He is so close I can smell the musky scent of the shampoo he used, his hair still damp from a shower. His temples pulse, tense, as he smooths the ointment across my hand, then covers it with gauze and secures it with tape. My stomach clenches and my whole body is aware of him as he lifts my arm again and wraps it with a long sports bandage.

"Jaycee . . . ," Carla says softly. Her eyes are full with concern, and I know it's for far more than the burn.

My eyes fall to my waist.

Gabe returns my arm to the table again and stands, then backs away.

I start to say something, I want to say something, but I realize looking at him, seeing the shock still lingering on Carla's face, that hiding a truth can cause just as much hurt as letting it all out.

Carla kneels in front of me in the spot where Gabe had been.

"Does Bryan know?"

I shake my head no and risk glancing at Gabe. He turns his head away. Heat rises in my chest, my face. I didn't know how lonely I could feel with someone standing right next to me.

"Okay . . . all right." She grabs my free hand and holds it between hers. "We'll figure this out. It'll be all right. You'll see. We'll get through this. Together."

17

My hand throbs the rest of the day, and the next day, and the next, but that's not half as bad as Gabe giving me the silent treatment. I can't tell if he's mad or hurt or disappointed, or all of those combined.

Yesterday, he saw me pull into my usual parking space and drove on past the diner. He didn't come back until I'd gotten out and gone inside. When I hand in an order, he passes it on to Hersch. If I'm coming to pick up a tray of orders, he turns back to the grill as soon as he sees me. And if I'm in the back room that also has the only staff bathroom in it, he avoids it as if it's been quarantined.

"Give him time," Carla says when she finds me in the

break room stewing over it all. She knows everything now, how I'm at least six, probably closer to seven months along, how I haven't had any prenatal care, how Mama doesn't know about the baby either, and how every day I am more terrified thinking about how this baby is going to have to come out of me and I'm going to have to decide what to do. "I've known you for years and I'm still trying to wrap my brain around it all."

"But you don't act like he does, like I have a *disease*." I fuss and mess and pull my hair up into a bun on top of my head.

"He's taken a liking to you."

"Well, he must've figured out he shouldn't have, that someone like him doesn't deserve somebody like me, someone who got pregnant by a no-good, bottom-feeding, fist-wielding fool. I guess I deserve whatever's coming to me for that."

Carla sits down next to me. "You don't deserve anything bad because of this. We've all sinned, sugar. Some sins are just . . . well, more obvious than others."

I can't help but roll my eyes. "This one's obvious, all right."

"Gabe probably just wishes you would've told him up front, like I wish you would've told me, is all. He'll come around."

"How was I supposed to tell him when I hadn't even told you?"

"Or Bryan."

"Or Bryan. Don't remind me." Elizabeth Blair's pinched face comes to mind.

Carla gives me a look I know means a lecture is coming. "Have you made a doctor's appointment yet?"

"No."

"You only have a handful of weeks left to work with."

"I know." She's offered to pay for the doctor visit. I have no excuse for not calling, except it's one more thing I'm afraid of, one step closer to this baby being born. At least while he's inside me he's safe. I'm safe. My eyes fill with tears. "All this crying. I never cried about anything 'cept Jayden until the last few weeks."

"It's the hormones, honey."

Gabe comes around the corner and nearly slides to a stop when he sees us sitting there. "Oh . . . um . . . sorry," he mumbles, then turns back around and heads back to the dining room.

"I sure hope he's got a big bladder," Carla says. "Could become a problem if he doesn't."

That gets us laughing, and now I've got tears of frustration and hilarity spilling over. I wipe my face and shake my head. "I don't know, Carla." The baby turns inside me and I lay my hands across my middle. Since I've first felt him move, it seems like he moves more every day. "Sudie said I have a choice, that I can give this child a chance. I've been thinking about that, how this baby could have two parents. How he could grow up not knowing the things I know. How Reverend Payne said sometimes God can do more with what we give him than with what we hope he gives us."

"Yes."

"But the other choice I have is raising him myself."

She nods. "You were so good to Jayden."

"If I was so good to him, then why is he gone?"

"Honey, that wasn't your fault."

"Wasn't it? I was all he had. And that wasn't enough."

"You're not your mama, Jaycee."

"Because I don't do heroin? I'm like her in every other way. I can't give this baby a house with a yard that I don't have to worry about him stepping on a dirty needle. I have to work, so I can't stay home with him. I can't be sure he's safe with somebody else watching him. And there's not a chance I'd trust leaving him with Bryan or his family."

"Dear Lord, help me help this girl." Carla directs her prayer to the ceiling.

"Last night, I found a bunch of websites. Adoption agencies." I'd been flipping through them on my phone. "Spent a good two hours reading profiles and visiting websites of couples wanting to adopt. Couples who promise care and nurturing, love and safety."

Carla turns serious. She leans toward me. Puts her hand on top of mine and gives it a squeeze. "I am here for you whatever you decide."

"I didn't know there were so many ways of going about it. That I can pick the family if I want."

She nods. "I've heard there's open adoptions and closed adoptions and everything in between."

The baby moves inside me again, and with each movement fear twists with love. Already he feels like he's mine. He feels like a chance I've got to prove I'm not Lila Givens, or a fate that will prove that I am. He feels like the only thing I have in the world that's ever been all my own. "I'm scared, Carla. Scared of keeping him, and scared of what it'd be like to let him go."

"I'm sure you are. But you're not alone. I'll see you through this. And Sudie. And Reverend Payne."

"That's another thing. How am I supposed to show my face at church?"

"Same way you have been. You go. You sit. You worship. Nothing's changed about what the Lord thinks of you."

I dab at my eyes again. "I doubt that."

"You know the stories," Carla says. "The woman at the well. The one who washed Jesus' feet with her tears. The bleeding woman who all she did was reach out and touch the edge of Jesus' robe. It's the folks who thought the Lord shouldn't love them that he made a point to love on the most."

The woman at the well. I am thirsty.

All you have to do is reach, the voice whispers to the place inside me that trembles. The voice that was with me when I was baptized. The voice I heard in my room the other night.

"I just . . . I didn't know I could love—and at the same time be afraid of—someone so much who I've never even met."

"I thought the same thing when I was carrying each of mine," Carla says. "It's hard to imagine they're separate little humans when they feel like they are so much a part of us."

"The more I feel him move, the more I wonder how I could possibly give him away."

"Well, now, that's one thing I know adoption isn't— you're not giving your child away. You'll always have him with you, whether in your heart or in your arms. All mine are gone halfway across the country, but there isn't a minute that ticks by that I'm not thinking of or praying for them. Adoption isn't about giving your child away. It's about giving your child life, Jaycee. Nothing will ever change the fact that you are his mother."

"I s'pose you're right."

"I know I'm right."

"But you got to raise your kids."

"I did. In that sense, I've got no right to compare myself to what you're going through. But I can tell you this: motherhood's one long grieving process. The only time you really have them is when they're inside you. Once they leave the womb, it's all about learning to let them go. When they take their first step, it's away from you, and every one after that until you launch them from the nest. Way I look at it, adoption is just a way you're trusting the Lord with him earlier than most. Took me a long time to realize that when I was kicking and screaming about letting my children go, what I was really fighting was trusting that God would take care of them. I had to learn to trust God with each of them, because holding on to them does nothing except cheat them out of the life they're supposed to live. Sooner or later, every mother has to do the same." She squeezes my hand again.

I imagine Jochebed leaning over baby Moses, tucking the linen blanket under his chin, kissing his dimpled knuckles, rubbing his head like I used to rub Jayden's until his eyes are too heavy to hold open and he sleeps, before she nudges the basket into the current of the river and lets the water take him. How in the world . . . ?

"Listen, it's not my place to tell you what to do. I'm here no matter what you decide. Why don't you take the rest of the afternoon off. I'll finish up."

"I'll be fine," I say, and I stand and smooth my apron over my bump, which seems all the more obvious now.

"It's a Wednesday. You know Wednesdays are our slow day. Besides that, I insist."

Gabe rounds the corner again. It is clear he is in a near panic about getting to the bathroom, but I am standing right in his way.

We're forced with having to look at each other, but neither of us say a word.

"Hooo-ey, it's gonna be a long few weeks if you two don't figure this out," Carla says.

She winks at me, then leaves the two of us in there alone staring at each other, until finally I push past him and leave.

I keep on walking right out the back door of the diner without looking back, and the heavy door slams shut. Only as I'm driving away do I chance taking a look in my rearview mirror to see if he followed me out.

He didn't.

But what I do see in that mirror are my eyes, which for the first time look like a woman's eyes, and not the scared girl who hid in her room from the junkies, or who drove Jayden to the hospital that horrific night, or who walked down Main Street with Bryan chasing in his car.

Sudie's right.

I have a choice.

And this baby deserves a chance.

18

The redtail takes two steps to the left, then a few to the right as I approach his cage. After a visit to the local veterinarian for an X-ray, we learned that along with a good concussion, he suffered a simple fracture on one of his long wing bones, which was good news. The wing was splinted and taped to his side to heal. He'll be spending a few weeks with us, well into spring at least.

He tilts his head as if questioning every move I make, watching to see what I'm up to next as I unwrap the thawed hunk of roadkill, one of a few dozen pieces of meat Sudie had in her freezer for her patients.

"It's what they eat half the time anyway," she explained

when I thought I was going to be sick the first time I watched her give it.

"Smartest of all the raptors," Sudie often reminds me, and I'm careful to interact as little as possible so he doesn't start to get attached to us. Redtails and deer, especially, are quick to bond with humans. And bonding doesn't do them any favors in the wild. Bonding with a rescue animal is a good way to get it killed by a human who doesn't know a tamed bird or fawn is coming at them to be friendly.

We have to work with him just enough for him to trust us to feed him and know we're not going to hurt him. But after that, we feed him and water him and leave him alone. He's curious more than anything now, and mostly calm.

"Don't let their calm fool you," Sudie always warns. "Wear the gloves every time."

I learned this the hard way with a kestrel. A couple years back we had a female we'd been rehabbing for weeks and she seemed almost tame, so I didn't bother wearing the gloves one afternoon when I'd been in a hurry to help feed her. Maybe she sensed my hurry. Maybe her keen watching figured out I'd let my guard down. I'd no more than pulled that cage door open an inch before she came grabbing at the half of a mouse I'd brought for her to eat, sinking her talons into the side of my arm so deep it'd required a couple of stitches and a tetanus shot at the clinic in town.

I don't take chances with caring for most critters now, not even the redtails. I pull the leather gloves on one at a time, careful not to move the bandage too much on my still-tender hand. I unlatch the door of the cage and set the carrion inside.

As much as I'd like to touch the feathers, to run my hand down the bird's back, to talk to it, I don't. I close the door quick and step back, quiet.

I jump when my phone bleeps with a text. You home?

It's Gabe. I pull the gloves off to text him back. At Sudie's. Feeding the hawk.

Three ellipses bounce at the bottom of the screen, indicating he's writing a reply.

Mind if I stop by?

If I say no, that I don't mind, I'm giving in to the silence between us. On the other hand, if I say yes, I do mind, well . . . I'm not so sure I'm willing to risk severing whatever hope I have of feeling again what I felt when he wrapped up my arm, when he pushed my hair back, when he looked in my eyes and I looked in his.

I start to type when I hear the crunch of tires on gravel.

Sudie went to the cemetery and she's not due back for a while. When I round the corner, I'm surprised to see who it is.

"Gabe Corwin. You didn't even give me a chance to answer. What if I'd said I minded?"

"That's what I was afraid of," he says, getting out of his car. "If you're half as stubborn as me—which it seems that you are—you would've told me not to come."

Relief rushes through me at the sight of him, at the fact he's here in front of me, looking right at me, but I can't let him see that. I put my hands on my hips and stand as tall as

I can, which I realize makes my baby bump, which I'm not even trying to hide anymore, stick out even farther under my T-shirt. "You're right. I would have. I have things to do."

"Well, I won't take up too much of your time." He stuffs his hands in his jeans pockets and steps toward me. "I wanted to tell you I'm sorry."

I cross my arms, as if trying to defend myself against the kindness in his eyes. It's not working.

"I'm sorry for the way I've been acting . . . about . . . well . . ."

"You mean the way you've been acting about me being pregnant?"

"Yeah. It's just . . . well . . . it was a surprise is all." He kicks at a bare spot in the grass. "It isn't right, us being in such close quarters and not talking to each other, trying not to look at each other. I thought maybe if I came here, if I could see you, that maybe, well, maybe at least we could work that out. Carla's right. Acting like this makes for awfully long days."

I can accept his kindness, or I can go on showing him I'm just fine without him. Like that redtail. He fussed and fluttered and threatened us with those talons until he realized we'd keep giving him food and a safe place to heal. I don't know for sure about Gabe and his intentions toward me, but I do know there's no way to find out without taking at least a little of what he's offering.

"I guess I'm sorry, too. I didn't exactly know how to tell you." My voice sounds small, weak.

"Sounds like it's uncharted territory for both of us."

"Yeah."

He runs one hand through his hair, and his cheeks are pinked up. He locks eyes with me. "I meant what I said the other day, when we were at your place."

"I guess learning about this is one way to get past cordial."

"It is." A grin breaks out across his face.

That dimple. The way his mouth turns up on one side when he smiles. The outline of his muscles beneath the heather-gray sweatshirt he wears with well-worn jeans. The way my heart burns inside my chest whenever I'm with him.

"You up for a little walk?" I say.

He tilts his head. "I thought you had things to do."

"Hmm, well, they can wait. I want to show you something."

I walk him across the meadow, back to where the craggy slope leads down to the creek. Flashes of yellow columbine and branches of volunteer forsythia mix with the bright green of the spring underbrush, which I push past. He breathes heavy behind me as we shinny over fallen tree trunks, up and over rocks and roots jutting across the trail, lightly worn and only by the steps of me and Sudie.

Oak. Sycamore. Maple. Sycamore. Ash. I recite the names of the trees as we pass them.

Suddenly the trees turn sideways and pain ricochets against my knees, my bandaged hand. I taste the grit of dirt.

I curse and pull my pants up over my knees, which sting from the shock of impact. They're not bleeding. My hand is still wrapped up. Glancing back at the trail, I see the root that caused me to fall, and curse again.

"Jaycee! You all right?" Gabe offers me his hand.

"I'll be fine." I try to get up myself, but the woods still look like they're moving. I sit back and run my hands over my belly, straining to sense if the fall hurt my baby. I'll go to the doctor, like I promised Carla. I will.

"Here. Let me help." Now both of his hands reach toward me.

I eye him for a second, but then am grateful for the boost. I brush the dirt off my pants and pick a few burrs off my bandaged hand. "I seem to be prone to accidents these days."

"I guess so! Sheesh. Should you even be traipsing through the woods like this?" he says.

"I'm pregnant, not sick."

"Right." He looks skeptical.

"Besides, where we're going is just up the bend." Nothing in my belly feels out of sorts. There's no pain like the one I had the other day.

"What's that smell?" Gabe scrunches his nose up.

I smell it too. Like a dead animal. "I don't think I landed on anything." I look around to make sure, and I see the cause of it. "Here. Look."

Several scaly plants that look like cream-colored pine-cones stick up from around the bottom of a nearby oak.

"What is that?"

"It's called squawroot. They are nasty smelling. Probably keeps them from being eaten. They only come up every four years."

"Are you serious?"

"Yeah, it's really weird. A good sign they're growing, though. Means the forest is healthy, despite all the ash trees dying."

"How do you know so much about plants and trees? And animals?"

"Sudie, mostly." I start down the path again, this time slower. My knee smarts.

"What's wrong with the ash trees?"

"You haven't heard about the borers?"

"Only thing I knew about trees before I met you was that I was glad if there was one to sit under during off innings when I played baseball."

Could we be any more different? I laugh and tell him all about how there didn't used to be emerald ash borers, until they came in on a shipment of some kind in Michigan and have been eating their way south ever since. The ash across Riverton and all along the Ohio River Valley started to show signs of dying the summer Jayden died. By last fall, whole tree lines full of them that had been green and thick were over half dead. "Can't see them, either. They're tiny and green, and they get underneath the bark and eat from the inside out. By the time the leaves start dropping, it's too late to save them. They say the only thing that'll stop them is when they kill all the ash and have nothing else to eat."

"Can't somebody spray them or something?"

"I guess not. I heard a couple places might have some kind of a preventative now, but it's too late for most of them. That great big tree by my trailer's an ash. One of a few I've seen not showing signs of dying yet. Probably too late for it, too. Besides, I probably couldn't afford whatever the treatment is anyway."

The trail turns and heads uphill to a set of worn steps and a bridge, too rickety to trust walking across any longer. "Used to be part of the state park. Still is, I guess. But they don't maintain it anymore."

"Pretty place," he says and scans the creek running below us, the hillsides with several big ash on their sides, the entire root system upturned along with them as they fell.

"Another one of my favorite spots."

"I can see why." He looks pensive.

"You haven't told me exactly why you came to Riverton."

"I don't know." He shrugs. "I thought it might be nice to live near the river."

I raise my eyebrow. "That's it?"

He shrugs again. "Columbus is a bigger town than this one, but I was tired of the same old same old. Tired of everyone knowing everything about me, thinking I'm the same person I've always been. You ever feel that way living here all your life?"

"Mmm-hmm." If he only knew that's one of the reasons I like him. Just like the kids I went to school with, he would have never sat with me in the cafeteria or paid me any attention if he knew the Jaycee Givens the rest of Riverton knows.

He leans against the fence and faces me. "I guess I felt like I just needed someplace where I could start new."

"That'd be nice, starting new." I look across the creek

valley, at the hawks circling above, at the sparrows hopping from branch to branch, at the squirrels circling up and down tree trunks, at the white snowdrops blooming in clusters, at the first bees gleaning nectar from the blooming clover at our feet. "That's what I like so much about the spring out here. All of this coming up from nothing."

For a while, our breathing is the only sound besides a cardinal calling across the way.

"I used to come here more often, before."

"Before?" he asks.

I push down a tightness in my throat. "The other day, at my place, you asked about my brother."

He straightens, waving a hand as if surrendering. "I'm sorry, I shouldn't have pried—"

"No, it's okay." It *is* okay. He can be trusted. And if he can't, I'd rather know now. "The other day, when you over-heard about this baby at the diner? I saw the look on your face and I realized keeping things from a friend can hurt worse than telling them outright. You might as well know the whole story."

He is silent as I tell him everything. About my father. About Mama and the drugs. About Jayden, him being born addicted. About the junkies coming in and out at all hours. About me being Jayden's one chance, about the rabbits who lost their mama and how I saved them but let my brother die.

When I finish, I turn and see that Gabe's face is wet with tears, which is peculiar because I don't seem to have any left to cry for myself.

"No wonder," he whispers.

"No wonder what?"

"No wonder you act the way you do." He reaches for my hand, and I let him take it.

"And how is that?"

"Jumpy. And scared."

"Knowing all this . . . it doesn't make you like me less?" I've been so afraid of what Gabe would think of me, that he'd leave me for sure. But if he looks at me different now, it's only with more affection. He doesn't act like he has pity for me as much as he has mercy, and I know plenty well the difference between the two. Pity's what folks at food pantries and shelters had on their faces when handing me and Mama a box of toilet paper or canned corn, or a stack of used clothing. Mercy's when someone acts like I'm just as human as they are despite the inhumane things happening to me.

"No," he says, looking out across the valley before looking straight into my eyes. "It makes me like you even more."

He reaches for me, but I pretend not to notice and start down the path. Heat rushes through me, the shame of my swollen belly all mixed up with the feelings I have for him. But I keep on walking. I have to, to hide the part of me that wants him with the part of me who knows better than to give my heart away to another man.

19

That Friday, I take the afternoon off work to see the doctor Carla's set me up with, and to help Sudie at the cemetery after that. The office is nice enough. Fancy, really. At least a dozen magazines on parenting and homemaking sit stacked on the granite countertop next to the sink. I cross my legs and try to rub the cold out of my arms. On the pale-blue wall is a framed print of a mother bathing a child.

The exam table is hard and awkward, especially through the thin paper gown they had me strip down and put on. Carla offered to come back with me, but I told her I'd be fine if she stays in the waiting room.

"You'll like Dr. Fitzgerald. He's so nice," she said.

My first reaction is to doubt whether he'll be nice to someone like me, unmarried and pregnant, but I figure it's my own shame making me feel that way. He probably sees unwed moms all the time. It is Riverton, after all.

There's a rap on the exam room door and, without giving me time to respond, a plump woman in purple scrubs pushes a little machine on wheels into the room.

"Ms. Givens?"

"Yes."

"I'm Paula, Dr. Fitzgerald's nurse. I'll be taking your vital signs, asking a few questions, and such before he comes in."

"All right."

Paula speaks softly and her touch is gentle as she takes my temperature, my blood pressure. She wears a simple gold cross around her neck that I notice as she presses her fingers against the inside of my wrist for my pulse. "How'd you hurt your hand?"

"Burned it on coffee. I'm a waitress. At the diner."

"Hmmm . . . That's a great little place. Maybe that's why you look familiar." She scribbles notes in my file. "Is this your first pregnancy?"

"Yes."

"And where have you been getting your prenatal care before this?"

"I . . . well . . ."

She looks up from her paperwork, the corners of her mouth turning downward. "You have been seeing someone before now, haven't you?"

I shake my head.

She looks as if she may say something, then hesitates. "Okay. Let's start with this. Do you remember the date of your last period?"

"September?"

"You're not sure?"

Not only have I calculated in my head too many times to count, but I remember Walmart was packed the last time I bought my monthly supplies, the aisles full of back-to-school shoppers and signs. I just don't want to admit I haven't seen a doctor before now.

"No, it was September," I say, avoiding her eyes. "I'm sure."

She grabs a paper wheel, a measurement tool of some kind, from the counter and turns it, adjusts it.

"That makes you about six, maybe six and a half months along."

I nod, trying not to let on at my shock at someone putting words to the whole situation. Trying not to think too much about how that means I really do only have a handful of weeks.

"Let's see how you measure."

I lie back on the table.

Paula stretches a cold measuring tape from my panty line up across my belly. She scribbles some more in the folder that's now on her lap. "Yep. Looks to be about twenty-eight weeks. Maybe even thirty. I'm sure Dr. Fitzgerald will want an ultrasound to confirm."

"An ultrasound?"

"Yes." She peers at me over the top of her bifocals, then reaches over and pats my thigh. "You'll get to see a picture of your baby today. We can tell you the sex, too, if you'd like." She hesitates. "Is there . . . would the father like to come watch when we do that?"

The ceiling light is too bright. Glaring. I close my eyes so she can't see the tears starting up, and shake my head. "No."

She pats my thigh again. "You can go ahead and sit up now. Dr. Fitzgerald will be in, in just a few minutes."

A few minutes feels like forever, the cold room, the magazines with smiling mothers and laughing babies, the silver tray with tubes and instruments set in neat rows on top, all of this making me feel like I'm watching this happen to someone else.

"Jaycee Givens," a voice booms.

Dr. Fitzgerald fills the room, a giant of a man dressed in light-blue scrubs and a long white coat, his name embroidered in bright-red cursive. He shakes my hand, his grip strong, sure.

"Paula told me a little bit about your history. So this is your first visit to a doctor? About this pregnancy?"

I nod.

His brow furrows. "We prefer to see patients for the first time around four to six weeks. The fact that you're around twenty-eight . . . well, it could be just fine. But we'll need to take some blood, run a few extra tests maybe you weren't expecting, along with an ultrasound. We'll do all that right here, so you don't have to worry about having to go anywhere else. But I need you to know, you need to see us regularly from here on out until this baby arrives."

He does seem kind, not like the nurse at the hospital who right away thought I was stupid when I brought Jayden in.

I nod again, fear beginning to gnaw at me. "Did I . . . I didn't hurt him . . . did I?"

"I don't see anything concerning yet, but like I said, we'll be running a few tests to be sure. Without a father in the picture . . . well, let's just say you're not the first young lady I've had to counsel about not coming in like this. Most of those turned out just fine, but it's not ideal. If something is wrong, we can often catch it early before it turns into something worse." He smiles. Yes, his eyes are kind. "Just promise to come back for the rest of the prenatal visits we're going to get scheduled for you, okay?"

I nod, determined to follow through with however many appointments I have left.

"Can Carla come back here?" I ask Paula, who's preparing the ultrasound machine.

"Is she your mother?"

"No." I think about the other mothers I saw sitting in the waiting room with their daughters. I think about Mama, sitting in jail. "Carla's the one who brought me here. She's my friend."

"All right." She leans into the hallway and tells someone to bring Carla back.

I lean back on the paper-covered table.

Paula puts a blanket across my naked legs and up over my privates, then squirts cold gel on my belly.

"Hey there. Everything okay?" Carla says, sliding past Paula and the machine. She comes alongside the exam table and grabs my hand. "You all right, darlin'?"

"I think so."

"This'll be cold. I'm sorry about that," Paula says, then presses the wand against my belly.

Whooshing and static come from the machine, followed by a pulsing sound.

"There it is."

A spot on the screen blinks in time with the *swish-swish-swish*. That's him.

That's my baby.

"Would you look at that," Carla whispers.

"Is that his hand? His arm?" I say, unable to take my eyes off the moving black-and-white parts of the screen.

"Mmm-hmm," Paula says, smiling. "And that curve there, that's his spine. This one here, that's his head. Oh . . . and . . . do you want to know if it's a boy or a girl?"

I look at Carla. "Do I?"

She shrugs. "It's up to you. But you've been calling him a 'him' all the time. Maybe you better get that confirmed."

"Okay. Tell me."

That's my baby.

Right there.

On the screen.

Paula presses the wand around, pushing it harder. "Okay . . . I think . . . yes, that's it."

I squint at the screen. "I can't tell a thing."

"Right there." She points. "Your hunch was right. It's definitely a baby boy."

I can't contain my giggling. Carla leans down, squeezes my cheeks, and kisses me square on the forehead.

A boy.

My baby is a boy.

Paula clicks away on the machine, and I try to memorize every move of the baby's hands, his arms, his legs.

"How's he look?"

"Technically, I'm not supposed to interpret these things. But I can tell you, all his measurements are right where they should be. He has all his arms and legs. His spine looks nice and straight. I think he looks pretty fine."

So I haven't hurt him.

Not yet anyway.

He is safe inside me, growing, living.

His heartbeat is small, but strong and fast, there on the screen, blinking right at me.

The heartbeats of those baby bunnies were strong and fast that summer night three years back, too. So strong, me and Sudie were able to eventually let them all go.

20

There's only one person who drives the two-toned, early eighties Cadillac that's pulling out of the cemetery as I turn in. Sudie asked if I'd like to come help her plant some annuals, and sitting on a cool patch of dirt, tucking in begonias and petunias, dianthus and coleus, sounds like a blessing. My belly's getting so swollen I can't do much else. It's only been two weeks since I went to the doctor, but it seems like the baby has grown a whole month's worth.

"What grave was Mr. Crawford visiting?" I ask Sudie, who's already planting a flat in the beds alongside the entrance. Jack, the cemetery dog, appears to be smiling as he pants contentedly under the nearby locust tree.

"Walter Crawford?" Sudie asks, not looking up from her work.

"Yeah. That was him, wasn't it? Just left? Can't miss that car he drives."

"Oh, I suppose it was him. I'm not sure. Maybe just passing through. It is a pretty place to visit in the spring."

She's right, planters filled with spring flowers, lilac bushes in full bloom, and rows of pink and white peonies spilling all over themselves. An exception would be the locust tree that appears budless compared to the other trees around. "Think that tree Jack's sitting under is okay?"

"It'll be all right. Just give 'em time."

"If you say so." Losing the ash trees is enough. The cemetery had already lost half a dozen when we counted last fall, leaving behind stumps big enough to spread out a whole church potluck. I bend down to pull a stray thistle from the flower bed, the whole root long, thin, and white as I slide it out of the ground. A cramp starts across my side and I stand to stretch.

"You all right, child?" Sudie sits back on her haunches and eyes me with concern. Her own face is damp with sweat, and a little pale despite the warm day. "Don't you overdo it."

I feel like telling her the same. "It's nothing. Just a growing pain. I asked the doctor about them."

"Glad you went to see him." She nods and goes right back to pulling, despite her breathing, which sounds a little ragged.

"I'm going to walk a bit, see if it goes away." Jack gets up on his aging legs and trots alongside me. We pass the Pinkett family plots, well-known for having the tallest monuments in the cemetery, a shrine to their successful socket wrench factory established by the patriarch, Cooper Pinkett. Cooper's marker is the tallest of all, complete with a gleaming granite socket wrench at the top. The factory closed a couple decades ago, but no one who visits the cemetery will forget it thanks to his foresight. Cooper's wife, Ada, is buried by his side, and spread out on either side of them are shorter stones engraved with the names of the next three generations of Pinketts, many of them still alive, an empty space where their death date will eventually be inscribed.

Before long, I'm standing over my father's grave and Jayden's next to it, Jack sniffing at the headstones. It's a nice spot, as far as plots go here, acres of farmland stretching out and a dandy breeze from the west. Most all the tree buds are bursting open, branches of weeping willows tinged with green. Little helicopter seeds twirl off a maple, and a robin, unmoving, peers at me from a nest tucked in one of the high crooks of its branches. Three-petaled blooms of trillium push up between rocks and out from the bottom of fallen trees along the fencerows bordering the cemetery. And across the way are six mounds of fresh-covered graves, the latest casualties of the heroin. The fact there were so many at one time made the national news. Riverton's fifteen minutes of fame. A ranger at the state park found them all dead inside their car, which they'd parked alongside the waterfalls there. The heroin they'd taken had been part of a bad batch, the newspaper said. Three more had died in a neighboring county, and nearly fifty patients in all had been treated for it at area hospitals. Gabe had been on duty and said it was a nightmare. One of the calls dispatch had assigned him to was from a four-year-old girl who knew something wasn't right with her mama and knew enough to call 911. He said while he'd been giving the mother the lifesaving Narcan, his partner had found a baby who'd been in his crib so long he was covered in stool and urine.

"Hey, Jayden." The modest headstone was a gift of the church, since he otherwise wouldn't have had one. The daffodil bulbs I planted last fall have already bloomed and folded for the season. The grass is green and the ground smooth over the top of him.

How can he really be here, in the ground, gone? How can any of what's happened to us be real? He never had a chance.

The baby flutters in my belly and I imagine one of the tiny arms or legs from the ultrasound, pushing and working against me.

Me and Bryan, what we did, it's not this baby's fault.

I wonder what my father would think, if he would've liked being a grandpa. And Jayden. How he would have surely loved having a little nephew to play with, to grow with.

"You'd have been the best uncle, Jayden." Two boys, running and playing in the meadow, catching fireflies and toads, growing tall and strong. But that wasn't meant to be. It isn't meant to be. At least not for Jayden.

But it can be for my baby. He can have a chance. I can

give him a chance. The meadow was once my kingdom. I can make it that for him, too. I won't make the kind of decisions Mama did. I won't be like that mother with the little girl and the baby in the back room.

Trust me.

The voice is as real as the wind playing through my hair, the leaves above me.

What do you mean, Lord? Trust you for what? To give me what I need to raise him alone? Or for me to give this baby to you? How am I supposed to do that, Lord? How am I supposed to let someone else raise him? Haven't I given enough?

I don't hear anything, let alone an answer.

"C'mon, Jack. Let's go."

By the time we get back to Sudie, she's finishing a second flat of red petunias.

"Better?" she asks.

"Better." I grab a flat of coleus, sit next to her, and pull a glove over my hand. The burn is scabbed over, but I still keep it wrapped. The little spade slides smooth and easy into the dark, rich earth. I pull out a single plant and gently separate its roots, tight and shaped like the square of the plastic container. "I've been looking at websites. About adoption."

"Mmm-hmm."

"I've been thinking about how you said I have a choice, that I can give this baby a chance."

"I did."

"Since I saw him on that ultrasound screen . . . it's hard to imagine giving him up, Sudie. Can't imagine someone else holding him and rocking him . . . I can't imagine someone loving him as much as me."

"That is hard to imagine." She pats another petunia into the soil. "But it happens all the time."

"I suppose that's true." I think about a family at church who recently brought an adopted baby girl home from China, how much they adore her. How her father swoops her up and sets her on his shoulders and she squeals with laughter. How I never had a chance to know my father like that. "'Sides that, this baby should have a daddy."

"A child needs a father, that's for certain." She stops what she's doing, sets back, and squints at me, the sun in her eyes. "Jaycee. If you're looking to me to make this decision for you, I won't."

I sigh long and loud. "I don't know if I can."

"You can. And you will, when the time comes. And if you're listening to the Lord."

I wonder if she sees things I can't, things like Saul did on the road to Damascus or the disciples who about near ran right into Jesus in the middle of the road after he rose again. "I don't think he talks to me like he talks to you."

She stands slow, her knees stiff and cracking. She grabs a thermos of lemonade and takes a drink, then offers it to me.

Beads of sweat collect under her nose, run down the side of her face. She pulls a faded red bandanna out of her pocket and wipes it away. "He doesn't speak like the world speaks. I've told you that." She looks over at the locust trees, branches cold and brown. "You know, you were asking about those locust trees. Every year they're some of the last ones to bud. And every year I worry about them. But every year I remind myself their buds already formed in the fall. Can't do much about what happens to them in the springtime. Just have to wait and trust the work the tree did the season before. You're in a wintertime of your life, child. The Lord knows *you* don't have the energy to do what you'll need to do, whatever that is, when it's time for that baby to come. But he's already been preparing you. He's already got you ready for spring."

"I don't *feel* ready for anything."

"You don't have to feel. You just have to know."

"That doesn't help either." I pluck a thistle from the bed and toss it into an empty flat where Sudie's been collecting other weeds to throw away. What would she know about giving away a baby?

Sudie exhales and sets a flat of begonias beside me. "Come on, child. I want to show you something."

She starts trudging and I heave myself up and follow her. Jack looks as weary as I feel as Sudie leads us toward one of the older sections of the cemetery, where a giant oak shades a smattering of thin white stones, the names and dates of Civil War veterans whittled nearly unreadable. Between these are gray stones, many with baby lambs and praying hands carved into them, most of them with dates of death in the 1870s when the cholera came and wiped out whole families and nearly the whole town. Shut the railroad down one summer, it was so bad.

When we get to a row of three flat grave markers we stop.

The names, which I've never stopped to notice, are etched on small, plain granite squares:

MARY

JOHN

SAMUEL

Behind them is a taller, wide granite stone with details listed:

MARY
JULY 31 – AUG. 20, 1972
AGE 21 DAYS

JOHN
JULY 8 – AUG. 26, 1973
AGE 1 MO. 18 DAYS

SAMUEL
JAN. 2 – JUNE 5, 1975
AGE 5 MO. 3 DAYS

CHILDREN OF E. R. & S. J. ADAMS

"We didn't have a chance to try again after Samuel," Sudie says.

We? These are *her* children? I stare at the names of the parents, where only initials are listed. I try to think of a time she's talked about a husband. Children. I can't.

To the right of the children's grave is another stone in matching granite, one I never paid that much attention to. A Vietnam veteran star is embedded above the name:

ERNEST RAWLINGS ADAMS
JUNE 14, 1949 – APRIL 4, 1975

And next to it, with an empty space for the date of death:

SUDELLE JANE
MARCH 14, 1952 –

Sudelle. "Sudie, I didn't know—"

"I know. It's been more than forty years. After a while, people stopped asking about them. And I stopped bringing them up. Easier than explaining everything."

"What happened?" I can't stop myself from asking, and I'm ashamed as soon as the words leave my mouth. Like I'm walking on forbidden ground. But it's *Sudie.* She had *three babies*? A *husband*?

A look comes over her I haven't seen before. Far away. Almost joyful, as if right now in front of us she's watching those three babies grown enough to be playing under the tree or picking her a dandelion bouquet. "They were perfect. All of them," she says. "The most beautiful babies you've ever seen."

The more Sudie talks about them, the more her countenance changes. The lines around her mouth soften. Her thin, worn lips fill out like the withered flats of flowers once we've watered them in. She pauses, looking up into the spring sky, crystal-blue and the sun angled in such a way that the leaves on the trees, the edges of the clouds all seem to glimmer. She closes her eyes and for a moment I think she's not well.

But soon she speaks again, this time with tears puddling in her saggy lids. "Each one lived a little longer than the one before. By the time Samuel came, I thought maybe he'd live. But it was the same thing, every time. They'd stop growing. The doctor, he tried to help. Different kind of milk, formula. Everything. They'd get fussier and fussier. They wouldn't hardly sleep. When they cried . . ."

She looks at me now, maybe recalling the way Jayden cried and wouldn't stop. "They were in *pain*. I kept bringing them to the doctor, asking him, begging him to help them, to stop the hurting. But nothing ever helped. Eventually they quieted, but then I knew . . . I knew the quiet meant they didn't have much longer. I wouldn't put them down . . . Ernie, he tried to get me to sleep, but I wouldn't sleep. I wouldn't let them go. Not until they passed. One minute I could feel their little lungs working, the next they'd stop and I knew. They were gone."

"Lord, have mercy."

"That's what I prayed. I suppose there's a fancy name for whatever ailed them, that it's something they can fix now. But it doesn't matter."

I can't stop comparing the date of Samuel's death with Ernie's. Two months apart.

As if she read my mind, Sudie says, "He never got to meet Samuel."

Just like my father. He never got to meet me.

"My, how we prayed for that child. Prayed like Hannah in the Bible prayed for her Samuel. Prayed the Lord would spare us from losing another. Ernie, he was home the spring before on leave. Left again for what was supposed to be a diplomatic mission. Something called Operation Babylift, I learned later. They knew the war was ending and they were working on ways to help the babies there. In Vietnam. He was on a plane that crashed carrying some of those babies. He would've been home in less than a month to see his own."

"It was an accident?"

She nods.

"You had to bury your husband and then . . . bury Samuel by yourself?"

She nods again, same faraway look in her eye, as if she can see something, as if she's a part of something I can't see that's happening right in front of her, something that's part of earth and part of heaven.

My heart hurts. I ask my next question as carefully as I can. I have no right to know about any of them, really, or about her reasons for never speaking of them. "But, Sudie," I say, reaching toward her slumped shoulder, "why didn't you tell me?"

"Oh, child. I'm sorry." For a moment, her face pales and

loses some of the otherworldly look. "You must think I'm terrible, never mentioning them before. It's not that I don't think about them. Truth is, they're so much a part of me I never stop thinking about them."

"I think I know what you mean."

Jayden's never far from my mind. Not even my father, really. I've just rearranged my life so that I can keep on going without them. And for the first time, I consider how Mama must've felt, losing my dad. Then Jayden.

"What is the Lord asking you to give up?"

Back when Jayden died, it took everything in me not to pull his tiny casket back up out of the dark hole when they lowered it in the ground. It's just not right, something so small. "How have you managed to go on?"

"Oh, I barely made it those first few months. Years, really. I worked odd jobs, cleaning people's homes mostly. Started taking in injured animals as a way to feel like I was helping something live. Spent so much free time at the cemetery they eventually offered me this job." She looks me square on. "It still hurts, child. I feel the holes of where they used to be in my heart every day. I'm just doing the best I can with what I have. And somehow, the Lord has repaid me for the years the locusts have eaten."

"But . . . why are you telling me all this now?"

"So you can see why I can't tell you what I think you should do. So you know how easy it would be for me to tell you to keep your baby. But so you also know life goes on if you decide to let go." She pauses, her eyes moving over each one of the stones, each one of the names. "You know, following those hearses in here, each time I felt what I thought Abraham must've felt when he was leading Isaac up the mountain. The Lord, he didn't save my babies, but he has saved me." She turns and starts walking back to where we have more work to do. "There's always letting go to do here on earth, Jaycee. But the Lord, he never lets go. And because of him, we never have to either."

21

I fill Jack's water bowl outside the cemetery work shed, and he laps at it, splattering it everywhere, and Sudie waves from atop the big riding mower halfway across the cemetery. We managed to plant four dozen plants without any pains returning to my belly, except the one gnawing at my stomach because it's craving a huge scoop of chocolate ice cream.

I'm due to meet Gabe at the Dairy Barn in twenty minutes, and the low-gas warning light gleams from the dashboard when I turn on the car. I forgot I needed gas. Good thing there's a station right near the Dairy Barn, the only one in town as a matter of fact, and a fact that riles up the guys at the diner like few other subjects. Even Hersch joins in on the complaining since the station owner, Bill Spradley, seems to enjoy gouging folks with his monopoly on the business. Closest gas station to town is ten miles to the interstate, or fifteen miles the other direction to the next town. But I suppose that's just the way it is in a small town.

Main Street is busy as it usually is on Friday evenings, folks a little happier with paychecks in their pockets and a week of work behind them. The gas station is quiet, though, as I pull up next to one of the pumps. The nozzle rattles as I put it into the gas tank, and I lean back against the car, warm from sitting in the sunshine all day. An older-model car rumbles by, the ground shaking under me from the souped-up woofers blaring. A passenger throws a cigarette butt out the window, the gleam of ashes tumbling in a trail behind it.

I'm inside paying when I hear the voice come up behind me to the second register.

"A box of Red Man and ten dollars in gas."

Fear burns down my spine and I try not to look back.

Bryan.

Maybe he hasn't seen me.

I haven't seen him since I've taken to not hiding my belly anymore. Should've known better than to let my guard down about running into him in this town.

"How you doin', Jaycee?"

I can feel his breath against the back of my neck and I

shiver. Takes all the courage I have to stand up straight and face him. "Bryan."

"Saw you leaving church the other day with some guy. Who is he?" He steps closer and I can smell the fresh tobacco stuffed inside his bottom lip.

My stomach turns. "None of your business."

"I remember when everything about you was my business, baby."

Icy fear shoots down my spine and weakens my knees. Why can't he leave me be?

The attendant, one of the crusty Spradley cousins who've been working here for generations, clears his throat. "That'll be $17.53, ma'am."

I fumble for my wallet and set two ten-dollar bills on the counter. When I turn, Bryan is staring at my belly.

"That what I think it is?" he sneers.

I cross my arms so quick I drop my wallet, change clanging and rolling everywhere. "It's nothin'." *Lord, help me. Please.* I bend to collect the pennies and dimes. I reach for a quarter near the candy display and he puts his steel-toed boot on my wrist, just under my hand bandage.

"Is it mine?"

I don't want to look up at him. I scan the store, already aware there's no way out of this.

"Get off of me!" I yank my hand back and scramble away from him, toward the door, and somehow manage to get on my feet again.

"Hey, now, you two be amiable. Don't need no trouble here," cousin Spradley says.

I use the moment to run out the door, gulping in the cool dusk air. I don't think I was breathing in there.

Help me, Lord.

The fluorescent lights flicker above my car, and I hear the bells on the station door jingle as Bryan follows me out.

Adrenaline pulses through me and I fumble for my keys. I feel him close behind me. When I try to open the car door, his hand is there holding it shut.

"Leave me alone." *Keep your voice strong. He hates weakness.* Like a coyote. Looks for the wounded deer, the struggling newborn calf in a farmer's midnight field. Weakness fuels the mean in him. I try to yank my car door open. If I can get it open I can get in and lock it and drive away.

But that's not to be. He grabs hold of my shoulder, turns me around, and shoves me against the car.

"I said, is it *mine?*"

The way he says *mine*, all hard and drawn out, feels like a noose tightening around my neck.

"What's the matter? You sleep with somebody else when you were sleeping with me? That it? Maybe you don't know whose it is. You little—"

"Stop it! I wasn't with anyone else. It's *yours*, Bryan. Okay? It's *your* baby. It's yours!" I regret the words as soon as I say them.

I've heard about blood rushing from someone's face but haven't actually seen it happen until now. Just as quickly, it turns red with rage like my words slapped him. He comes at me in an instant, so close I feel the heat from his mouth, his neck. He grabs hold of my arms. His fingers dig in deep. "Don't you raise your voice at me. Especially while you're carrying *my baby*."

I feel like the hurt rabbits me and Sudie save, the way they look up at us from their crate, eyes black and darting around full of fear, no way for them to know we mean them no harm. Difference is, Bryan *does* mean harm.

He turns all calm. Scary calm. Except for the fingers still digging into my bones. "I miss us, Jaycee," he says, letting go of one arm to push a stray piece of hair back from my face. "Don't you miss us?"

"He botherin' you, Jaycee?" Another man's voice.

Gabe.

"Who are you?" Bryan sneers and lets go of my shoulder.

I scurry away and run behind Gabe. "This is that boy you were asking about—the one you saw me leaving church with." I hadn't heard his car, or any car, pull into the station. *Thank you, Lord.*

Bryan squints at Gabe, then puffs out his chest and smirks. "Oh, yeah. You're that new guy. The one from the diner." He locks his eyes on me. "Didn't take long for you to find a new guy, did it, Jaycee?"

"You all right?" Gabe asks me over his shoulder.

"Fine."

He nods, then rears back and sinks his fist right into the middle of Bryan's face.

Bryan careens into the gas pump, loses his balance, and lands on his behind on the asphalt. He dabs at the corner of his mouth, which is split and bleeding.

"I believe the young lady was saying she'd like to leave." Gabe says as Bryan struggles to get up off the ground.

"C'mon, Gabe," I say. "I'm all right." I lower my voice to a whisper, the thought of Bryan's wrestling abilities on my mind. "He's not worth it."

"Yeah, but you are," Gabe says to me, his eyes not leaving Bryan's face for a second.

"No, she ain't," Bryan snorts, then shoots tobacco spittle out of the corner of his mouth at me before shoving past Gabe and heading toward his car. He sneers over his shoulder. "You can have that piece of trash. And her baby, too." He revs the engine a few times, squealing the tires, stopping the car hard near us. His eyes leer down to my belly and back up at me again, eyes so full of hate I have to look away. "Don't be coming to me for money, you hear?"

That gives me the gumption to look at him again. Right then I know sure as I've been about anything in my life that I have to let this baby go. That I have to make a way for him to live safe and free. I glare right back into his dark and bitter eyes without flinching. "You don't have to worry about that. I'm giving him up. *For adoption.* Only thing I'll ever need from you again is a signature."

"That right?" He revs the engine, wipes a new trickle of blood from his mouth. Calm comes across his face, then anger, just as quick. "We'll see about that."

What's he mean? That he wants this baby? Surely not. Horror turns my stomach. "I hate you!" I scream at the glaring red taillights of Bryan's car as he drives away. I clench my belly, as if somehow I can draw it further into myself and away from this nightmare, then sink into Gabe's arms. My knees are weak, from fear and from relief at Gabe being there.

"You sure you're okay?" His breath is warm on the top of my head as I lean against him.

"I will be."

22

Chocolate ice cream puddles around the ridge of my cone. The sign on the front of the Dairy Barn flickers, and the air is so still, feels like we're on a movie set instead of Main Street Riverton. Gabe takes his two scoops of butter pecan on a sugar cone from the attendant, a teenage boy who smiles shyly and averts his eyes from customers, and we sit on a concrete bench at one of several red-topped tables. Nearby, a mother helps her little girl with dark curls with her rainbow ice cream, and a glob of it lands in the middle of her princess T-shirt. Her father lifts it off with his finger and eats it, then lovingly taps her nose.

"Thank you," I say to Gabe.

"You're welcome."

"Not just for the ice cream."

"I know."

I shift my weight at a sudden twinge in my side, but that doesn't help much. It aches the same as it did at the cemetery, and when I run my free hand across my middle it feels tight.

"What is it?" Gabe asks, butter pecan dripping down the side of his cone.

"It's pulling. And it's hard."

He reaches toward me, and I jump.

"Sorry," he says.

"Me too. I jump at the littlest thing. Here." I take his hand and hold it against my belly.

"Is that a contraction?"

"I don't know. Maybe." A foot or an arm rolls underneath where his hand rests. "Did you feel that?"

His face, bright with surprise, gives me the answer. "Does it hurt when he does that?"

"No." I laugh and press his hand tighter against me. The way he looks at me and something about the blinking lights, the way my skin feels hot where he's touching me, the way our thighs rest against each other . . . something about this almost feels right, him and me and this baby inside. But this isn't Gabe's baby. And I meant what I said to Bryan. I *know* I have to let this baby go—to protect him as much from me as from the Blair family. Chocolate ice cream runs down my hand and drips to the ground. When I go to take another bite, another pain comes, sharp and low. "That pulling sure does, though."

His brow furrows. "We better get you home." He shakes his head, then surprises me by cursing about Bryan. "What's wrong with him anyway?"

"I don't know," I breathe.

Gabe puts his hand on my back, as if trying to steady me through the pain.

"There's always been talk about that family. Talk about the way his dad treats his wrestlers. What happened with another girl Bryan used to date." I think about Elizabeth glaring at me, whether at church or across the checkout lanes at the Walmart or passing each other on the road into town. "Seems like anger's just something that runs through that family."

"You're pretty brave, you know that?"

"Brave?" Pain stifles my laugh to a chuckle. "I'm not brave. It's like Sudie says. I'm just doing the best I can with what I have."

"Whatever the reason . . . I've seen too many women stay with men like that. It only gets worse." He takes a napkin and touches it to the side of my mouth. "You're a messy ice cream eater."

"Am I?"

"You are." He dabs at the other side. "Why don't you leave your car here? Let me take you home."

"That'd be fine." I'm not up to being alone, for one thing. For another, I'm not up to being away from him.

It's not even nine o'clock when he pulls up alongside my trailer. He shuts off the engine and the song of hundreds of bullfrogs, mating in the nearby low spots in the meadow, fills the car.

"I love that sound," he says.

"Me too." The moon hangs low, surrounded by a thick haze. "Storms are coming. S'posed to get a lot of rain the next few days." The thought crosses my mind of me and Gabe and this baby, the three of us on my front stoop . . . then another summer after this, me and Gabe watching a toddler dressed in bib overalls, wobbling across the yard chasing after fireflies. I shake my head to get the thought out of my mind.

"Still hurting?"

"No. I think I'll walk a bit, see if that doesn't help ease this pulling. It helped earlier today. I've got the mail to get besides."

"Mind if I join you?"

"I was hoping you might."

The sky darkens to black above the trailer park as we walk around the horseshoe drive. Clouds cover the moon, the stars. We pass Sudie's, and soft yellow squares of light from her windows reflect off the pale-gray gravel. A breeze comes and rustles white seeds from the cottonwood like snow. I remember trying to catch them as a little girl as they swirled around Mama pinning sheets to the clothesline. I'd catch one and run back to show it to her, and back then, she'd stop what she was doing and pull me tight to her chest, then we'd sit awhile on the warm grass and she'd teach me to hold a piece of crabgrass between my thumbs and blow to make a whistle, or how to pop the heads off dandelions, or how to get helicopter seeds from the maple tree to spin. I still recall the smell of the borax on her hands, cracked from always scrubbing something, and the way the whole world had seemed safe and right. I was a princess, and the trees, the yard, the meadow were my kingdom then.

A door creaks and Virginia Johnson emerges from her trailer, glass bottles clanging against each other inside the trash bag she carries down the redwood steps.

"At least she's not throwing them at her husband," Gabe whispers, and we dissolve into laughter.

Dewey's always been a drinker, a habit Virginia most likely enables since Dewey passed out is a heck of a lot better than Dewey sober. Doesn't matter if they're on food stamps like me and Mama were. They'd find a way to sell the food and buy their beer and cigarettes with the cash. She traipses down the path toward the community Dumpster, where the evidence of all our low-income lives intertwine, the stench of alcohol, diapers of toddlers who too often wander alone, their bellies swollen from diets consisting of gas-station snacks.

Not every residence has problems. Take Shawnie and Tim. They go to church and take care of their lot and keep themselves clean, same as Sudie and me, now that Mama's gone. Problem with that is they're so responsible they get put in charge of things like calling the trash company when the Dumpster overflows, mowing the common areas because they're the only ones with a working lawn mower, and calling the police when the late-night domestic situations get out of hand or someone overdoses again.

"You asked me once if I have dreams."

"Yeah."

"Well, I do. I have dreams of getting out of here."

"Here's not so bad."

I look at him as if he's off his rocker. "Anyplace is better than here. We're invisible here."

"That's not true."

"Isn't it? Think about it. When people tell stories, write books, make movies, make the news, they don't tell about people like me, people like the six out at the graveyard with fresh mounds of dirt over them, people like Sudie—who have the kindest and best hearts in the world but who don't matter because we're small and poor and people think that means we're dumb and don't matter. And if they do tell those stories, nobody wants to hear them. No one sees people like me."

He stops in his tracks and takes my hand. "I see you."

I can't help but giggle. "That's noble of you, Gabe. C'mon." I start walking again.

He gives me a look of exasperation. "Is that why you're giving your baby up for adoption?"

It is the most direct question he's ever asked about my predicament.

"No . . ." But is it? "I mean . . . what I said to Bryan . . . I don't know." I study his face to see what he thinks of my fickle uncertainty, and he does not appear to be bothered, but rather sturdy, like no matter what I say he'd be sure as ever that the sun rises in the morning. I'm not used to sturdy. "Sudie and Carla, they say I have a choice. A choice to give my baby a chance."

He kicks at a rusty bottle cap. "Seems to me he'd have a chance either way."

"What do you mean?"

"Seems to me . . ." He hesitates, as if searching for the right words. "He'd have a chance whether you keep him or give him away. Any child would be blessed to have a mama like you."

"You think I should keep him?"

He stops walking again, and his eyes search mine. "I don't know. But I'll be here for you either way."

I think about the mom and dad with the little girl with the dark curls at the Dairy Barn, how I felt the ache of wanting something like that with Gabe. Had he felt that too? Not that it matters. That's not a reason to keep this baby. I sigh and start off down the drive again. The pulling in my belly starts up again, and I try to massage it away. "A child would *not* be blessed to have me," I say over my shoulder.

"Is that why you're going with adoption? What happened to your brother—that wasn't your fault, Jaycee."

I shake my head. "He had a chance. Not much of one, but he had one. And I let him down."

"It was an impossible situation, Jaycee. You were doing the best you could. It'd be different with your own."

"Would it? How? I don't have anything more to give him than Mama did."

"You don't do heroin."

"Mama didn't always do heroin. She was even married, which is more than I am. But my dad died before I was born. She had to find work. Ended up being an aide at a nursing home. I remember she liked it well enough, until she hurt her back. Couldn't get the pain medicine she needed."

"That's not going to happen to you."

We get to the mailboxes and stop. The sweet smell of honeysuckle hangs in the air, and the bush is thick and high, the vines wrapped around the posts and up onto the make-shift roof that covers them.

"Maybe not, but it's everywhere, Gabe. You saw it the other night when you found that baby in its crib."

"What makes you think he's not going to be exposed to it with a different family? In a different place? Just because they're married and live in a nicer part of town, that doesn't mean it'll be perfect."

"No, but it'll be a heck of a lot better than it is here."

"But you have good friends. A home. A church. *Me* . . ."

"*You?*" As much as I like him, I don't know. . . .

"Yeah. Me. You can trust me, Jaycee."

"You hardly know me."

"I know enough."

"Really? What's my favorite color?"

"Yellow."

"How'd you know that? I never told you."

"That first day in the diner. I watched you tying those yellow ribbons on the bottles with the daisies."

"Well, you don't know my favorite book. And it's not *Watership Down*."

"No, it's not. Your favorite book is that romance novel that was on your shelf. That one that had the lighthouse and the couple on the front."

"How in the world did you know that?"

"I saw it on your bookshelf. It was the one with the most worn-out spine."

"So you notice things. Fine. But what about when things get hard, Gabe? What about when my mama gets out of jail? What about if I keep this baby and there's Bryan and his family? What if I don't keep this baby? What about the fact that this life, this hard life, it's like Bryan's family and the anger, one generation after the other. Would I have you then?"

"I know about hard, Jaycee."

"What's been so hard about your life? Really. I'd like to know."

"Everybody's got problems. Some you just can't see. You think because I have a nice car, my school's paid for, that I can't understand what you've been through. And you're right, I don't know what it's like to lose a brother, to see the things you've seen, to have done the things you've done. Maybe my life has been a little boring compared to yours. But that doesn't mean I can't love you."

Love?

By the look on his face, he's as surprised as I am at the word, huge and real and hanging out there right in front of us.

"Doesn't mean you *can*, either."

"If that's true, if you really mean that, then you're judging me as much as you think I'm judging you, which I'm not."

"Really? Tell me honestly. What'd you think the first time you drove into this trailer park in your shiny blue Jeep?"

He shoves his hands into his pockets. "Ashamed."

"Why?"

"Because I know I've been blessed with much. I know I haven't had to suffer, not like you or anybody around here has." He waves a hand at the trailers behind us. "I don't know why some folks are born like me and why some are born like you, and why where we're from decides half our lives for us before we're old enough to know we can do things different from the way our parents or our grandparents have always done them. All I know is, love is bigger than all this. At least, it can be. So every time I drive my shiny Jeep in here, I feel ashamed because I know when people see it they think the same thing you do—that I'm some jerk who thinks he's better than them, that I can't understand them, and worst of all, that I'm not capable of loving them."

Loving.

That's twice now he's mentioned it. And twice now that I'm wanting to run. Instead I turn to the mailbox and make a racket rattling the key around until the door swings open. A couple of bills. Mailers. But no letter from Mama.

The dim light over the mailboxes makes the envelopes look dingy, yellowed.

"Nothing around here ever changes, Gabe."

"Doesn't mean it can't."

I don't argue with him, though I have plenty more I can say to prove him wrong. It is for that reason I try to push the thought of me and him and this baby, together, out of my mind as we head back to my place in silence. At least the walking has helped ease the pain in my belly. I let him kiss the top of my head when he says good night and watch his taillights shine as he drives off until the night swallows them up.

Maybe Gabe's right. Maybe things can change.

Maybe it's time I write Mama a letter.

∼

Dear Mama,

I was helping Sudie at the cemetery today. Did you know about her husband and babies? I can't believe how she gets along after losing all that.

It made me think of you, Mama.

You're right that nothing can bring Jayden back, or make everything that's happened in these last few years go away. But I've been thinking about one of Reverend Payne's sermons a lot. He said sometimes God shows his faithfulness not by what he brings to our life, but by what he takes out of it. Then he asked us what the Lord is asking us to give up.

I think he might be asking me to give up being so mad at you.

Jaycee

23

"Doctor says I'm measuring about thirty-four weeks," I say to Sudie outside at the elevator cage, where the hawk eyes us and, in particular, the breakfast of dead mice in my hand. He's getting stronger every day, and today she's moving him to the long flight cage. It's release day for the turtle, too.

"Not much longer then. What'd he say about your pains?"

"Says they're probably from stress. Wants me sitting every chance I can at the diner. Carla doesn't want me to work, but I can't afford not to. Besides that, I haven't had any more for over a week now."

Sudie nods, the space suddenly and unusually awkward between us.

Guilt twinges through me. She wouldn't take any chances with a baby. Not after what she's been through. I change the subject. "My prison visitor permissions went through."

"Good. You should see your mama before you have the baby. And with Mother's Day coming up . . ." She pulls on her falconer's gloves, thick and long and wide leather up to her elbows.

"I haven't told her yet. I just . . . I didn't know how to tell her in a letter."

Sudie stops fiddling with the gloves. "She needs to know."

"I know, but after everything . . . I didn't feel like she deserved to know."

The hawk blinks and cocks his head, taking in every movement. Sudie tosses a towel over him and wraps him tight so he can't grab her and fight her with his talons. She carries the bundle of him to the flight cage and sets him inside, quick to close the door before he wriggles himself out from under the towel.

"Can't rely on feelings all the time. You know that. You're only hurting yourself when you don't forgive," Sudie says to me. She kneels down just inside the cage and nudges the hawk to step off her arm and onto the ground. "'Sides that, there's a girl that lingers within a woman, no matter how old she gets, that never gives up the hope of pleasing her mother."

I know she's right about that, too, but I don't let on. As much as I try not to think about Mama in prison, about the things she did that got her there, about the letters we've been trading this summer, the closer I get to having this baby, the more I think about her. The more I wonder how she managed to raise me as a single mama. She'd kept my baby things. Wrote in her journal that she dreamed of having a little girl like me and how grateful she was to have me. I wonder what she'd say I should do, now that she's sober.

"Were you close to your mama?"

"Didn't have a chance to be. She died when I was little."

"I'm so sorry." Isn't there a limit to how much one person should be allowed to lose? "How can you be so sure about God after all you've been through? Aren't you angry at him?"

She looks at me, her brow furrowing for a moment. Her brow smooths with her answer. "Yes. Yes, I was. For a long time I was very mad at him. I didn't want to have to be like Abraham, giving up my husband, my babies, like it was some kind of test to see if I loved God more. I didn't want anything to do with a God like that."

"What changed?"

"I did." She quickly comes out of the flight cage and closes the door behind herself, and I know by the way she begins trudging back to her trailer that she intends this to be a sufficient answer to my question. She turns her head and says over her shoulder, "You mind feeding those raccoons for me? Let 'em out to play a bit?"

A state policeman delivered a gaze of five raccoon kits to her a couple weeks ago, after a farmer noticed the mother wasn't coming back to the nest. They'd been old enough to lap up the special formula and baby cereal, and had moved on to moistened cat food she kept sealed tight and locked in a plastic bin outside the long, pine-framed screened-in cage at the edge of the woods. I take the bag of cat food and see their little banded faces bobbing and peering at me coming toward them. They sniff at the bag and chirp, rolling around and playing at my feet as I duck inside the cage and fill their bowl, pouring in just enough water for the cat food to soak up and get soggy. They eat as if they haven't eaten in days, though I know they ate the night before. When I'm finished, I keep the door open so they can venture out and play a little. Sudie sits on a stump next to the hawk cage, and soon the kits mosey out of the cage and are playing at our feet. Once they're out, they'll follow Sudie everywhere, like ducklings after their mama.

"Oh, sure, you're cute now," Sudie says to them, shaking her head.

I know what she means. We'll keep them and help them learn to forage for their own food, but we'll be sure to release them when they're five or six months old. Any longer than that, they get spoiled to humans, for one thing. And for another, they get vicious when their hormones kick in, which makes them not cute at all.

"Gabe going with you to let the turtle go this afternoon?"

"He is. I'm expecting him anytime now."

"He's a nice young man." Her eyes gleam.

"I suppose he is."

She nudges me and laughs.

"Oh, of course he's wonderful. But I can't let anything get in the way of whatever it is I need to do for this baby."

She nods. "Unless this thing is something the Lord is using to help you make your decision."

I think about the little family we saw at the Dairy Barn. About my life here, life with Mama. About Dewey Johnson. About the fresh graves at Sudie's cemetery. About Bryan and the ache in my bones when he gripped my arms. I think about the websites I've been looking at of parents wanting to adopt, the way these couples have arranged their whole lives to welcome a child, together, some of them with other children, and all of them with homes that look safe and loving and whole. Families who pray every day for a birth mom and baby they haven't even met. "I don't know, Sudie."

"Listen," she says as a female jay calls in a tree above us. A male replies from many yards away. "Listen for the Lord. He may not send pillars of fire or clouds of smoke like he did for the Israelites, but he sends his Spirit. Listen for it, and you'll know what to do when the time comes."

When she stands, I see sweat stains the pits and back of her shirt. It's not that hot out. Not for that much sweating.

"You feeling okay, Sudie?"

"Fine. I'm fine." She waves off my concern and trudges around to the front of the trailer, the five little kits scrambling and tumbling at her feet.

"Maybe you should see a doctor to make sure?"

She raises an eyebrow at me. "No way. No doctors for me. All they'll do is tell me I'm not eating right and I'm not exercising enough, neither of which I am willing to make changes to at my age."

One thing about Sudie, she's as stubborn as she is kind.

Gabe's blue Jeep appears down the drive as we're about to go inside. The soft top is off, and the radio is playing one of the popular country songs. "Ladies." He tips his baseball cap at us and hops out. "So where's this turtle?"

Sudie's breathing sounds raspy as we follow her inside and she fusses over getting the turtle out of his cage. She spreads newspaper on the table and sets him on it, along with a couple of containers of car touch-up paint.

"I thought you aren't supposed to paint turtle shells," Gabe says.

"You're not. Unless they've been fixed with Bondo like this one and need to be camouflaged." Sudie hunches over the turtle and covers the Bondo with dark-green paint.

"Where are we going to let him go?" he asks.

"Same place he was found. Off Old Mill Road, near the bridge over Big Clifty Creek."

"Do you always let them go where you found them?"

"We do," I answer. "They have a better chance of surviving when they're back where they started. Their instincts help them remember where to find food, mates."

"So we'll eventually let the hawk go back where I hit him?"

"We will."

"I think I'm going to visit my mama on Sunday," I say to Gabe as the Jeep rolls to a stop beside the Clifty Creek Bridge. "Mother's Day and all."

He switches off the car and turns to me. "You sure about that?"

I can't blame him for asking. He's seen the way I act when I get her letters. "I need to tell her about this baby. Besides that, Sudie says the only person unforgiveness hurts is me."

"Sudie's a wise lady."

"Might be a good time to go since the pains seem to have gone."

He nods, then reaches for my hand. "You shouldn't go alone. What if she upsets you and they come back? Besides that, it's not a short drive."

"Gabe, you don't have to . . ." The baby turns inside me. And yet, part of me feels like I'm taking advantage of him being so nice. If he's doing this because he wants more than friendship . . .

"I know I don't have to." He looks at me as if he senses my larger concern. "Look, Jaycee, I know it'll be a long time before you're ready to make any big life decisions beyond what you're doing with the baby. But I want you to know I'm offering this, I'm doing these things for you, because I want to. Not because I expect anything back."

"But—"

"*But* nothing. Right now, just remember I'm a friend who cares about you—cares about you quite a bit—and I'm not going anywhere."

"Well . . . thank you."

"Now, I'm not gonna lie. If someday you think you

might feel more for me than friendship, that would be a fine day indeed."

That grin. For a moment I think I might let him kiss me. But a semi barrels by, and the force of it shakes that thought right out of me.

Gabe opens his door. "C'mon. Let's get this turtle to where she needs to go."

"Sudie says turtles only wander an acre or two around where they live," I say as we traipse down the incline toward the swollen creek. "And they have such a strong sense of home, you have to bring them back right where you found them. Otherwise, they'll do anything, including crossing roads and getting hit again, to get back. That's why we have to be sure to release them where we found them."

"Didn't this one get found up by the road?"

"Yes, but we can't leave her there. Sudie said her nose was pointed this way, so we'll take her this way."

"What about hawks? They have to fly more than a couple acres. How do you know where to take them?"

"Best bet is to take them where they were found." I step over an old tree fallen on its side. "Redtails mate for life. Don't you remember the one we saw watching us the day you hit it?"

"Oh, yeah, now that you mention it."

"It was sitting up in a giant cottonwood. Watching everything we did. I think that was his mate."

"How can you tell it's a male?"

"Just a hunch. Besides that, the one that was watching was a lot bigger than ours. Females are a lot bigger than the males."

We're at the edge of the creek, wide and high from the wet spring. Cardinals call, *boo-kee boo-kee boo-kee*, and a couple of bullfrogs banter in the tall grass and new green brush. "Looks like as good a place as any." I lift the turtle from the box and set her on the ground, on a soft bed of dried leaves which crunches beneath her. She's tucked tight in her shell without any indication of wanting to come out.

"Now what?"

"Watch."

The turtle slowly pokes her nose, then the top of her head out of the shell, and before long it's stepping slowly in the direction of the creek and away from the busy road.

Gabe and I are halfway back to the road when he grabs my arm and stops me. I'm off balance for a moment, the weight of my belly more awkward every day.

"Sorry," he says apologetically. "But look." He points to I don't know what. At least not at first. "Over there. At the base of that tree."

I still don't see anything, but then there's movement. The twitch of a round black nose. The glimmer of a round black eye. "Oh, it's a fawn!"

"It's not moving. Is it hurt?"

At the sound of his whisper, the fawn ducks its head, pressing itself as close to the ground as it can.

"I don't think so. . . . Oh, Gabe, I've never seen one before. At least not like this."

He steps toward it.

"Don't . . ." I tug on his T-shirt.

"How will we know if it's okay?"

"It's okay. I'm sure it is."

"Then where's the mother?"

"The mother leaves it alone during the day. The babies, they don't have a scent, so they're safer apart from the mother. People find them and bring them to rehabbers all the time thinking they're orphaned, but most of the time they're not. Same thing with baby rabbits."

"God sure thought of everything, didn't he?"

I smile. That's what Sudie always says. Dappled sunlight filters through the tree branches above the fawn, creating spots of light on the ground all around it. A perfect match to the spots of white across its back.

"I do believe he did."

24

Knowing about Sudie losing her mama when she was little and later losing her three babies, thinking about the change in Mama in her letters, and most of all, carrying this baby inside me, makes Mother's Day feel completely different than it's ever felt before. We navigate around the larger-than-usual crowd headed into Riverton Community Church. Little girls run circles around their mamas in matching dresses, little boys in bow ties ride in the crook of their daddies' arms, Sue and Athena Gilbert grip the arms of their shaky mama, white-haired and back bent halfway over her walker.

"Sudie . . ." I nod toward the church entrance. Elizabeth Blair is there with Bryan and his father and sister. I quick look away to avoid her glare. My belly feels heavier than ever when I see Reverend Payne standing at the doors and greeting everyone as Veda and Trina hand all the mothers pink roses on their way inside. Everyone has known about my pregnancy for weeks. But maybe because it's Mother's Day, I don't know, I feel ashamed all over again. Reverend Payne and the church have done so much for me over the years. I should have known better. There's a limit to mercy, after all.

"It's all right, child." Sudie seems to sense what I'm thinking. She hooks her hand around my arm, and the spring sun catches on her pearls.

The Blairs file in well ahead of us. Surely Bryan hasn't told his parents about me and this baby. But what if he has? My face burns as we move up the steps, the proper mothers taking their roses, husbands kissing them on the cheek, children clinging to their legs.

One by one, folks wade into the river ahead of me, my stomach clenching at the thought of coming up wet in front of everybody or my nose plugging up or choking on the water . . . I half walk, half swim out to Reverend Payne . . . hands strong but gentle to steady me . . . Mama and Sudie . . . tears of pride running down their faces.

"Jaycee," Reverend Payne says. "Sudie. You ladies are looking lovely today."

Sudie squeezes my arm.

I look for a dove to come down like it did for Jesus and John the Baptist, but none does . . .

Veda holds out a rose and I hesitate to take it. "For you," she says, extending it closer to my hands.

"Jaycee," Reverend Payne says, taking the rose from Veda. "The rose is for you." His eyes are focused, knowing. Kind.

I feel the old go and the new come as Reverend Payne and the deacons float me back and under and bring me up out of the water . . .

I love you, the voice says.

But I'm a mess, Lord.

I'm your strength.

But I don't know what to do, Lord.

Be still and know.

But I'm scared, Lord.

I am with you always.

Help me, Lord.

Trust me.

I look down the church steps and see folks watching me, folks like Hersch and his wife. Jim Thompson from the town funeral home, who helped me with Jayden's arrangements. Carla and her husband. And at the base of the steps, Gabe. He winks and gives me his biggest smile.

The crowd along the riverbank claps and cheers . . . we all hold hands in a big circle and sing . . .

My baby moves inside me, and I turn to Reverend Payne. "Thank you," I say, and take the rose, the stem smooth, the thorns trimmed away.

"See?" Sudie whispers in my ear as we head into the sanctuary.

The chancel and steps to the pulpit are filled with vases overflowing with fresh-cut lilacs and daisies, lilies and tulips. Ida Lambert powers through an upbeat version of "Day by Day," followed by an emotional performance of "You Raise Me Up" by one of the high school girls. The children's choir sings, their cherubic faces pink with pride as they scamper into the congregation afterward to present their mothers with pink carnations.

"Thank you, Ida," Reverend Payne says, then turns to the congregation. "Mother's Day is a day to be celebrated for certain. All over America we're celebrating the ones who raised us, the ones who bandaged skinned knees, the ones who tucked us in at night, the ones whose love is unconditional and whose work is interminable, whose lives exemplify all the standards of Proverbs 31. But there's something in Proverbs chapter 31 that isn't often talked about. That's verses 8 and 9:

> *"Speak up for those who cannot speak for themselves;*
> *ensure justice for those being crushed.*
> *Yes, speak up for the poor and helpless,*
> *and see that they get justice.*

"I find it intriguing that these two verses that talk about the voiceless and those being crushed, the poor and the helpless, that these two verses show up right before the exposition of what we hold up as a standard for women. Don't you?"

The congregation responds with a few nods and the sound of folks rustling their bulletins.

"So I'd like to change Mother's Day up a bit this year. I'd like to talk about the mothers we won't see at our Sunday brunch, the ones who were reluctant to take a rose today, the ones who refused to take one at all, though Veda and Trina and I did our best to assure every woman in this room they do indeed deserve a rose."

That was almost me.

"There are those in this room whose wombs ache for a child, or for a child they've lost. Those who felt crushed by broken mothers, single mothers from decades ago and among us now who are ostracized and feel alone. Those who sit among us who dread this day every year, because for them, Mother's Day feels like a scab peeled from a wound that never heals. Or those who feel that because they are not mothers, they are somehow less or incomplete, unchosen, unseen."

Gabe gives my hand a quick squeeze and lets go again. Reverend Payne goes on with his sermon, and I scan the audience and think on so many of the stories I know. I wonder if Sue and Athena Gilbert, unmarried and childless, feel incomplete. I wonder about Carla, with her children spread all over the country and none of them here to celebrate her. I wonder about the mothers of the children buried out at the cemetery, the ones who buried child after child after child during the cholera outbreaks, or like Sudie, for reasons she'll never know. I think about my own broken mama sitting in prison this morning with one baby in the ground, and me . . .

She still has me.

"In past years, we've had mothers stand," Reverend

Payne's words draw me back. "There's nothing essentially wrong with that practice. But today, I want *all of us to stand*. Because we all came from a mother. We all have lost or will lose a mother. Some of us have been loved by mothers, and others of us have been hurt by them. And while some of us may not be mothers in the traditional sense of the word, we are all made in the image of God, who, while most often portrayed as a father, is also described as having a love for us like that of a mother . . . one who cannot forget us any more than a mother can forget the child who has nursed at her breast, one who covers us with his feathers and shelters us with his wings, who protects us when earthly mothers do not. One who hears us when we are voiceless, one who ensures eternal justice for those who are crushed, one who fulfills our deepest needs.

"I want all of us to stand this morning to acknowledge that the origin and the fulfillment of love—of who we are— is not through our mother or father, not through genes or ancestry or human legacy, but through the grace and perfect love of Jesus Christ. We're all lost, but found in him. We're all poor and helpless, but he is the Great Rescuer. Whether you are grieving or celebrating today, he redeems and restores it all."

The familiar chords of "Amazing Grace" fill the room as we all stand and Ida leads us in singing the hymn. I glance at Sudie, whose face is wet with tears, same today as I imagine it was when she buried her children. I think about how the Lord blessed me with Sudie long before I ever realized the injustices of Mama, how he must've been watching over me . . . how we're all adopted . . .

What is the Lord asking you to give up?

Help me, Lord.

Trust me.

❧

We're halfway back to the car when I feel a bony hand close tight around my arm.

Elizabeth Blair. Coach Blair stands behind her. They're both scowling, her dark eyes steeled with their usual disdain for me. And behind them, Bryan, his face red and trying his best not to look at me, with his sister. The cocky anger he showed that night at the gas station seems to have been replaced by something else—something that looks almost like regret.

He must have told them about the baby.

My legs feel like noodles under me and I grab on to Sudie's hand so hard I'm surprised her fingers don't turn purple.

Help me, Lord. Please. Help me.

Trust me.

Mrs. Blair steps so close to me I'd fall down without Gabe and Sudie next to me. I try not to inhale the venom she spews. "I know that's my grandchild you're carrying," she says.

"Elizabeth," Sudie says.

Mrs. Blair waves her off. "Bryan told us everything. I told him a long time ago to stay away from girls like you, but he didn't listen. Well, *you're* going to listen. If you think I'm going to allow a junkie's daughter—"

"Elizabeth." Sudie's voice rises.

Mrs. Blair doesn't flinch. "—to raise my grandchild, you are sorely mistaken. I am not going to lose the one good thing to come from your relationship." Elizabeth takes a deep breath as if bracing herself for the next statement. But to my surprise, the harsh lines of anger on her face sag into grief. "There's been others, you know. Girls who took care of the situation before it came to this. Grandchildren I'll never see."

"I've lost babies too," Sudie offers. "Can't make things right by doing something that's wrong."

A breeze flips back the chiffon sleeves of Elizabeth's dress, and there are the bruises. Bruises in the same place where Bryan used to grab hold of me. Bruises his daddy must've taught him how to make. *Evil don't stop until someone makes it, until someone speaks up for the ones who can't speak for themselves, does it, Lord?*

I can hear Gabe next to me breathing slow and sure. Sudie tightens her grip on my hand.

Elizabeth pauses, as if she might actually be considering what Sudie said. "The baby is my only chance at redeeming this mess. You can expect papers—paternal custody papers—from Walter Crawford."

I can't stand looking at Elizabeth's pinched-up face another minute. Gabe and Sudie look nearly as blindsided as I feel. Knowing Elizabeth has always been capable of such nastiness does not soften the blow of it. Beyond her, along the horizon, are trees thick with leaves, except for the ash among them. The center branches of the towering old ash are showing their fate, completely stripped as the insects bore away deep inside. My heart steels against Elizabeth's anger, and I let go of Sudie's hand, my own curling into a fist.

"Ensure justice for those being crushed. Yes, speak up for the poor and helpless . . ."

"This baby is not your only chance," I say, surprised at the strength of my own voice. "This baby isn't my chance, either. The only chance that matters here is that the baby gets one of its own. Away from you and Bryan. Away from Riverton. And away from me."

Elizabeth crosses her arms, a smug smirk on her face. "You're wrong about that. Expect those papers, Jaycee. There isn't a thing you can do to stop us." She turns and stomps away. Coach Blair follows her after giving me a bone-chilling glare.

"You're shaking, Jaycee," Gabe says, and puts his arm around me.

Whatever strength I had to stand up to her is gone, and I bury my face in his chest. "She can't do this. She can't. I have rights too."

I feel Sudie's arms around me. "Don't you worry about her, child. The Lord will fight for you and this baby. You only need to be still."

"Be still?" I turn and wipe my eyes. "How am I supposed to be still? She's got Walter Crawford and everything. The only thing worse than giving this baby to strangers would be for it to be raised by them."

"C'mon," Gabe says gently. "We need to get going to make visiting hours. We can talk this over in the car."

25

"This baby's going crazy inside me." I press my hands against my belly and feel the bumps and pushing. I'm worried about the pain coming back, so I try to focus on breathing slow. Calming down. "I think he's doing somersaults."

"Can't blame him for that," Gabe says, one eye on the road and the other looking at me sidelong with concern. "You're not having pains, are you?"

"No."

"You sure you're up to seeing your mom after all this?"

"No. I'm not sure. But I can't see how I can put it off, either. Might not be another chance before this baby comes, and if I give him up . . . or if Elizabeth manages to take him . . ."

"She's not going to be able to take him."

"How do you know?"

"There was a case in my hometown a few years back. Real nasty. Grandmother was trying to sue for custody, and the judge dismissed the case. It can't happen, especially if Bryan isn't interested in the baby. He's the only one who could try to get custody."

"What if his mama makes him? You saw the look on her face."

Gabe rolls his eyes. "It's *Bryan*. I don't get the impression he's the kind of guy who's gonna fight for anything that'll get in the way of his life. Besides, even if he did, he'd probably have to prove you're unfit, which means he'd have to get through me and Sudie and a whole lot of other people who can prove just the opposite about you."

"I hope you're right." I rest my head back on the seat and focus on an old, soft country song on the radio, one I know the words to without thinking about them. We are miles out of Riverton now. The roads open up into straight, flat country and a patchwork of fresh turned and sprouting fields, and my eyes feel heavier with the rhythmic passing of fence posts and tree lines, and my thoughts drift back to Mama, how she'd sit on the couch with a ratty afghan around her shoulders and watch entertainment programs on the TV about Whitney Houston or Anna Nicole Smith, Michael Jackson or Tammy Faye, and she'd weep. She'd cry over the folks fighting on *Jerry Springer*, or at the Kardashians when they started going round with each other, or the housewives of Orange County when they got too catty. Mama had a curious ability to cry along with famous people and people she never met, but never once did I see her shed a tear for me. Not for Jayden, either. Not when I cried myself to sleep when we had nothing to eat for dinner. Not when kids wouldn't play with me on account of where we live. But then I think about Sudie and all she's lost. She doesn't have much either. I've been giving Mama such a hard time for so long, I wonder if I've been missing how much she's hurting too. Maybe there isn't time for tears when it takes all you got to get through the days. And I wonder what she's going to say about this baby.

I roll down the window of the car a crack and breathe in the fresh air, praying it relieves the nausea creeping up in my throat. We're about halfway to the prison located in the next county over, and visitors are allowed for thirty minutes. White lines of the road sweep past the car with an awkward cadence, each pulling me closer to Mama.

"You all right?" Gabe asks, turn signal ticking as he pulls off onto the prison exit.

I nod and swallow another gulp of air like I'm coming up for breath in a swimming pool. "Stomach's just a little upset."

"Not much farther."

Five more miles of country road to the east and the high fencing edged in two feet of razor wire begins. The boxy shape of the prison looms in the distance. At the entrance, we stop at the guard booth. They write down our names and who we're visiting, then wave us through. Gabe steers the car down the gravel drive and parks behind ten or fifteen other cars, and we follow a smattering of other droopy-shouldered visitors to the front doors, where a grim-faced correction officer lets us all in. Inside the lobby we wait for another officer, dressed in the same uniform with the same gun, Taser, baton, and bottle of pepper spray holstered on his hip, to call our names. He pats down several of the male visitors, but nods me on through the metal detector.

When I'm led into the community visitation room, I pick a table in the back corner. The fumes from Pine-Sol and other cleaning chemicals are thick, and I have to swallow hard to keep from gagging. A young prisoner kisses and tickles twin toddler boys in overalls while her visitor, a young man who looks like he might be their father, watches with a scowl on his face. Another woman, skin so dark and so smooth she couldn't have been much older than a teenager, sits across from an older woman in her Sunday dress and hat who dabs at her eyes with a tissue. Another, her arms sleeved with tattoos, argues pretty loud with the man who sits across from her, the back of his neck dark, dark red—from anger or the sun or both.

A buzzer sounds, the prison-side door of the visitation room opens, and the guard lets in a slight, slumped woman. He points her in my direction.

Mama.

26

She looks better than I thought she would. Instead of the bony, sunken-faced heroin addict I'd said good-bye to in the courtroom, Mama has regained some fullness to her cheeks. The gray, saggy circles are gone from under her eyes. She appears showered and clean.

When she sees me, she stops. Her eyes fill with tears.

And to my surprise, mine do too.

Mama pulls out a chair across the table from me and sits down. The bright-orange jumpsuit casts a strange glow on her sallow skin, but her fingernails are pink instead of stained black from soot and filth. She reaches out and covers my folded hands with hers. "Jaycee, I . . ."

"Happy Mother's Day, Mama," I say, taking advantage of her hesitation.

"You look so good, Jaycee."

I feel tears pricking my own eyes as a couple slide down her cheek. I wipe them away quick. "Thanks, Mama. You do too."

She shakes her head. "No, I don't. I look awful. Besides that, orange is not my best color."

I smile for a moment, before I notice her elbows, bony, resting on the table. *She is fragile.* The realization overwhelms me. Not pity, but mercy.

The same mercy the Lord's been giving to me.

We've both been thirsty.

The baby kicks, and I'm glad I'm sitting down so I can keep my baby hidden from her, for now.

"How is home?"

"It's okay. Got it all cleaned up. Bud and Larry from church, you'd be amazed how they helped fix it up. Painted the walls. Helped lay down new carpet."

She nods. "How is Sudie? Shawnie and Tim? The others?"

"They're all good."

"And the diner?"

"Good, too."

At the table next to us, a plain man visits with a woman with her hair cropped short and blunt. She leans across the table toward him as if she's hanging on his every word. He has his Bible open and holds a polished wooden cross.

The baby turns inside me. I stare at my own hands, empty,

nails bitten to nubs. They begin to blur as tears fill my eyes. The voices in the visiting room rise and fall like waves pounding against a seashore, as if one person reaches out and the other pushes back.

"What is it, Jaycee?"

I look up and see real concern in her eyes. A look I've been longing for, more than I even realized. "There's something I have to tell you." I push my chair back from the table and wrap my arms around my belly.

"Oh, darlin' . . ." She gets up and runs around the table and throws her arms around me. From the corner of my eye, I see one of the guards start toward us, but I wave at him to let him know it's okay.

My heart and everything I've been holding in for so long crumples. "I don't know what to do, Mama." The words come out all desperate and ugly like the tears and now the snot running down my face.

"Jaycee—" She pulls back and brushes a stray strand of hair away from my eyes.

"I was so mad at you when they took you away. I was so glad you were gone." I think about the first letter I tried to write her, how angry I was. And how glad I am that I tore it up. "But all this—" I motion toward my belly and suck in air between sobs. "When it comes down to it, I need a mother . . . I need you to help me know . . . how to be a mother."

She's crying about as hard as I am now, the two of us a hot mess. I'm sure the others in the room are starting to stare, but I don't care.

"Well, I'm not so sure I'm the best one to help you with that." She looks away.

It's my turn to reach toward her. "I remember, Mama. I remember you and me when I was little, before you got hurt. I remember who you were, Mama. Who *we* were. That's the Mama I need."

She shakes her head and pulls away from me, then sits in the chair next to me. "I've done a lot of thinking in here. Not much else to do besides think. I've thought about everything that happened to us, everything that led up to losing . . . to losing Jayden." Tears gather fresh in her eyes. "I just don't know if I'll ever be the person you remember again."

I nod, grateful for her honesty.

There is one more thing.

"Mama, I need to ask you something."

"Anything."

"Why didn't you just quit? Stop using the heroin? Didn't you love us enough to quit?"

"I love you and I loved your brother, that's for certain." A visitor at the next table hands us a couple of travel packages of tissues, and Mama dabs at her eyes. "You have to understand, when I was high . . . what the smack did . . . for the first time since your father died, the world was beautiful. I was beautiful. Everything was beautiful. And I was so tired of fighting the pain and the ugly and the hard of life. I never stopped loving you. Problem was, I loved the heroin more."

The words sting. I think of Gabe in the waiting room and am so grateful he is here. I have plenty more to say and ask, but a pulling starts in my belly and I shift in my seat.

"Everything all right?" she says, concern washing over her face.

"It's just a pain. It'll pass."

"You shouldn't have come—if I'd have known you were pregnant, I wouldn't have asked you—"

"It's all right. I wanted to come. Really." I rub my hands up and down my belly, and slowly the pain subsides.

"I remember those feelings, the way every twinge made me worry. You and your brother, the way you moved inside me." She smiles softly. "I ever tell you about the day you were born?"

"No."

"Sudie took me to the hospital when I was laboring with you."

"Sudie?"

"Yes. Sudie. She stayed with me the whole time. You came out all gooey and wide-eyed, your hands and feet still purple like they weren't quite ready to come out and work just yet. They laid you on my belly, you looked up at me with all the expectations in the world, and I knew I couldn't meet them. Not without your dad. I also knew that I loved you more than I knew it was possible to love.

"After you were born, I worked as hard as I could to give you things I didn't have, but I always felt like it wasn't enough. I hated that we were poor. I hated when you started to realize we were poor too. When I hurt my back, started taking those pills, all the shame I had about not giving you what you needed, about horrible things I'd done . . ."

"Mama. I don't need to know—"

"What I'm trying to say is while I had a choice about the heroin, back when I had you, I didn't think I had a choice about how I raised you. I was stuck there in that trailer, and all I could see was you being stuck there too."

"Why didn't you give me up for adoption?"

"I didn't think about it at the time. Besides that, the second I saw you . . . there's no way I could have even if I'd wanted to. You were all I had. You were the only part of your father I had left, and we were in it together. I loved every second of taking care of you. But when I look at you now—" her eyes puddle with tears again—"I see that giving you up might've been the best thing that could've happened to you." She shakes her head. "I'm sorry for that."

"The rose is for you," Reverend Payne said. . . . His eyes were kind. . . . I felt the old go and the new come as he brought me up out of the water . . . and Mama was there holding my hand, singing next to me. . . .

Maybe mercy is the rose I'm supposed to give Mama today.

"I didn't think you cared about me anymore, Mama."

"I never stopped caring. Never stopped loving you for a second. I hated myself. And heroin was the only thing that made me feel better. But those are my burdens, not yours. I passed them on to you, and I didn't even know it until I've been stuck in here with all the time in the world to think about it. You can give your baby—my grandbaby . . ." She chokes up. "You can break the cycle and give him a chance."

A chance. I can give this baby a chance.

"So you really never thought about giving me away?" I ask again.

"No. Never. "

"Because that's what I need your help with, Mama. I think . . . I *know* . . . I'm giving this baby up for adoption."

She starts to say something, then stops. She studies my face and starts to say something again.

"Am I a horrible person? I mean, what kind of a mother gives up her own child?"

"No. You are not a horrible person," she says, without pausing a second to think about it. She scoots her chair closer to me and takes hold of my hands. Her eyes are stern now, but soft with something I haven't seen in them in a long, long time. Something that reminds me of when she'd take me to the park and swing alongside me, or when she spent hours teaching me how to tie my shoes. Something that reminds me of the kindness in Sudie's eyes when I went running to her trailer on cold, dark nights. "If that's what you feel the Lord is telling you to do, that's what you need to do. And that's a decision that's not bad or good or anything, except for loving a child deep enough to trust it to the Lord. You can do better than I did, Jaycee. You can do better for you, and for that baby. You become what you're not willing to give up, whether you know you're hanging on to it white-knuckled or not."

"But how do I know giving him up is giving him the right chance, Mama?"

She thinks on that for a moment. "You remember the story about those two women, both claiming to be the baby's mother and fighting over it in front of King Solomon?"

I nod. "He said he was going to cut the baby in half."

"And that's how he figured out who the real mama was. The one who was willing to give up the child so that it could survive."

Elizabeth Blair comes to mind, and I tell Mama about the scene in front of the church. "She says she can get custody. That if she can prove me unfit—"

Mama puts a hand up. "Now wait just a minute. Folks can say what they want about the things I done, but no one can say anything about you."

"I don't think she sees it that way. And besides that, they've got money. Lots of money. They used it against Mary Ashby. I know they'd use it the same against me. Against this baby."

Mama shakes her head. She knows I'm right. The Ashbys weren't even poor, by comparison to us.

"We don't stand a chance against folks like the Blairs," I say.

"You're right. We don't. But we've got the Lord."

I start to argue with her. Where was the Lord when Jayden died? And when my father died, for that matter? But then I look at her, the way her eyes are bright for the first time in years even though she's in the middle of a concrete room. I think about the miracle of that, right in front of me, and

I begin to understand the living water Jesus was offering at the well, how he wanted that woman to trust him to change her life, how he wanted to take away the pain in her soul. I pour my own heart out to Mama then. Everything about Bryan. I tell her the good, too, about Sudie and the animals. About Gabe. And somehow in the middle of all that telling, I realize it is in the pouring out that I am filled. I realize he is making a way for me and Mama, and if that's true, he can make a way for this baby, too.

Me and Mama, we sit there in silence for a good long while, holding on to each other for the first time, and letting go, too, our lives intertwined, like so many mothers and daughters I suppose, like sweet honeysuckle vines weaving themselves into inseparable knots on a barbed-wire fence.

A buzzer sounds, signaling the end of visiting hours. I stand and take a step toward the exit, then pause at Mama's side. I lean down and hug her one more time.

"I love you, Mama."

"I love you, too, Jaycee." She gives my hand one last squeeze before I walk away.

"You take care now," the guard says, opening the steel door for me.

The weight of it slams shut, and I jump. My belly tightens in response. I take Gabe's hand, and we drive the whole way home in silence.

27

"There you go, little nuggets."

The raccoon kits tumble over each other to get at the bowl of cat food I set inside their cage. Sudie texted earlier. Says she isn't feeling well. Would I mind feeding the critters for her? Of course I don't.

Dark skies line the horizon to the west, and the meadow is strangely quiet for this time of the morning. Weatherman says to expect days of rain, something the valley is most certainly not in need of since this spring's been wet already. The trapeze inside the flight cage creaks, but not from a breeze. Rather, the hawk is on it. He keeps his eye right on me as I toss a couple pieces of mouse into his cage. The trapeze swings as he spreads his wings out, stretching one, then the other, and he balances himself without faltering so I know it's near time to let him go.

Before heading into the diner, I check on Sudie, lift the blinds in her front room, where a passel of baby opossums nuzzle together under the special heat lamp. A local police officer brought them in after finding the mother alongside the road, having had the wisdom to check if she had babies in her pouch before shoveling her carcass into the woods.

"Sudie?" I say in the direction of her darkened room.

"I'm okay, child," she finally replies. "Just slow moving. Thank you kindly for helping me."

"Of course . . . but are you sure you're feeling okay to handle the rest?"

Her voice is raspy. The young opossums, eyes closed and still hairless, will die without frequent attention and feedings.

"Fine, fine. I been up with them through the night. I can do it through the day." She coughs hard. "Come sit by me a minute. Tell me about the visit to see your mother."

My eyes adjust to the dark, helped by the new light pouring in through the front windows, and I sit on the bed next to Sudie, who lies beneath a quilt that looks to be handmade. The room is neat but spare, except for the corner where there is a tall, narrow curio cabinet painted white with gilded handles. The piece is nicer than anything else in her place. Makes me wonder where it came from. Something unwanted at a flea market? Something her late husband's family passed down?

"So how was it?" Sudie asks, interrupting my wondering.

"So, you were right."

"Really?" Her eyes widen. "And how's that?"

"Well, I found out forgiving isn't as bad as I thought it might be."

A knowing grin comes over her face. "And?"

"And . . . while not everything that happens is good, the Lord can take the things that happen to us and work them into something good down the road."

"Amen to that." She grins even wider, reaches a calloused hand toward mine.

"I am scared, though."

"Scared of what?"

"Elizabeth Blair. Those custody papers. They haven't come yet. What if she's right? What if she can take my baby? What if she can keep me from giving him a better chance than I ever had?"

"That sounds like an awful lot of what-ifs for someone who just said the Lord can work things for good."

"But, Sudie—"

"*But* nothin'. Listen here. The Lord promised we will have trouble in this world. But he also said he'd be right there with us. The way I figure it, you can sit and worry all day long about Elizabeth Blair and those what-ifs, or you can trust that God loves that baby more than you could even imagine and spend these last weeks in peace about that. There's always gonna be what-ifs. Shadrach, Meshach, and Abednego probably had plenty of what-ifs when they walked into the fire. Daniel was probably thinking about what-ifs when he walked into the lions' den. And I'm pretty sure Moses' mother was thinking about what-ifs when she set him in that basket and pushed it into the river. Point is, they trusted God with the what-ifs. And God delivered them."

"I don't need a sermon right now, Sudie." Tears prick at my eyes. Surely she knows those old Bible stories feel pretty impossible when the hard is here and now.

We sit there for a while in the darkened room until her breathing evens out. I am about to get up and leave her be when she starts coughing something fierce, wheezing hard as she tries to catch her breath.

I fetch a glass of fresh water from the kitchen. "Let me call Mary Beth to take care of the animals," I say as she takes the cup from my hand. Mary Beth is younger, and she has a husband who works along with her, the two of them licensed wildlife rehabbers the next county over. She's always happy to take in Sudie's overflow in the height of the summer and anytime she needs help.

Sudie doesn't reply right away, which tells me she is considering this. And if she's feeling bad enough to consider it, she's feeling awfully bad.

"That might be all right," she says finally, her voice faltering.

I fill an oversize plastic cup with ice and Sprite and take it to her room. Her lips are cracked and the skin under her eyes blue and sunken. "Please go to the doctor, or at least call him. I'm sure Shawnie or Tim, even Gabe, would come drive you there."

"Pshaw. I'm fine. Nothin' the doctor can do for a virus. That's probably what it is. Just gotta ride it out."

I'm not so sure. She's been so tired, and this bug doesn't help. When I leave her place, I can't help but think about how I left Jayden alone too. It takes all I have to drive away.

I call Mary Beth first on my way to the diner, and she agrees to come pick up the baby opossums and to check on the other critters inside and feed them while she's there. Not only does this help Sudie out, it makes me feel better knowing Sudie won't be alone all day. After we work out those details, I call Gabe.

"I don't know what's wrong with her. She's not been right all spring." I tell him about her sweating spells, her energy that seems to be dwindling by the week. "She won't go to the doctor, Gabe. Maybe if you came by she'd let you take her blood pressure or somethin'?"

"I'll do that," he says. He's coming in at lunchtime, scheduled to close. "You think tomorrow's soon enough?"

"I think so." *I hope so.*

"It's been a long night. Three Narcan runs. Two nursing home runs, and one of them dead before we got there. Then a heart attack at the Waffle House out by the interstate. I didn't sit down once 'cept when we were driving to the next call." He pauses. Country music plays on his radio in the background. "You know, the hospital's still seeing cases of the flu," he says. "Say the mild winter gave it a late start."

"Maybe that's all it is, then." Come to think of it, folks have been coming into the diner coughing all over the place. I picked up the last two afternoons and closings because Carla was home fevering and coughing too. My windshield wipers move to the music playing on my own radio as they wipe away a misty rain. I rest my hand where I can feel the baby kicking. "Let's hope that's all it is."

When I get to the diner, the smell of fresh-baked cinnamon rolls fills the air, and the place is already buzzing with customers. Mothers and preschoolers fill nearly all the tables, a playgroup from one of the bigger churches that meets here sometimes on Wednesday mornings.

I recognize a couple of the mothers from high school, girls who'd sat on the stage in the auditorium on awards day every spring, collecting ribbons and certificates for perfect attendance and honor roll grades. Girls who waited until they were married before getting pregnant. Girls who don't have to work during the day because their husbands make plenty as plant managers or schoolteachers or commuting to the city for work. Girls who wear clothes I see in the windows at the local boutique. Girls who have second babies strapped in car seats and hanging over their elbows when they come in, and some of them carrying third legitimate babies in bellies swollen big as mine.

I take their orders of cinnamon rolls for the toddlers, eggs and sometimes oatmeal and decaffeinated lattes for themselves. I imagine their children playing and giggling, toys spread across hardwood-floored living rooms of their three-bedroom tract houses in the new neighborhoods outside town, not floors that bow under their feet when they walk across them or walls that had to have the smoke scrubbed out of them. Girls whose babies have a chance without having to make a decision like that baby mother who stood before King Solomon . . . without having to make a decision like me.

Every day the question of what I'm going to do about this baby feels like a gleaming sword hanging above my heart, threatening to slice me and my baby in two. And although the visit to Mama brought me some comfort, Elizabeth Blair's threat won't leave my mind.

Twenty minutes into the shift my feet already ache. Feels like one of the baby's feet or maybe an arm is lodged under my ribs. Rain falls steady outside, running in little rivers down the diner windowpanes. Hersch flips orders and scrapes the grill in a comforting cadence. The mothers and preschoolers trickle out except for a trio whose children are coloring quietly and happily in another booth. Some of the lunch regulars shuffle in, including Shorty Smith and his brood from the tool factory and Bud and Larry the handymen. Reubens are popular on this rainy day, and Hersch pushes mounds of steaming corned beef around next to Shorty's three over-easy eggs to go with his no-butter English muffin.

By the time Gabe comes in, my side aches. If my belly felt any heavier it'd be dragging on the floor. I meet him in the break room and see that his face is drawn and somber, a sign of the stress of his late night. "You all right?"

"I am now," he says, smiling for me.

"It sure is a gray day."

He nods. "You're not overdoing it around here, are you?"

"No." The ache in my groin warns me this is not a completely honest answer. I ignore it. "I'm worried about Sudie."

"Let me get through this shift. I'll check on her first thing in the morning," he says, putting on his apron, then stepping to the sink to scrub his arms, his hands.

"All right."

The day drags on, and as the lunch crowd tapers off, a group comes in asking for a table for eight. Administrators from the university, by the look of it. Several of them wear brushed-gold name tags stating their department: admissions, financial aid, multicultural student life.

"It's his birthday," one of the women whispers in my ear, nodding to a tall black gentleman wearing a bow tie with his suit. "Do you have any chocolate cake today?"

"I'll see what I can do." I wink, doing my best not to let them see that I am tired and want nothing more than to go home, check on Sudie, and put my feet up.

"When are you due?" she asks kindly, not like Anna Rose's mother. For as highfalutin as the students and their families can be, most of the folks who work at the university, professors included, are pretty down-to-earth. Living in Riverton year-round takes away a bit of the novelty of us townies, I suppose, and they eventually realize we aren't all charity cases.

Working at Riverton College becomes just a job to them like any job becomes after time, and a square of land with a house on it is just a square of land.

"I got about a month left." I smile, hoping she doesn't ask the next question. But she does.

"Do you know if it's a boy or a girl?"

"It's a boy."

"Do you have names picked out?"

I shake my head. She doesn't know I won't let myself pick a name, like Sudie won't let me pick names for any of the rescues.

"Well, spring is a wonderful time to have a baby. Good to get outside and walk. Beautiful time of the year."

"Yes, ma'am." Coming from her, and since my secret is out, I take her encouragement to heart. I follow her to the two tables Gabe has pushed together and where the other seven are already seated.

"Anything I can get y'all to drink while you're looking over the menus?"

They rattle off requests for iced tea and diet sodas, a couple of them content with the glasses of ice water Gabe fills behind the counter.

"There any chocolate cake left?" I lean hard against one of the counter stools and hand Gabe the drink order. The pull in my groin feels stronger, and along with it, a familiar knot in my back.

Gabe places the other glasses on the tray next to the waters.

Hersch sprays and wipes down the counter where Shorty

and his friends sat. Carla sits in the break room, her back to us, the adding machine zipping out lines of totals and tallies.

"Should be. Why don't you take a break." He eyes me as I rub my belly, which is hard and tight.

"I'd be fine if it didn't feel like somebody's shoving a baseball into my lower back."

"Let me take that tray out to them. I can get their orders. Me and Hersch can get this." He looks at Hersch, who turns and nods at me.

"I can get these drinks, if you can get the rest. And if you're sure you don't mind."

"You are one stubborn lady." He grins.

I hoist the tray up and over my arm like I've done hundreds of times before, and I'm halfway to the table when pain sears across my pelvis. The tray, the glasses, everything crashes to the ground in a numbing roar, and I'm paralyzed by the squeezing spasm.

"Jaycee—" Gabe is next to me in a second.

"Somethin's not right."

28

My right arm aches where a paramedic shoved a needle into it to give me intravenous fluids. Above me, a monitor bleeps the regular rhythm of my heart. And next to me, the baby's heartbeat whooshes through a speaker on another monitor.

A hand pushes the curtain back from the door of the emergency department room, and Dr. Fitzgerald appears.

"Hey there, missy, what do we have going on here?" His voice booms, and I'm sure whatever patients are the least bit conscious can hear him. The whoosh of the baby's monitor gets louder as he fiddles with a couple of knobs, then inspects the strap the nurses placed across my belly.

"Good news is, baby looks great. The nurses who checked you, they said your water's intact, and you don't have any bleeding."

"No, sir."

"Are you still having pain?"

"A little." I try not to wince. "But nothing like I had at work. It was bad. Really bad."

"Contractions don't usually feel too good." He winks, then his face gets serious. "That's what's happening, Jaycee. You're having contractions." He looks at the baby monitor again. "In fact, you're having a small one right now. Can you feel it?"

It's nothing compared to what I felt when I fell, but when I touch my belly, it's hard as it's ever been. "Not really. Just tight."

He nods, then inspects the bags of fluid hanging on the pole next to the bed. "I've asked them to keep you on a little bit of medicine here to slow down how often you have those contractions. This little guy needs a few more weeks before I'd be comfortable letting him come out. We'll keep you here a day or two and see if this doesn't help. Sometimes it does. Sometimes we have to keep people longer."

"Longer?" I push myself up higher and look at Gabe, his face wrinkled with worry. "I'm supposed to work. And Sudie. She needs my help."

"Hush," Gabe scolds. "I'll see about Sudie. And you know Carla won't let you work a lick once she hears about this."

"You really should listen to this guy," Dr. Fitzgerald says. "I think he might have a bit of a crush on you."

I roll my eyes but can't help but notice the adorable blush rising into Gabe's cheeks. He's right about Carla not letting me work. She'd said as much when the paramedics wheeled me out of the diner on a stretcher. Said she'd pay me anyway. But I can't stand the thought of that.

Dr. Fitzgerald puts a hand on my leg and pats me, as I imagine a father might pat his own daughter. "Let's take this one day at a time. Everything else looks just like it's supposed to look, besides the contractions. We'll do what we can to see if you can get back to the things you need to get back to. But right now, we need to be conservative about all this. Okay, kiddo?"

Kiddo. No one's called me that before. I imagine my real father might have, if I'd had the chance to know him. "Okay. Thank you, Dr. Fitzgerald."

"You're welcome." He gives Gabe's shoulder a squeeze on the way out of the room.

Three days later, Gabe brings me home. The trailer is quiet, especially with the windows closed, since I leave them open as often as I can, and there is a faint trace of the old smells I worked so hard to scrub out of the walls and floors.

"I stocked you up," Gabe says.

The counters are full of fresh snacks and drinks. "You did! Oh, thank you!" I take a big red apple from the collection of fruit, next to a giant bag of peanuts in the shell, fresh bread, and my favorite chocolate chip cookies on the counter. In the fridge, there's milk and lunch meat, yogurt, and more. "You didn't have to do all this."

"You're right, I didn't have to. I wanted to. Remember?" Gabe crosses his arms and raises an eyebrow at me, obviously referring to our previous conversation when we let the turtle loose. "Besides that, I was standing there when the doctor said bed rest, Jaycee. How you gonna get to the store when you're on bed rest?"

"I don't know. I coulda figured it out."

"Right," he says sarcastically. "Now why don't you figure yourself on over to the couch there and put your feet up already." He's already set it up with pillows and a blanket from my room, my Bible, a stack of new magazines on the side table, and on top of it all, the tattered copy of the North Carolina romance novel.

I smile at him, the way the one dimple on his left cheek lingers as he watches me settle myself and turn on the TV.

The evening news comes on.

"We've got flash-flood warnings all across the region tonight, with things not expected to get any better in at least the next twenty-four to forty-eight hours." A weathergirl with straight-edged, long brown hair and a form-fitting dress sweeps her arm across the screen. Huge blotches of green and red mark the areas where the most rain is falling. Riverton is right in the middle of it.

"Heard Chief say on the radio they're going to have to start closing some roads. Mudslides along some of the valley roads. You're high enough here you won't see flooding, but the roads leading out of here, I'm not so sure about them." He runs his hands through his hair.

"I'll be fine."

"I don't care if they do close them. I'll find a way in here if you need me."

"Doctor says the pains should stay away—"

"As long as you mind what he says and don't get up. He doesn't know how stubborn you are."

I think about Jayden. About the names of Sudie's babies. *Mary. John. Samuel.* Their names etched deep into the cold hard granite. "I'm gonna mind."

"I hope so."

"I *will*, Gabe. By the way, how was Sudie when you saw her earlier?"

"She was fine, especially since Mary Beth came and took the opossums. I brought her a few groceries too. Told her about a couple of the guys at the station willing to mow and keep tabs on the cemetery until she's better."

"She appreciated that, I'm sure."

"She did, although she was a little hesitant about the guys."

"She's particular about things there, that's for certain."

"She wouldn't let Mary Beth take her newest patient, a big brown bat with a concussion in an aquarium on the middle of her kitchen table."

I laugh. "Sounds about right."

"And she's managing to get outside to the hawk and raccoons without any trouble."

"That's a good sign. They're all almost ready to release anyway. How does she look? Is she eating?"

"She looks all right. Checked her blood pressure and it's high, but she won't call the doctor . . . won't let anybody call for her, either."

I sigh. "That's no surprise. Talk about stubborn."

"Yeah, talk about stubborn." He pats my nose with his finger. "Promise me you'll stay put, little missy. I gotta work at the station the next two days. On call between those."

"I will."

"And you'll call if you need anything? Even if you feel the littlest twinge? If I'm in the middle of something, I'll send a separate truck."

"I will."

He leans down and kisses me on the top of the head. Warmth runs through me. To feel loved for who I am and not what somebody can take from me is something. I never thought that kind of love was meant for me.

On the corner of the side table, next to the magazines, is my mail, and I sort through it, the same old mailers, a couple of utility bills. And a thick white envelope, official letterhead from Walter Crawford, JD, CPA.

I don't know which is pounding harder, my heart or the rain outside as I tear it open. Lightning brightens the room, then the TV flickers and thunder rumbles low and long, rattling the walls of the trailer as I read words like *plaintiff* and *defendant*, *the Court* and *establishing paternity* and *filing for custody*. It is signed by Mr. Crawford, "on behalf of Bryan Blair."

A pain shoots across my belly and I drop the papers, sending them flying all over the floor.

Dear Lord, please. Help me. The baby can't come early. Bryan can't have this baby. . . .

The pain eases, and I quick text Gabe and send him a photograph of the front page of the document. What am I going to do?

I try to rub the rest of the pain out of my side, praying it's stretching and not a contraction. I don't have money for a lawyer. And it doesn't matter if half the town stands up for me—which it wouldn't. With Mama in jail and what happened to Jayden, all a judge is going to see is that. Nobody needs to tell me the whole world is stacked against me in this.

I rub my belly and breathe through the pain, which lingers low like a warning that it's sure to come again. I search the internet for what the letter means, what my options are, but all I can find are websites of lawyers who seem awfully anxious to take cases.

My phone vibrates with Gabe's reply. It'll be okay. Trust me. Trust him? Really? What can he do?

Every time I pray, the Lord says to trust him, too, but nothing seems to be getting any better. The Blairs have money and a house that doesn't have rust stains in a neighborhood with swing sets and sidewalks, all of that able to hide—or at least make people look away from—the finger-shaped bruises on Elizabeth Blair's arms and who knows where else. They don't have a list of court records on the public websites. They never lost a child to heroin.

Trust me.

That's not helping! Tell me something else, Lord! I want to scream.

Trust me with your child, the voice says again.

How? I don't know how to trust anything, Lord, let alone you.

I get up, but only to turn off the TV, to use the bathroom, and to get a tall glass of ice water to last me the next few hours.

When I sit back down, the Bible Sudie gave me at my baptism is sitting on the table, reminding me of Sudie lecturing me about trusting the Lord too. I try to ignore it, but something keeps nudging at me to open it. Something. Or *Someone.*

It's not going to help, Lord. I know all about your peace that passes understanding, how I'm supposed to "be still and know," and yes, how I'm supposed to trust you with all my heart and lean not on my own understanding. I've been trying to acknowledge you in all my ways, and nothing's helping. Things just keep getting more complicated. Nothing in the Bible's going to help.

Still, I flip through the pages, worn from years. Sudie had gone through and highlighted all her favorite verses in it before she gave it to me, so plenty catch my eye.

A trio of pressed pansies fall out when I get to one page, right in the middle of the Psalms. Verse 103:17 is highlighted.

But from everlasting to everlasting
    the LORD's love is with those who fear him,
    and his righteousness with their children's children—

Their children's children.

But why would Sudie highlight this, after all her children passed?

What righteousness has she been left with?

Unchanging love.

What's that mean, Lord?

Love—my love—is bigger than what you can see.

Bigger how?

Everlasting.

Not if Bryan and his mother have anything to do with it, Lord.

I'm bigger than the Blairs, too.

I figure God is big enough to take me rolling my eyes at him, then.

I set the Bible down and scroll through my phone, searching for anything I can find on paternity laws and maternity laws. I don't understand most of it. And what I do understand is on lawyer websites, pop-ups asking for my name and address so they can con me into hiring them.

One thing I do find, on a government website.

It says custody can't be challenged or decided until after a baby is born. The baby belongs to the mother until proven she can't raise the child.

If this is true, then I have a little time.

Not much, but a little.

Questions and worries roll through my head and my heart like the thunder that keeps rumbling across the sky and the sheets of rain slapping angry against the sides of the trailer, and I fall in and out of a fitful sleep, but sleep that is at least free from any more pains.

29

The racket of feral cats wakes me in the gray early morning, and I struggle to hoist myself up to sitting, my belly like an anvil weighing me down. Outside my window, the whole world looks blue in the rain-drenched dawn.

Although the rain has dwindled to a light sprinkle, at least for now, flood warnings flash across all the local TV channels, and the news is all about places being swallowed up by the high and ruthless currents. Radar maps show more rain is coming, too. The only saving grace about Shady Acres is it sits at the highest point in a section of the county cut by rivers and streams. Across the meadow, folks aren't so lucky. Sandy Creek carries water from the high cliff waterfall and curves around the back of Shady Acres before heading downhill and turning into a torrent alongside the next trailer park down the road. I can't recall a time the water's ever been this high, and I'm shocked to see the steely reflection of water in the distance where grass and crops once surrounded those trailers. These rains are devastating.

Small and thin, the cries start up again, baby kittens or raccoons under the trailer, most likely.

I can't take it anymore.

When I open the door, the air smells faintly like dead fish and rotten earth turned over by the floodwaters filling the valley. I wish I'd put on flip-flops as I pad down the steps and onto the soaked ground. I bend down to look under the trailer where it sounds like the cries are coming from, but it's still too dark to see anything very well. If it's a raccoon, I don't want to rile up the mother and have her charge and bite me. Mama raccoons are far from the friendly little fur balls over in the cage at Sudie's.

I go back inside and skip the flip-flops, pulling on my rain boots instead. I grab a flashlight from the kitchen, my creaky steps across the trailer floor halting the cries momentarily.

Back outside, the water-laden ground squishes under my feet as I tiptoe around the edge of the trailer and try not to step on branches or anything that will make a sudden noise. Eventually the cries start up again pretty close to where I'm standing. I bend as best I can and shine the flashlight under the trailer again, jumping back as one of the gray feral tabby cats skitters out and hightails it into the meadow. It's been chasing a black-and-white female around for some time, and when I shine the light again it reflects green off the retinas of her wide and crazy-looking eyes.

The cat hunches over the catch at its feet, and at first I figure it's a mouse or vole. When I look closer, I see the cat's white muzzle is covered in bright-red blood. Shining the light on the kill I see it's not a vole at all, but a newborn kitten.

Lord, have mercy.

She's eatin' her babies alive.

"Stop it! Get outta there!"

She hardly moves except to hiss before she drops her head and tears at the still-squirming baby kitten's neck. I search for a stick or a rock or anything to get her to stop, finally grabbing a broom from inside. I thrash it back and forth under the trailer until mama cat runs out, hissing the whole way out to the weeds where the gray tabby ran.

That doesn't stop me from beating my stick, though. I just keep beating and beating and beating the ground, my whole body shaking.

"Why? Why would she do that?" I scream, maybe at God, maybe at the whole of nature itself. "If you care so much about the sparrows—" I start beating the side of the giant ash, idle and unyielding to my blows—"why'd you let this happen? Those babies weren't doing nothing but trying to live!"

Tears stuffed up me pour out and I let them, mixing with the rain until I don't have any tears left. I weep for the kittens and for Jayden. For the people in the next trailer park over who had nothing to start with and who have less than nothing now. For Mama and the heroin that came to town and's been eating the heart out of all of us. For the threat of those papers Elizabeth had to have forced Bryan's hand to. And for my baby, heavy and sagging under the film of my soaking-wet nightgown.

From behind the screen door my cell phone rings, and I trudge up the red-stained steps to get it.

Gabe's name flashes across the top.

"Hey." I barely manage to speak between sobs, and I try unsuccessfully to cover the speaker so he can't hear them.

"What's wrong? You okay?"

"Yes," I squeak. "I mean, no."

"Is it the pains? Did they come back? You're supposed to call—"

"No, no, it's not the pains."

"Then what is it?"

"I just . . . this cat . . . it was eating its babies . . ."

"Eating its babies?"

"Yeah . . . and . . . it was so awful . . . Gabe . . . I'm sorry . . ."

"You got nothing to be sorry for. That sounds horrific."

"Sudie told me once they do that when they're stressed," I sob.

"This weather's enough to stress out the best of us. Roads around you are closed, at least two of the three, like I thought they might be. Completely submerged. They've got boats out rescuing people all over the valley, and the rain's still coming down. That park near you? Some of the guys from the department were over there earlier pulling people out with motorboats. Said metal aprons were everywhere, washed clear off the bottom of their trailers. A couple of trailers closest to the creek are completely submerged. Three of them were lifted up entirely by the currents and laid to rest half a mile downstream. Whatever's left is going to be covered in silt and mud. Most of the town is shut down, including the diner. Folks just can't get anywhere right now. . . ." A voice from dispatch crackles in the background. "Jaycee, you sure you and the baby are okay?"

"I'm fine . . . really. I'm just . . . having a moment, I guess."

"Well, you're entitled. And probably past due."

"I guess you're right." That makes me chuckle, until my throat tightens up again. "It's so good to hear your voice. I mean . . . I know you were just here last night, but . . ."

"It's good to hear you, too."

If he only knew the ache that won't quit lingering in the middle of my chest when he's not around.

"Weather service says things should ease up, maybe even sunshine by the end of the day. But it'll take more than that for the roads to dry out."

"I'm not supposed to get up anyway." He'd have a fit if he saw me in my soaking-wet nightgown, palms of my hands still stinging from beating at the earth with the broom.

"Right. Just stay put. I'll get out there as soon as I can."

I'm worried about Sudie, over there alone. I'll call her, but first I decide to take a hot bath. Surely lying in the tub is enough like bed rest to be all right.

I get in and watch the water rise until my belly is like an

island in the middle of the mounds of bubbles. For a little while I let myself imagine for the hundredth time what it would be like if this was me and Gabe's baby. If he was my husband and I was his wife. If we could just run away like I used to want to run away, to the ocean, where no one could find us and we could have one of those lives where we sit in chunky white wood chairs on a porch that faces the sea.

Sudie doesn't answer when I call her cell phone. Not when I try the landline, either. Maybe she turned the ringer off. But she never does that, especially when the weather's bad. Doesn't want to miss a call about an animal rescue. Everything in me says to check on her, but I can't risk the pains coming, especially not after this morning. Besides that, the rain has started up again and is relentless.

I decide to call Shawnie and Tim.

Shawnie answers. "Ye-lo?"

If Gabe thinks my southern Indiana accent is bad, he ought to hear hers. "Shawnie, it's Jaycee. Have you seen Sudie out today?"

"Not in this mess."

"Right. Well, she has the hawk and the raccoons that need feeding out back. I just thought—"

"Think maybe we oughta check on her?"

"She hasn't been feeling well lately. I'm worried. I'd check on her myself, but I'm on bed rest. Pretty strict."

"Oh, honey, I'm sorry to hear that. Do I need to check on you, too?"

"No, no, I'm fine. If you could check on Sudie, though, that'd be kind."

"Okay. Tim's here too. Couldn't get into work even if he wanted to. Same with most folks, I think."

"My friend's an EMT. Says they're having to use boats to rescue folks all over the county."

"Won't be a surprise if we see the forest animals starting to line up two by two then, now will it?"

"No, it won't," I laugh.

"All right, then, Jaycee, I'll go check on our Sudie and call you as soon as I see that she's okay."

30

Gabe was kind enough to boil eggs as part of the things he left me, and I grab a couple along with a big cup of water and head back to the couch to wait. The lunch hour news is on, and the station from Cincinnati shows devastation in the remote areas, a couple of those near Riverton. Video footage shows folks stranded on rooftops, and a county hospital is being evacuated because the water is flooding the entire first floor.

I jump when the phone rings.

"Jaycee?" Shawnie says on the other end. "She's not answering the door."

Fear burns in the pit of my stomach.

Something's wrong.

Bed rest or not, I've got to get over there.

I throw on a pair of maternity jeans that are getting too small for me and an old T-shirt and my rain boots. Walter Crawford's letter lying half-open on the side table catches my eye as I step outside, adding to my collection of gnawing fears. I type a text to Gabe: Something's wrong with Sudie. I'm going over there. The whole way over to Sudie's, I try to shush the voice in my head telling me I'm supposed to be on bed rest.

The rain is coming straight down again. The clouds above are an angry gray. I can see the end of the hawk's cage from the front of Sudie's trailer, and he is sitting there on his trapeze, his eyes fixed on me as if he knows something is very wrong too.

Shawnie is waiting for me on Sudie's stoop, where the front porch light beside her flickers. Sudie always turns it off in the mornings. Doesn't like to waste electricity.

"I did see her out yesterday morning tending the critters," Shawnie says. "But I can't recall that I've seen her since."

The house is quiet—too quiet.

"Sudie?" I call, and rattle the doorknob. "We can let ourselves in. I have a key."

Inside, everything in the front room looks yellow, the only light from outside pushing its way in through closed, worn-out blinds. Blinds she always opens when she wakes up in the mornings. The big brown bat hangs unmoving, except for when it blinks its eyes, in its glass aquarium. A couple of dirty plates are on the counter. She never leaves dishes on the counter. The stove clock clicks, and I'm afraid to say anything that will break the silence.

"Sudie?" Shawnie says.

There's no movement from the bedroom, sepia and still.

"Something's not right. . . ." Panic burns fierce in the pit of my stomach as Shawnie and I look at each other, neither of us wanting to go on. I force my legs to move, each step heavy and weak, toward the bedroom.

She's napping.

Lord, please let her be napping.

Thoughts of Sudie over the last few weeks flood my head, the way she was sweating so much at the cemetery, the way her skin stayed pale despite long hours in the sun, the way she'd get out of breath after a few steps. She always had some kind of excuse.

"Sudie?" My voice sounds weak, thin. *"Sudie?"*

Standing at the threshold of her room I see her, lying on her side, her body in a zigzag shape under the blanket. I don't have to step further to know she's gone. The floor is hard against my knees as I crumple. "No . . . no . . . NO! You can't go! You can't!" I wrap my arms around my belly and hear myself scream, as if it's not me but someone I'm watching.

Shawnie steps around me and I watch in horror as she pulls back a corner of the sheet. She presses her fingers under Sudie's chin, then turns to me and nods.

I get up and run to her lifeless body then. I can't help it. I have to see her. Her dusky, ashen face is flaccid, her arm is hanging half off the bed, her palm is outstretched and open as if even in death she wants to offer an embrace.

"We need an ambulance in Shady Acres . . . or maybe just the coroner," Shawnie says to a 911 operator. "Yes, I'm sure. I checked her pulse. She's been cold awhile," she continues. "Yes. Yes, I understand. There's no hurry. Yes. Thank you."

The two of us make our way back to the front room, bonded by the sick fear that comes in the presence of death, and we wait. I text Gabe: She's gone.

Who?

Sudie.

What?! How?

I don't know. I think her heart gave out.

I'm in the middle of a run. I'll be there as soon as I can.

"What makes you think it was her heart?" Shawnie asks, her eyes bloodshot from crying. Tim is here now, sitting with us too.

I tell them about how Sudie'd been acting, but more than that, about how I think the burden of forty years carrying the loss of her babies and her husband had to have finally caught up with her. She had her joy in the Lord, to be sure. But that kind of loss would break anyone. The Lord himself wept when Lazarus died, even though he was able to bring his friend back to life. The rest of us don't have the luxury of that.

An ambulance finally arrives, along with a police car.

Then the coroner.

Then the funeral home.

I can only assume they followed each other in on the one county road still open.

The Walsh and Thompson funeral home is the only one in town, and one or the other of them, Ike Walsh or Jim Thompson, make it a point to personally come to retrieve the bodies of their clients. Jim was the one who'd come to the hospital to get Jayden's body.

Ike comes for Sudie. He steps into the house, nods at me and Shawnie, then heads to the bedroom, where he spends several minutes before reappearing.

"She surely was a saint, Ms. Sudie," he says. Light reflects off the bottom half of his heavily corrected bifocals, and he pulls a handkerchief out of his pocket and wipes sweat off his near-bald head, speckled with age spots. He looks directly at me. "She has everything planned. Picked it out and paid for it a long time ago."

"I've seen the plot," I say, unsure of whether he knows me or not. "Her husband and babies been waiting a long time for her there."

He nods, then motions a young man to come in with the stretcher.

I cringe at the body bag, packaged like something you'd buy at a convenience store, set on top of the dark-red velvet drape.

The rain has tapered off enough to go outside, just in time to see Gabe's Jeep coming down the drive.

"I came as soon as I could," he says, breathless. Tears shine in his eyes, which makes them even more blue.

"Gabe." I feel his strong arms around me, the baby safe between us.

He keeps hold of my hand the whole time the officials do their job. Ike and the young man steer the cart awkwardly out of the trailer. It doesn't seem like it's really her zipped up in there as they push it into the end of the hearse.

"I can't stand thinking about her body cold and alone in the back of there."

"Me either," says Shawnie.

Gabe shakes Tim's, then Shawnie's hand. "Thank you for helping Jaycee."

"You're welcome. You should get her home, don't you think? This ain't exactly bed rest."

"I'm fine," I say. "Really. The bat needs water and some mealworms, probably."

"I can take care of that," Shawnie says. "I'll call Mary Beth and see if she can take some of the critters. She doesn't have a flying cage like Sudie does to handle the hawk, though."

"I can—"

"Would you stop?" Shawnie chides. "I can take care of him, too. I've seen Sudie feed him those mice." She shudders. "I hate those things, but I don't mind feeding him if I have to. Temporarily."

"Actually, I don't think you'll have to for long. He's pretty much ready for release. Sudie said so the other day. Been catching live mice over a week now."

"Wait, I have to feed him live mice?"

I laugh. Feels good to laugh a little. "I think he'll be fine if you prefer to use the dead ones a day or two. Anyway, he doesn't favor that wing anymore at all when he flies." I turn to Gabe. "We can let him go. I wouldn't be up for long to do that. It's just a car ride away."

"We'll see about that," Gabe says.

"The raccoons are on straight cat food now," I say. "Don't forget about them."

"How *many* raccoons?"

Shawnie's visible trepidation makes us all laugh this time.

"A half a dozen. They're babies. Don't worry. They're cute."

"Mmm-hmm," she says, crossing her arms. "Nothing else, is there? No snakes? I don't do snakes."

"No. That's it, besides the bat."

"Let's get you home," Gabe says, taking my hand again.

"Wait. There's something I have to get."

I find it beside the sink, the green bottle. The dandelions are still fresh in the top of it. She must've picked them just yesterday.

We say good-bye to Shawnie and Tim, then walk slow back to my place. The rain has stopped, the clouds thinning except for a few wispy low gray ones that float fast over our heads. Over the meadow, there's a break where streams of sunlight angle to the ground.

"I always think that's heaven coming down when I see the sun breaking through the clouds like that. . . . What's that hymn?" I start humming, and Gabe recognizes it, starts singing the words.

"Swing low, sweet chariot . . ."

"Coming for to carry me home . . ." I smile and the tears come flooding out again. "That was one of her favorites. She loved the old songs. The old hymns."

Gabe sets his arm around my waist to steady me, our steps in sync as we walk up my drive. "She loved *you*, Jaycee."

"I know." I wipe my face. Gabe follows me inside the trailer.

"You feeling okay?"

"I don't know." I shake my head. "I think I've been crying all day."

"No pains though, right?"

"No. No pains. I just hurt here." I put my hand over my chest.

Inside the trailer, he makes sure I force down a sandwich, along with an apple he slices up for me. When I finish that he scoops me up in his arms, big belly and all, and sets me gently on the couch. "There. You stay put. I'll stay as long as you need."

"What about the flooding? Don't they need you at the station?"

"I told Chief what happened, how you're on bed rest. He told me to go on and take as long as I need."

"Thank you."

He smiles, fluffs the pillows behind me, and picks up my feet, arranging them on the couch.

"I'm so tired, Gabe."

"I know. I'm not going anywhere. Try and get some sleep."

"You don't have to stay," I say, not wanting to be a burden, but at the same time knowing if he leaves I might fall apart.

AMY K. SORRELLS

"I'm staying, Jaycee. That's all there is to it. You just lost your best friend. Besides that, somebody needs to make sure you stay put on this couch."

His eyes are filled with so much kindness, tired or not, I can't argue with him. All I can do is nod.

Gabe grabs the TV remote with his free hand and flips through the channels until he settles on a show about fixing up homes, and despite Sudie's passing, I fall into a deep and dreamless sleep. When morning comes, he is still here, watching as I wake up.

31

The next few days are a blur.

Sudie doesn't have any living relatives. At least she picked out her own casket and paid for a burial plot back when her husband, Ernest, passed, so the only decision I have to make is what clothes to give the undertakers. That isn't too hard. Sudie was not a fussy woman, except for her unwavering insistence on wearing a dress to church. I choose a navy-blue one with a starched white collar, the one I remember her wearing to the wedding of one of Shawnie and Tim's children a few years back.

It is when I'm in her room choosing that dress that I dare to look in her curio cabinet.

The veil between life and death feels thin when rummaging through a dead person's private things. I shiver when I pull open the bottom drawer. The smell of must and age is strong as I search out a pair of clean pantyhose. I can't imagine putting pantyhose on a dead person, since putting them on when you're alive is hard enough, but I am certain Sudie would insist on wearing them. I hold them up and stretch them out to make sure they don't have any runs in them. Sudie put up with a lot, but never a run in her hose.

Next drawer up are all her skivvies. I can't say for certain whether she'd care about wearing these, but a clean pair's got to be better than the ones she's got on now.

The drawer above that holds a few old scarves and socks, and above that, costume jewelry, thick Bakelite necklaces and bangles, the kind people wore in the seventies.

I smile. Sudie had style.

The very top of the cabinet lifts up, and inside is an indigo velvet-lined and sectioned space with rings and earrings and more delicate necklaces, including three lockets, each containing a lock of hair.

Mary, John, and Samuel. The only evidence I've ever seen of their sweet lives.

I take them out and set them on top of the pile for the funeral home. She would want these to go with her.

I'm about to close the top when I see her strand of pearls.

I remember the first time Sudie had me help her fasten them before church.

"You know the story about the pearl in the Bible, don't

you, Jaycee?" she asked as I fitted the clasp together at the back of her neck, her thick hair pulled up and pinned into her trademark braided bun.

"No."

The pearls shimmered in the morning sunlight streaming through her window, each one perfect and round and with a hint of pink. I watched her adjust the strand around her neck. Her dress was the color of lilacs with tiny little pleats all around the skirt that made it swish when she walked, and thick black shoes with a strap that buckled across the top. My own shoes were the sneakers I wore every day, the same ones with the plastic edges cracked and peeling back in places.

Even then Sudie had animals, and she had feedings to do before we left. She lifted one of three abandoned fledgling sparrows from its makeshift nest of shredded rags and tenderly began to feed it. "Well, then, let me tell you." The sparrow opened its mouth and nearly inhaled the mixture, which she had to feed them every couple of hours. "There was a man. He was a merchant, and he sailed his ship all over the world looking for pearls to buy and sell. He'd seen plenty of pearls, thousands and thousands, and so none of them really impressed him anymore. But one day, while he was at the pearl market, he found one that stood out from the rest of them. He couldn't believe no one else had claimed it, it was so much more beautiful than the rest. So, you know what he did?"

I shook my head.

"He went and sold all he had just so he could buy that

precious pearl." She ran her finger across the sparrow's fuzzy head and placed it back in the nest.

"That's how much God loves *us*, child."

I imagine Sudie and Ernest, young and in love, out to dinner on Main Street, maybe. Strolling hand in hand by a jewelry store, Sudie eyeing the pearls, him saving up for the pearls, giving them to her for Christmas, or maybe their anniversary.

I put them in the bag of things for the funeral home.

At the cemetery, the begonias and coleus and petunias have grown thick and strong from all the rain, and the leaves of the locust trees have all come out. Slowly folks gather around the grave site and the casket, set precariously on top of the lowering device over the four-by-five black hole in the earth. Inches of soil are the only thing separating her and Ernest and those babies now, and as heartbroken as I am, I can feel the rightness of that. Even Jack, sitting on his rain-soaked haunches alongside the gravestone, seems to sense the victory in this.

The fields around the cemetery are overflowing with bright-yellow ragwort stretched out to the horizon, and I imagine them as streets of gold. There's a lot I don't understand about the Lord, about what happens between the last breath and when he raises us up out of the grave. But I know that times like these, when the ragwort is in all its splendor as if it wants to celebrate Sudie's homecoming too, are when the veil thins and he gives us a glimpse into the great mystery so we can know, as much as it's possible to know, that the grave is not a cold, black ending but a welcoming place to finally find rest from the hard things of this life.

Several rows over, a woman kneels on one of the fresh graves of the young people who died from the bad heroin. She doesn't seem to care that her knees are sunk deep into the thick, soft mud. I wonder if the veil ever thins for her.

My rubber boots sink into the waterlogged green grass. Setting chairs out here was not an option because of all the rain, so I was careful to keep my feet up as long as I could at home to ward off any contractions that might be tempted to come with having to stand here this afternoon.

Gabe is on one side of me, Carla and her husband on the other, and it seems like the whole church is here to see Sudie off, except, thank goodness, for the Blairs. Jim Thompson and Ike Walsh stand stoic at the head of the casket. Reverend Payne is dressed in full robes and holds his weathered Bible in both hands. Veda and Trina ordered the finest spray of flowers for the top of the casket—lavender roses and larkspur, lilacs, lilies, and freesia—and they have tea and finger foods waiting for everyone back at the church. Shawnie and Tim are here, along with several other neighbors, including a surprisingly sober Dewey Johnson dressed in an ill-fitting suit with Virginia standing next to him, her hand curled around his elbow.

Reverend Payne clears his throat, and the hushed voices still. A lone tractor hums low in a distant field. Red-winged blackbirds trill from their perches along the fencerow, and two mourning doves trade calls. Over my shoulder I hear the footsteps of a latecomer, and when I turn I see it's Walter Crawford and he's looking straight at me.

Those court papers.

Lord, help me.

"'God places the lonely in families,'" Reverend Payne reads, the Bible splayed out in his hands. "'He sets the prisoners free and gives them joy.' Psalm 68:6. The word of our Lord."

He scans the small crowd of us, taking the time to look at each face. "I picked that verse because some might say Sudie was alone, and the four graves around her would confirm that observation—were it not for each of you, and were it not for the fact that the Lord demonstrated this promise of placing the lonely into families in Sudie's life. I remember well the days we buried her children, her husband. They were dark and difficult days. I'm really not sure I've had any as difficult as that." He pauses, his chin trembling. "But seeing how the Lord surrounded her, placed her in a new family, the family of this church . . . Well, I can tell you that is indeed what set her free and gave her the joy we all knew her to have."

A mumbling of amens rolls across the group, and the reverend goes on to talk all about how much Sudie loved her church family, how much she loved the family of critters she cared for and restored, how much she loved the land and the seasons.

"God places the lonely in families."

The baby kicks inside me.

"He sets the prisoners free."

My mind wanders away from this spot, away from the feeling of Walter Crawford's eyes staring at the back of my head, and to the far corner of the cemetery. I can just see the edge of Jayden's headstone.

The day we buried him, Sudie and Shorty dug the grave themselves. The sky had been clear, a brief morning rain washing away the hot and sticky summer air. We'd marveled at a swirl of wind that passed over us, whipping up a mess of leaves that seemed to hover around the site. Jack had jumped and growled, barked and mouthed at the tiny twister as if it were playing with him, and he was playing with it. The veil lifted for me in that moment, and while some might argue it's not biblical to think such things, I know it was God's way of letting me know Jayden was free and running with joy on streets of gold, even right here in this cemetery playing with old Jack, and that I was not alone, either.

You're not alone now, he says to me. *I place everyone right where they need to be.*

But where does this baby need to be, Lord?

I'm jolted from my thoughts and prayer by Reverend Payne saying my name.

"If there's anyone Sudie cared about, it's Jaycee here, who was like a daughter to her. And her good friend Walter."

Walter Crawford? I think back at the times I've seen them talking at church. That day I saw him driving out of the cemetery. I figured the pink in her cheeks was on account of her being hot, but maybe not.

Sudie, you sly girl. I grin until I remember those custody papers sitting in my living room. But wait . . . if they were such good friends, what had she known about those? What if he was using Sudie to build a case . . . ? But that's ridiculous. Isn't it?

"Thank you both for your friendship with Sudie."

I nod and feel my face heating red. I am sure Walter is staring at my head even harder. Thank goodness Gabe takes my hand.

"In the last few weeks, Sudie didn't feel well, and I think perhaps she knew this day was coming. She and I talked more and more frequently about how she couldn't wait to see her husband and her children. But all that was secondary to her anticipation of meeting our Lord."

More mmm-hmms and amens, and across the way, I see Hersch. The corner of his mouth turns up so slightly someone else might have missed it, and he nods at me. Carla slides her arm around my waist and gives me a squeeze.

"There's just one hymn Sudie asked that we sing. Ida, would you be kind enough to start us off?"

Ida looks slightly lost without the security of her big organ, but she gives the pitches and begins:

"Why should I feel discouraged? Why should the shadows come?"

The rest of us join in, tentative and unsure of ourselves and the raggedy-ness of our meager voices in the big open space around us.

*"Why should my heart be lonely, and long for heav'n
    and home,
When Jesus is my portion? My constant friend is he:
His eye is on the sparrow, and I know he watches me;
His eye is on the sparrow, and I know he watches me."*

As the machine lowers Sudie's casket into the ground, Reverend Payne reads from Revelation, the chapter at the end where it says God wipes away all our tears, that death is no more, that we won't have to mourn or cry or hurt anymore when we get to heaven.

Maybe Sudie kept that green bottle—the one I set by my sink and put a stem off a lilac bush in before I left this morning—to remember this promise, too. Not just to collect her tears, but to know someday she wouldn't have any more.

A hawk circles overhead, soaring on the breeze without even bending its wings as we file past the edge of Sudie's grave, tossing in rose petals distributed to us by Trina Bishop. Little Clifty Creek shimmers gold on the far horizon, and I realize living life with arms and a heart wide open is a choice, that accepting the Lord's grace and trusting him is a risk worth taking because he is always watching over us, and that where we've come from isn't near as important as knowing who we belong to.

I am thinking on all this when Mr. Crawford approaches.

"I know this isn't the time or place," he says, turning his felt hat in his hands, "but do you have a moment?"

My heart feels like it's beating in my throat.

"What's this about?" Carla says.

"Custody papers," I say, my voice barely a whisper. "The Blairs. Bryan. He sent me papers saying he's going to file for custody."

"Is this true, Crawford?" Carla eyes him.

"It's true," I say to her, then turn back to Mr. Crawford. "If you were Sudie's friend, if you really cared about her, then you have to help me. Please. Don't let the Blairs take my baby. Please, Mr. Crawford." The heat of shame rushes through me as I realize how desperate I must sound.

"Jaycee," Gabe says softly.

"Can they really do that?" Carla asks.

"Unfortunately, they can." Mr. Crawford turns to me and averts his eyes, turning his hat in his hands again before looking back up at me. "What I wanted to say is that Bryan's mother was there."

"What?"

He clears his throat. "When Mr. Blair came to see me, he came with his mother. It was obvious she was running the show, that he was reluctant."

"He couldn't have been that reluctant. He went through with it." I try to keep my voice down, but a couple of folks turn their heads as they walk by us toward their cars.

"Sure he did," Carla sneers. "He's spineless. Especially around his parents."

Mr. Crawford edges closer to us. "There is a way," he says quietly.

"What? How? I can't afford a lawyer of my own." My stomach churns with feelings of helplessness.

"If Bryan decided to give up his rights, that would make the other documents null and void."

"He's not going to do that," I say, my voice cracking. "There's no way. Not now. Not with the way his mom is, keeping him on such a tight leash."

"Mr. Crawford, with all due respect, I'm not sure what you're saying is very helpful," Gabe says.

"Gabe's right," Carla says. "It's not right to get Jaycee's hopes up about something that isn't likely to happen."

"That's not my intention." Mr. Crawford reaches out and sets his hand kindly on my forearm. His pale-blue eyes, outlined by deep and upturned wrinkles, look deep into mine. "I'm not saying he will give up his rights. I don't know the young man, other than what I saw when they came to my office. If Mrs. Blair hadn't been there . . . I'm just saying, if he states he's willing to give up his rights, that's a way, God willing."

I nod and run my hand across my belly. "God willing," I say, tears puddling in my eyes.

Mr. Crawford says good-bye and heads toward his car, leaving me there with Gabe and Carla, and her husband by her side.

I look back toward where Sudie lies in that closed-up casket and try hard to pray like she might've prayed, about how the Lord can help me walk straight into a fire without getting burned, about how he can lead me right through a den full of lions without getting eaten alive, about how he can help me keep believing the rising waters threatening my baby will somehow set him free.

32

"You sure he's ready?" Gabe asks.

"I'm sure."

A bean field rolls and curves out toward a thick tree line at the spot on State Road 62 where Gabe steers his Jeep to a stop on the berm. In the backseat, the hawk is quiet in the travel cage, as if he has no recollection of the wide-open air he used to float on, wings hanging on the breeze, the whole sky his.

I get out and hand Gabe Sudie's long leather gloves. He's come a long way from being scared to death of the creature just a couple months ago, enough so that he is able to do the handling of the hawk since I'm not even supposed to be out

295

here. But I insisted on coming. I can't stand sitting home. Nothing to do but worry about every twinge in my belly, or about how in the world to keep the Blairs from getting custody of my baby, or if by some miracle they don't, how I'll manage to give him up for adoption.

The hawk watches us, intent, with his amber eyes. When I open the metal door of the crate, he steps one way, then the other, before I toss the towel over the top of him and quick bundle him up. Once he's wrapped snug, I step aside so Gabe can pull the bundle of him out and cradle him, sure to hold the talons tight together.

"Let's head that way." I nod in the direction of the giant cottonwood where I saw the female on the day we rescued him.

We step over the pale-blue chicory, purple corn thistle, and yellow pilot weed, the earth rough and uneven under our feet, and very soggy though it's been three full days of sunshine since the rains stopped. Gabe's more worried about me than holding the hawk as I step, awkward from my swollen body.

"I can feel his heart beating," he says, grinning.

"Let's stop here."

The enormous cottonwood is a few yards away, far enough for him to fly to, but close enough that we can watch him if that's where he chooses to land.

I look at Gabe and he looks at me.

"You ready?" he asks, both of us aware of the deeper meaning of the question.

I nod.

While maintaining his hold on the hawk's talons, he takes the towel off the top of him. The hawk tilts his head one way, then the other, as if he's trying to reorient to a place he remembers. I hope this is true. Before we have time to blink, he stretches his wings and thrusts himself up and out of Gabe's grip, pushing and beating the air back with his wings, flying straight and without a hint of injury to the wing, until he reaches the cover of the cottonwood.

"Adoption isn't about giving your child away," Carla had said. *"It's about giving your child life . . . nothing will ever change the fact that you are his mother. . . . You'll always have him with you, whether in your heart or in your arms. . . ."*

I don't even realize I'm crying until Gabe asks if I'm okay.

"He belongs here. Did you see him? He knows this is his home."

Will my baby know the same thing with his new family, Lord?

Trust me.

I'm trying, Lord.

Anything is possible with my help, he whispers. *I have never forsaken you. Nor will I forsake the child within you.*

My baby rolls and kicks inside me, and we stand there for a while just watching the hawk perched on a high limb of the tree. We would never know he's there if we hadn't watched him land there ourselves.

Gabe finally breaks the silence. "You know, you remind me of that hawk a little."

We turn and head back to the car.

"How's that?"

"You've overcome a lot."

"I guess." I shrug. "I've seen plenty of folks who've had it worse."

"Maybe so. But here's the thing: the whole time I've been learning about your story, I've seen some things maybe you haven't."

"What do you mean?"

"I've seen the way God's taken care of you. The way he sent you Sudie a long time ago. Hersch watching out for you. Me showing up at the gas station when I did. Heck, me catching you that first day when you tripped over the sidewalk, and everything in between. Those things aren't coincidence."

"They might be."

"Would you put your stubborn away for a minute and let me finish?" He grabs my hand. "I think God wants you to know he has a plan for all of this. Not just a plan for your baby, but a plan for you, too."

I never thought about any of this being in God's plans *for me*. Always felt like life was just something happening to me for no good reason. But if the Lord was working so many bad things out lately like Mama and me, well . . . "Maybe you're right, Gabe."

"I'm always right," he says, trying to hide a grin.

We get in the car and are about to pull away when I see them on the horizon, two hawks circling, just floating together on the high currents of wind, crossing in front and then behind each other, turning and returning and free.

"Think that's them?" Gabe asks.

"I'm sure of it."

33

"Mmmmmmhhh . . ." I can't keep quiet as my lower back cramps into a knot in the middle of the refrigerated foods section at the Walmart.

"I don't know about this, Jaycee. If you're hurting that bad, we better get back and put your feet up." Carla eyes me with concern as she tosses several yogurts into the cart.

"Dr. Fitzgerald said I could try." I'd seen him the day before. Since I'm thirty-nine weeks along, he says the baby will be fine if I go into labor, so I'm free to get up and about.

"Emphasis on the word *try*."

"It's the first big pain I've had since Sudie's funeral. It's not like I'm going on a jog. I'm *fine*."

She eyes me again. "If you say so."

I force myself to straighten, the knot easing up a little. "Even if it means having this baby in the middle of the canned-food aisle, I've got to get a couple new pairs of stretch pants. Nothing fits anymore. Besides that, I can't stand one more day of looking at the walls of that trailer, nothing to do but worry about those custody papers and everything else."

"Well, Walmart might not appreciate it if you drop that baby right here on their floor. Stretch pants are one-size-fits-all. I could've picked a pair up for you if you weren't so stubborn."

"I like to think of it as *determined*."

We head to the clothing department and flip through racks of clothes. I hold up a ruffled crop top and giggle, despite another pain ramping up. "Think this'd cover it?"

Carla raises an eyebrow and laughs.

The pain twists its way around to the front of my belly, low and so tight I have to grab hold of a wobbly rack of clothes to keep myself from sitting down right then and there. "Maybe you're right . . . about this being too much."

"All right. Take a minute. Breathe through it." She puts her hands on my shoulders.

"Do you think it's started?"

"I don't know. Let's see how long between this and the next one." She checks her watch. "It's 1:17."

The pain subsides and I put my hands under my belly as if that'll help hold it up as we walk toward the front of the store. Tears prick my eyes as another pain twists in my back, taking my breath away.

"You okay, young lady?" An older woman, her too-large blue Walmart vest hanging over her humped back, asks as I stop and lean on our cart.

"She's okay," Carla answers for me.

"You take care of yourself . . . and that baby, you hear?"

I hear.

No longer caring about the stretch pants, we leave the cart behind and head toward the doors. I fall into the front seat of Carla's car, never more grateful to get off my feet. That is, until I feel the next pain come. I lean forward and push against the dashboard to offset the pain, but nothing helps.

"I don't think you're going to need those stretch pants. It's 1:22. That's five minutes—a little less, really. We're going to the hospital."

Carla starts the car and squeals out of the parking lot.

"Take it easy."

"I love you, Jaycee Givens, but not enough for you to mess my car up giving birth in it. So no, I will not take it easy."

We both burst out laughing at the craziness of it all as she weaves through town, past the diner and Spradley's gas station, past the old homes and the river and the college, past the state park, and out to the state road that winds and curves to the hospital. Past the place where Mama put the crosses. The same road I drove with Jayden, clinging to life by only a thread in the backseat. What if this is the last time I'm on this road with my baby? What if the Blairs find out I'm in labor?

I don't have time to worry about that for long. A new pain wrings and twists inside me, reminding me of Sudie squeezing water out of clothes before hanging them on her line outside to dry.

"Can . . . you go . . . faster?"

"Not if you want to get there in one piece." She pats my leg. "Hang on, darlin'. Just about ten more minutes or so."

We pass the familiar stretches of corn and bean fields, farmhouses and trailers, strip malls, schools, and then finally the white sign with big red letters: *E-M-E-R-G-E-N-C-Y.*

Carla veers the car under the Ambulance Only entrance, throws the door open, and hollers, "We're having a baby here!"

A woman in blue scrubs approaches where I sit, still holding on to the dash. She's followed by another woman pushing a wheelchair.

"Can you make it to this chair?" the first woman says.

The distance is only a few feet, but it looks like miles. I swing one leg out, then the other. "I think so." I manage to stand, and a gush of warm liquid drenches my crotch, my thighs.

"Oh, honey," the one holding the wheelchair says, "I guess you *are* having a baby today."

34

"Where's the anesthesiologist?" Carla barks at the nurses.

The emergency room workers took me up a special elevator directly to the labor and delivery unit. The benefit of this is that they have me strapped to a monitor in seconds, just like the one Dr. Fitzgerald has in his office that shows the baby's heartbeat. I listen as they poke my arm and take blood and start fluids.

"His heart sounds strong," I say to the nurses. It's as much a question searching for reassurance as it is a statement.

An older nurse with amiable eyes studies the monitors for a moment. She pats my hand and smiles. "It does."

"The anesthesiologist is finishing up with another patient

down the hall," another nurse says in a voice that sounds a lot like she's sassing Carla for asking. "He'll be here next."

"I hope so," Carla says.

They probably think she's my mother.

I don't have the energy to explain who she is with the pains the way they are. I try and focus on splashes of green and blue light dancing on the wall, afternoon sunlight coming through the window and reflecting off someone's stethoscope, maybe a monitor. Feels like I'm watching somebody else moaning and carrying on as I fall back against the bed after the next contraction.

"Here's a little medicine to take the edge off." A third nurse pushes a syringe full of something into the tube sticking in my arm, and warmth soon flows all over me. Her highlighted brown hair is pulled up in a knot, and she looks hardly older than me. Reminds me of one of the nurses who took care of Jayden. "I'm Amanda. I'll be with you the rest of the day."

Better her than the one with the sass.

The next contraction is brutal, but at least I am able to breathe through it and rest easier as it subsides.

"Did you text Gabe?" I ask Carla, who has moved in from the doorway and is standing beside me.

"Yep. He says he's on his way."

"I told him he didn't have to be here for this, but he insisted."

"Well of course he did, honey."

He doesn't have to. He wants to.

"Well, well, well. Looks like we're going to have a baby today," Dr. Fitzgerald's voice booms.

I grin with relief at the sight of his huge smile, his hulky frame.

A dark-skinned doctor I don't recognize slips into the room behind him.

"'Bout time you showed up, Patel," Dr. Fitzgerald says over his shoulder, then turns to me. "Let's get you more comfortable, whatta you say?"

I nod and grip the side rails of the bed as I feel another contraction coming on.

"Let's sit you up," one of the nurses says.

How in the world am I supposed to sit up when I feel like I'm tearing in two? But with her help and Carla's, I'm able to. They lean me over a bedside table and the anesthesiologist, Dr. Patel, gets to work on the epidural. He scrubs a low spot on my back with something cold, followed by a sharp pain and then pressure. The discomfort is minimal compared to the pain searing through my pelvis. When he's finished, I lay back down and soon feel more warmth of medication washing over my belly, which is soon numb to the pain of the contractions I see rising and falling on the monitor.

"You've got a ways to go," Dr. Fitzgerald says after doing a quick pelvic exam. "You're at about five centimeters, half effaced."

"What's that mean?"

"Means you're about halfway there. And that you got an epidural in time to do this comfortably."

"Halfway? That's it?" All that pain . . .

"First babies can be stubborn sometimes. Don't worry. Everything's going perfectly. I'll be back when it's time." He pats my shoulders and leaves the room.

The nurses gather everything up around me and wheel me to another room, this one much larger. On one wall is a bassinet for the baby and monitors just for him. And there's a whirlpool tub in the corner.

"What's that for?" I ask the older nurse.

"Some women choose to have their babies in the water." She shrugs.

I can't imagine.

"It's good you have that epidural now," another nurse says as the three of them work together to hoist me from the cart onto a bigger bed. They put a catheter in me so I don't have to get up to use the bathroom, adjust the monitor stretched across my belly, and take my vital signs one more time. "Try to get some rest while the contractions do their work."

Amanda, the nurse who reminds me of the one Jayden had, adjusts a couple of pumps and monitors, pats my other shoulder, and follows the other two out of the room.

Another worker in a different color of scrubs comes in with a cup of ice chips and Carla behind her.

"Don't eat these all at once," the aide says. "They're just here to wet your whistle." She straightens things up on my bedside table, adjusts the blinds, fluffs the pillows behind my head. "What else can I do to help you be more comfortable?"

"I think I'm fine." If being scared to death doesn't count, I'm fine.

"If you think of anything you need, just press your call light. I'm right outside your door. The nurses are watching the baby's monitor and your contractions at all times."

"You sure you're all right?" Carla asks when we are finally alone.

"Better than I was, pain-wise anyway. This epidural is amazing."

"They are definitely God's gift to women. I had one with three of the four of mine. The last one came so fast I didn't have time to get one with him. That might be why we didn't have any more after him."

We laugh at that, laughter I'm glad for considering everything that's happened the last couple of hours. With the pain mostly gone, the realization of what's happening hits me. Even more so half an hour later when the next white coat–clad woman enters the room.

"Hi, Jaycee. I'm Donna Howard. I'm not sure if you remember me—"

"I remember," I say before she can finish. How could I forget her as the social worker who was there when Jayden died? I look at Carla, who sees what must be dread on my face and scoots closer to the bed to grab my hand.

"Dr. Fitzgerald's office let me know you're here. It's my understanding that you've been considering placing your baby for adoption?"

"Dr. Fitzgerald's office? I don't remember . . . I'm not sure . . ."

Carla squeezes my hand.

Help me, Lord.

Trust me, he says.

"I understand. I'm not here to tell you what to decide. I'm just here to tell you that I'm aware that you have discussed adoption as an option, and that if in fact you do decide to pursue that direction I'm here to help. I see every mother who might be considering that as soon as I can after they're admitted."

"Okay." I consider telling her about the custody papers, but then decide against it. What could she possibly do to help with that? What can anyone do?

She steps closer to the bed. "I'm sorry about what happened to Jayden."

She remembers his name. It's been so long since I've heard someone say his name out loud. Tears fill my eyes.

"I'll help you any way I can, whatever you decide," she says, then turns and walks out of the room.

"Ms. Givens?" The nurse with the highlighted hair pulled up in the bun steps hesitantly toward the bed.

I hadn't noticed her come into the room.

"I'm sorry, I overheard what Donna was saying to you. About adoption?"

I search her face, unsure of her intent. Her makeup is applied like the pictures in magazines, her eyebrows shaped and filled. Her nails shine a soft pink, a gel manicure if I've ever seen one. Probably thinking I'm just another trailer trash girl who slept with everybody I could and wants to rub it in my face.

"This might be a terrible time to say this—really, please stop me if it is. It's just that, well, sometimes I think the Lord . . ."

I can tell she feels awkward since she's my nurse, but I can't help but want to hear what she has to say. "It's okay. Go on."

"My best friend and her husband—they've been trying to have a baby for years. Of course she's my best friend, but even if she wasn't, anybody can tell you they're the kindest, most loving couple around."

"You'll know when the time comes," Sudie said, *"if you're listening for the Lord."*

"Do they live here?" Worry shoots through me.

"No, they don't. But they've got a website." She hesitates again, as if she's worried about overstepping. "I'll just write it down so you can look at it if you want to." She scribbles the web address on the back of a paper towel and hands it to me, a look of apology and hope at the same time on her pretty face. "Like Donna said, I'm not trying to tell you what I think you should do. I'm really not. But here it is, just in case."

I made a way through the waters.

"Isaiah 43," I say to Carla after the nurse leaves the room.

"What one's that?"

"About God making a way. I highlighted that in my Bible the day Reverend Payne mentioned it in his sermon. The one about Moses' mother setting him in the river. How I remember it now, I have no idea."

Carla smiles, a knowing smile. "The Holy Spirit. He reminds us of the things the Lord teaches us."

"I want to believe that, but Bryan . . . those custody papers."

"Just because Elizabeth Blair dragged Bryan by the ears to Walter Crawford's office doesn't mean she's going to get her way."

I think about Walter Crawford, the look in his eyes when we were standing beside Sudie's grave, what he said about Bryan giving up his rights and how that would trump the papers his mom coerced him into signing.

"Bryan'll never go around his mom."

"You never know. Miracles can happen," she says, with what seems to be a twinkle in her eye.

"I'm tired of hoping for miracles, Carla." I shake my head and reach for the scrap of paper the nurse left. "Why even get my hopes up?"

Reluctantly, I type the website address into my cell phone.

The first photograph that appears on my screen is of a couple, arms around each other, standing on a beach with the sun rising over the ocean behind them.

The ocean.

"Look at this, Carla." I motion her to come look at the web page with me. "My baby could live by the ocean with a mom and a dad like this."

A few scrolls and clicks later, and Carla and I learn that they are in their late twenties, that they dated a couple years before they got married, that they both have big, close extended families. The woman, Michelle, is a psychologist. The man, Joe, is a carpenter who owns his own business and renovates houses. They live year-round in a beach community . . . *in North Carolina* . . . and their work schedules would allow one of them to be home with my baby all the time. They love to explore. To celebrate holidays. To cook. They have two dogs and love animals (except for cats, they note). They have a house in a neighborhood with sidewalks and good schools, and a nursery already decorated and ready.

But what really gets my attention is their letter.

Dear Birth Mother,

Thank you for giving us a chance. Because that's what we want to do for your baby. We want to give him/her the chance you've been praying for, for him/her. We know that you are the person who has chosen to give him/her life, and that nothing will ever change that bond between the two of you. We also suspect that you're reading about us because you are considering giving him/her up for adoption.

We want to assure you that to us, adoption is not about you giving us a child. Adoption is about you choosing to trust the Lord with him/her, for a chance to have a life that you, for whatever reason, are not able to give, and that we promise to provide by His grace.

We have been praying for you before you even visited our page, that the Lord will give all of us wisdom and

strength, and that you will know your decision is the
highest love one person can have for another. Most of
all, we pray that the Lord will give you peace in every
step of your journey.

Love,
Joe and Michelle

"Listen for the Lord," Sudie said. *"Listen and you'll know*
what to do when the time comes."

Problem is, even if I know what I need to do, I can't do anything if Bryan gets custody.

35

I wake from a fitful sleep to extraordinary pressure rising through the effects of the epidural.

"Carla . . ."

She's fallen asleep too, in the chair next to me.

"Carla!"

She jolts awake. "What is it, hon?"

"I don't know. I think . . . I need to *do* something . . . I think I need to push!"

She scrambles to find the nurse call button, and soon a handful of nurses are in the room.

"I'll call Dr. Fitzgerald," one says.

"I need to check you," says another, flinging back the

sheet and spreading wide my numb and floppy legs. "She's at ten. Fully effaced."

A flurry of activity begins as nurses come in and out, tearing blue paper wrapping off boxes of supplies, turning lights on above the nearby baby bassinet, adjusting bags of fluid running into me.

"Jaycee," Gabe says, skidding into the room.

"You have great timing," I say.

"It's time?"

"It's time."

He scoots by the nurses and wraps his arms around me. "I love you. It's okay. Everything's going to be okay."

"I didn't have time . . . I'm not ready."

"I don't know if anyone's ever ready," Dr. Fitzgerald laughs. He extends a hand toward Gabe. "You must be the significant other."

Gabe steps back and looks to me to affirm this.

"He is."

"I'm not sure where that leaves me." Carla winks. "You want me to stay, honey?"

"Yes." I turn to Dr. Fitzgerald. "Is that okay? Can they both stay?"

"Absolutely," he says, smiling at us all. "Whatta you say we have a baby, then?"

An hour later I'm still pushing.

Gabe and Carla's shirts are stained with sweat from holding

my legs. I am sure Gabe had no idea what he was in for when he offered to stay with me, but the nurses put them both to work. Good thing he's an EMT.

"Now I know what Aaron and Hur must have felt like holding up Moses' arms at the battle against the Amalekites," Carla quips.

"Your jokes are awful," Gabe says to her.

I fake a tired laugh.

Dr. Fitzgerald does not look pleased.

Lights on the baby's monitor are flashing and alarms keep ringing.

"Is something wrong?" I say to Dr. Fitzgerald. "What's wrong?"

The lights and alarms sound again, and two more nurses rush into the room.

"Notify the team. OR. Now," he says, his brow furrowed with worry.

One nurse tells me to put my legs down and another straps an oxygen mask across my face.

Like the mask they put on Jayden.

Panic rises inside me.

Lord, help my baby. Don't let me lose my baby.

The team of workers push Gabe and Carla aside and pull the side rails of my bed up, then rush me out of the room and down the hall to another room that's cold and bright and top to bottom white tile. Everyone is putting masks and gowns on.

I want to sit up and see what's happening, but I can't move. The epidural has me numbed. The strap is still across my belly. The people in masks appear on either side of my bed and count to three, and I feel them pulling me from my bed to a narrow table. It's so skinny I'm sure I'm going to fall off until they put more belts across me and splay my arms out onto arm boards on either side of the table like a cross. People put more stickers on my chest.

"What's happening? Someone tell me what's happening!"

No one answers.

"Gabe? Gabe! Where's Gabe?"

"Shhh—shhh-shh. It's okay." Dr. Patel suddenly appears next to my head with a tall cart full of drawers and monitors. "They have to get the baby out now. You have to have a C-section." He points to a screen. "Look. There. That's your baby's heartbeat. It's slow, but it's there. We will take good care of you. We will take good care of your baby." He pushes a syringe full of clear liquid into my IV. "This will help you relax."

I don't want to relax. I try to argue, but the medicine soon makes me not care.

Help me, Lord. Help me. Please. Help my baby.

Trust me.

My breath fogs up the mask that covers my nose and mouth. Warmth runs up my arm and I see Dr. Patel pushing another syringe full of something into me, something that makes me feel sleepy. I struggle to stay awake.

Gabe appears next to me. He's wearing a white paper suit, a blue paper shower cap on his head. His eyes are wet with tears. "I love you. It's going to be okay," he says.

Someone puts a screen of fabric between my chest and my belly. I feel pushing and pressure on my belly, and my entire body jostles with the force of whatever Dr. Fitzgerald and the other staff are doing.

"It's a boy!" someone hollers.

Or do they? Am I dreaming?

"A boy?" I ask. My tongue feels huge in my mouth.

"A boy," Gabe repeats, tears falling freely now. He leans down and kisses my forehead.

More jostling and pressure on my belly.

The room is quiet.

Too quiet.

"Why isn't he crying?"

Gabe looks across the room. "They're cleaning him up. . . . It's okay."

I don't believe him, but then I hear the cry. Even through the fog of all the medicine, I can't keep back the sobs.

A nurse comes from around the curtain holding him, wrapped snug in a soft, striped blanket. She holds him against my shoulder, my face, so I can feel him and see him, and I can't believe he's here.

He's here.

And he's the most beautiful thing I've ever seen in my whole entire life.

"Congratulations, Mama," Dr. Fitzgerald says, peeking over the top of the curtain. "You both did great. Cord around his neck caused a bit of a scare, but it's all good now."

"Thank you."

"He's beautiful," says Dr. Patel, pausing to look at him before getting back to tweaking knobs on his machine and fiddling with all the vials on top of his cart.

"He's perfect," says Gabe.

Something breaks loose inside me, something I can't name. I didn't think I could love anyone more than I loved Jayden, but this is different. This is my baby.

My child.

My son.

"What is the Lord asking you to give up?"

Help me, Lord.

Trust me.

I feel his breath against my face, see the quick rise and fall of his chest, and I wonder what it must feel like to take in air for the very first time. To see light for the first time. To feel air for the first time. Fine, velvety hair covers this side of his face, his back, and he has a thin layer of dark hair, like my own, on his head. Every finger, every toe, every curl of his ears, the round edges of his nose, every single part of him *is* perfect.

One look at his inky-blue eyes, glazed with the first sight of life, and I know I have to let him go. I have to give him a better life. Better than growing up in a trailer in a town with a mama and a daddy who can't stand each other, better than growing up with the feeling that no matter what he accomplishes, folks still look at him like he's stupid or no good because they know that's the kind of people he came from. I feel it with an urgency right then and I know. I have to set him free.

God willing.

The photo of the couple on the beach fills my mind, the ocean and the sunrise, brilliant, behind them.

My next thought is of my mama. "Gabe, could you call the prison? Have them get a message to my mother. Have them tell her she has a grandson."

36

My baby stirs and searches for my breast. I unsnap the hospital gown and lift my breast to his mouth. He shakes his little head back and forth until he feels it in his mouth and finally latches. It seems as if he's always known this rhythm.

"Isn't it something he just knows?" I say to Gabe, who is watching us from an armchair next to the window.

"It is," he says.

Light from the parking lot and streets outside the window create angled shadows in my hospital room, dark except for that and the soft glow of the TV that Gabe has turned to a sports channel.

"You're beautiful," Gabe says.

No one has ever told me that. And I certainly don't feel very beautiful, my hair a mess, my belly saggy and stitched up, my face puffy from all the fluids they gave me.

"You're beautiful," he says again.

I can't help blushing. "Stop."

"No. I'm never going to stop telling you that."

I grin at him. Imagine for the hundredth time it's the three of us back at my place, or a brand-new place Gabe's picked out for us. A real house, where we can live together. But mostly I imagine me and Gabe, just the two of us and the memory of my baby, and three green soda bottles holding fresh flowers by our little kitchen sink. One for Sudie. One for Jayden. And one for him.

The rattle of a blood pressure machine on wheels approaches and a new nurse comes in the room, older and heavyset and sighing as if this is the hardest thing she's had to do all day. She fiddles with the machine, the pump next to me, and the bags of fluids attached to it without looking at me or saying hello.

Gabe clears his throat a little too loud. "Are you the new night nurse?"

I try to hide a giggle.

"I'm Sue," she sighs, and finally looks at me and the baby at my breast. "Oh," she gasps.

"Oh what?" I say.

"What are you doing that for?"

"What?"

She pinches up her mouth and puts her hands on her

hips. "Why, that breastfeeding. We don't recommend it for mothers who've chosen adoption. He probably shouldn't even be in here."

I look down and watch his tiny chin and cheeks tugging, swallowing, tugging, swallowing. I don't even know what to say to her. Shame comes and sits beside me, laughing and mocking same as always, whether in third grade watching the taillights of a white Mercedes headed out of Shady Acres, seeing Mama strung out and walking toward me in the middle school cafeteria, or at the register of the diner with the loudmouth mother smirking at me. I have the urge to rip the tube out of my arm and run out of this room, to find a bus to the east and the Carolina coast, where no one would know me or where I came from, and where I could live with my baby forever. Except for Bryan. And those papers. Nausea washes over me. I haven't had time to think about that with everything happening so fast.

Help me, Lord.

Trust me.

"Why not?" Gabe asks her, a hint of anger behind his words.

"Can't let yourself get all attached if he's going to belong to someone else."

Something rises inside me, something that feels like the way a mother raccoon arches and hisses when something gets too close to her nest of kits. "I haven't decided *anything* yet." At least not as far as she's concerned.

Sue's eyes widen, then scrunch up all mean and narrow. "Suit yourself."

She is not gentle as she slaps a blood pressure cuff around my arm, pokes the thermometer in my mouth, and whips the sheets back to press on my belly and check my pad. "Do you need anything for pain?" she asks, not bothering to pull the sheet back up.

"I'm fine. Thank you."

She spins on her heel.

"Oh, Nurse, this water pitcher is empty. And I think—" Gabe leans down, where a bag hangs off the bed—"yeah, the urine bag needs emptied."

She huffs out of the room and it takes everything we can to keep our laughing quiet so she doesn't hear us.

My baby's latch slackens, and I wipe drops of milk from the corner of his sweet mouth. I set him on one of the hospital blankets and crisscross the corners over his bony little arms and legs. They're shaking, I imagine from what must be the dizzying feeling of being free and undone outside my womb. He calms once he's wrapped snug and cradled snug in my arms.

A nursing assistant brings in some water and drains my urine bag. When she's finished, she comes and leans over me, peeking at my baby, sleeping sound. I'm expecting another chastising.

"He sure is something," she says. No chastising at all.

"Thank you, Hannah," I say after reading her name tag.

She smiles, then straightens my linens and collects the trash on her way out the door.

Gabe and I are left in the quiet again, the three of us. As

much as we laughed at Sue, her words still sting. I can't help but think of the reason why Sudie never let me name any of the rescue animals.

Releasing them is hard enough without getting too attached. . . .

37

"Good morning, sleepyheads," a cheery nurse says in the shade-drawn dim of my room.

I'm relieved to see the day shift has arrived, and that it's the nurse with the highlights in her hair who gave me the website of her friend.

"I'm Amanda. I don't know if you remember me from yesterday."

Amanda. "I remember."

Feels like neither of us want to bring up her friend or the website. The silence feels awkward as she goes about checking my stitches, my vital signs, then checking my baby.

"He's just perfect, isn't he?" she says, measuring his head, turning him over, and checking his back.

He winces and whines at the cold and the shock of being stretched out and touched, but soon settles again when she swaddles him up.

"I think so." I glance at Gabe, curled in the recliner beside me. He nods at me encouragingly. "I checked out your friend's website."

Amanda appears relieved that I've brought it up, but also hesitant. She waits for me to say more.

"Your friends . . . they're the ones. I know they're supposed to be the ones."

Her eyes fill with tears, and it's clear she's trying her best to hold back her emotions. "Do you want me to let Donna know?"

I nod. "But you need to know . . . the baby's father . . . he sent me papers. Paternal custody papers."

"Oh . . . wow . . ." She stops herself, and it looks like she has some of the same feelings I have about that. "Okay, I'll let Donna know that, too."

Maybe Donna *could* do something to help. At this point, I'm willing to try anything.

Amanda takes out my catheter and helps me to the bathroom for the first time. Most of the feeling is back, and my belly smarts. She offers me pain medicine, but I refuse anything more than a Tylenol.

"Might help you get around better if you take something stronger," she says as she watches me wince and hold a pillow tight to my belly to brace against the pain.

I shake my head. I'm tempted to tell her that's how Mama

got started. A little of the strong stuff to help with her back pain. Then a little more. Then a little more. Then the doctor wouldn't give her any more prescriptions. Then she got desperate. Then she found heroin. Then Jayden. Then this. I'll take whatever pain I have to over that.

She runs and gets me an ice pack, and soon the cold eases the sting of the incision. She hands me my baby and I marvel all over again at his eyelashes, his long, thin fingers splayed out in contentment, his little mouth, open just enough that I can smell his sweet, new breath.

"Anything else I can do for you?"

"I think we're good."

An aide walks in with my breakfast tray and sets it up for me. Sausage, a stack of pancakes bigger than my head, fresh fruit, and orange juice in a pretty glass. Fanciest meal I've ever had.

"Amanda?" I say as she starts out of the room.

"Yeah?"

"Please pray?"

She gives me a kind and knowing smile. "I've been praying since I met you yesterday."

~

I'm texting with Carla about what I should do when there's a knock on my door.

"There's a visitor here for you," an aide says. "An older gentleman. Says his name is Walter Crawford?"

My gut clenches and instinctively I pull my baby closer.

Gabe had to go to work at the station.

Carla's at the diner.

No one's here to help me.

Trust me.

I'm trying, Lord. I'm scared.

"The Lord will fight for you and this baby. You only need to be still," Sudie had said.

Lord, please let that be true. Mr. Crawford was kind at the cemetery. Whatever news he has . . .

Trust me.

I take in a deep breath. "Okay," I say to the aide. "You can send him in."

Walter Crawford holds his hat in one hand and a briefcase in the other. I look at his permanent pout, his stocky frame, and try to imagine him and Sudie having a thing together. I suppose he is kinda cute, in an Alfred Hitchcock-y way. At the very least, the thought helps calm my nerves enough to keep me from wanting to climb out of this bed and run out the doors.

"Ms. Givens."

"You can call me Jaycee."

Now he's the one taking a deep breath.

I brace myself for what I'm sure he's going to say. I imagine Elizabeth glaring at me, a smug look of victory on her face in a cold old courtroom. I imagine having to place my baby in Bryan's arms, his angry eyes. My arms ache as if they're still bruised.

"When we last spoke, I told you how there was a way to overturn the original custody papers."

I nod. He's going to tell me it's too late. It's over. *Don't cry. You can't cry.*

My baby squirms, turns his head. He'll be hungry soon.

Mr. Crawford's pout turns into a slight smile. He reaches into his briefcase and hands me a file. "Here."

I open it and scan the document, hardly believing my eyes.

VOLUNTARY RELINQUISHMENT OF PARENTAL RIGHTS

Comes now in person, <u>Bryan Blair</u>, born <u>August 12, 1995</u>, acknowledges that he/she is the legal or alleged father (or is charged as being the legal or alleged father) or mother of _____, born <u>June 14, 2018</u>, in River County, Riverton, Indiana. The said <u>Bryan Blair</u>, does hereby in writing expressly consent and agree to the termination of his/her parental rights concerning the above-said child.

I hereby transfer the custody of the said child to the <u>office of Walter Crawford, Attorney-at-Law in Riverton, Indiana,</u> in order for that agency to make an appropriate placement for the child in accordance with the law. I swear and/or affirm that my signature to this document has been freely given without coercion, duress, or the exercise of undue influence.

I read it again.

And again.

"Relinquishment?" I say to Walter.

"It's official. He's giving up his parental rights."

I scour the document, checking every signature line. Bryan has already signed his name on all of them.

I look at Walter, and he nods, face pink with unmistakable joy.

"What did you do?"

He holds his hand up. "I can assure you, I didn't do anything at all. Unless of course you count prayer. Mr. Blair came to my office late yesterday afternoon. I was packing up to leave. Almost missed him. He asked if I would draw up this document and deliver it to you. He asked us to make sure the other ones are destroyed. My secretary was there as a witness. He was completely lucid. And, I might add, *confident* of his decision."

My phone blinks with another text from Carla.

Carla. *That twinkle she had in her eye.*

Bryan signed the papers, I type, and hit Send. Did you have something to do with this?

Ellipses appear at the bottom of the screen.

When her text appears, it's three emojis: praying hands, a smiley face with a zipper for a mouth, and a smiley face that's winking.

I don't care what she said or did to convince Bryan. All that matters is that it's true. The Lord did fight for me. By sending me people like Carla and Amanda, Donna, and even

Mr. Crawford at just the right times. He fought for me, and most of all, for my baby.

"What do I need to do?" I say to Mr. Crawford.

He leans toward me and points to the blank lines below where Bryan has signed. "Sign in all those same places."

When I'm finished, I start to hand him the paper.

"There's one more thing."

I scan the document, looking for any spaces I missed. I don't see any.

"Right there," he points. "You have to give him *a name*."

38

River Samuel Givens.

My heart has known his name for weeks.

My hesitation about putting it on paper comes not from the fear of attachment—it's far too late to avoid that. No, it comes from the piece of me that still, after everything, thinks I don't deserve to give him a name.

"It's okay," Walter encourages. "You *are* his mother, after all."

I'm his mother.

I *am* his mother.

God knit River together inside of *me*.

He made something out of nothing, stringing cells together one at a time deep inside me to shape his sweet nose, to sculpt each finger and toe, to knit every fiber of his heart that beats and every part of his lungs that breathe. River is fearfully and wonderfully made, and there is no place he can go that will ever change this. I am the first page, the best page, of River's story in a book the Lord is only beginning to write for him. Reverend Payne said Moses' mother didn't give him up because she didn't love him. She gave him up because she *did* love him. She gave him up to protect him and to save his life. And he went on to save the Israelites. An entire people. An entire nation.

"Sometimes God shows his faithfulness not by what he brings to our life, but by what he takes out of it; not by what he gives us, but by the joy we receive from what we let go of and give to him," Reverend Payne said.

I pick up the pen and press it against the page, and I pray through every curve and turn of the letters . . .

River. *Thank you, Lord.* Samuel. *Save him, Lord.* Givens. *Bless him, Lord.*

Trust me.

Okay.

I don't know how a heart can be empty and full at the same time, but that's what mine feels like as I give the signed paper back to Walter. Empty because there's nothing left to stop what I know I have to do. Full because I know it is good and right and God is in it.

Walter leaves and I put on the call light.

Amanda comes to answer it.

"Tell Joe and Michelle. Tell them they have a son who is waiting here for them."

39

Donna Howard has been working with Walter to draw up the rest of the necessary adoption papers. The fact that I had a C-section means I can stay at the hospital during all of this, which allows me to stay with River. Although Joe and Michelle Moore are more than gracious in their willingness to communicate with me, we all decide together that we will only meet face-to-face one time, when I put River in their arms. Not before, and not after. For all our sakes. They're due to arrive midafternoon.

There's a knock on my door.

"Come in."

"Hey, you," Carla says from behind a large galvanized vase

full of meadow wildflowers. "Thought you might like having these around, this being the day and all."

"I still can't believe Bryan signed those papers."

"Mmm-hmm," she says, humming as she fiddles with and arranges the flowers.

"Will you ever tell me what happened?"

She looks at me from the corner of her eye. "Nope. But don't worry. I didn't do anything that caused the boy any harm."

Before I can get any more out of her, Dr. Fitzgerald bounds into the room.

"I came to see you one more time, brave little lady," he says.

"Thank you," I say as he stands beside my bed.

"It's been a pleasure."

"Thank you . . . for not acting like something was wrong with me. For not judging me."

He appears to think on that for a moment before saying simply, "You're welcome." He passes Gabe, who's carrying a cup of my favorite coffee, on the way out.

"How are you holding up?" Gabe sets the coffee on the table beside me.

"I didn't sleep all night long. I couldn't. I've just been staring at him, trying to memorize every part of him, everything he does, all the noises he makes. . . . Did you see he has a spot here on the crown of his head where his hair grows in a swirl?"

"I didn't." He kisses the top of River's head, then mine. "You do good work, Mama."

Someday, Gabe. Lord willing, someday maybe this could be you and me and a baby of our own. I don't dare say it out loud, but I have a pretty good hunch he's thinking the same thing.

The Reds are growing on Gabe, and he settles in to watch them play the Padres on TV while I nurse River for what will probably be the last time. I take pictures of him until my phone says it's full. I kiss his hands, each finger, each foot, his lips—shaped like a perfect rosebud—and the curve of his little round chin, even though I did the same thing a thousand times last night. I inhale the sweet scent of him, the fragrance of baby wash still lingering on him from his first bath. I giggle when he gets the hiccoughs and weep when I hold him against me and feel every rise and fall of his chest as I burp him.

"I love you, River Samuel. I will always, always love you. I'm your mama. Do you know that? *Your mama . . .*"

River and I both startle as the door clatters open.

Donna Howard walks in. "They're here."

Fresh tears fall and I lean my face against the feather-soft hair of River's head.

"Are you sure you don't want me to go with you?" Gabe asks, his own eyes watering up.

I shake my head and take a deep breath. "No. I'll be okay. I have to do this myself."

He comes to the bed and wraps his arms around both of us. He whispers in my ear. "I'll be *right here* when you get back."

"Thank you. For everything, Gabe. Thank you."

"Oh, wait—I almost forgot." He reaches in his pocket and pulls out his cell phone. "There's something you need to see."

When he hits Play on the screen, it's a videogram from Mama. "Congratulations, Jaycee. River is the most perfect name. What we talked about . . . if you decide to go through with it . . . I want you to know . . . love means laying down your own life, your own wants and needs, for someone else's. I didn't do that for you too well. . . ."

I can see her chin is quivering, despite the grainy video.

"But I know if you decide on adoption, you'll be doing it out of the deepest kind of love. The love of a mother for her child. The kind of love that trusts the Lord with her child. The kind of love I didn't know existed before I saw you, and that I nearly lost forever."

Donna, who's looking on, gives me a knowing smile. "Are you ready?"

"I am now."

40

"Can't I walk?" I say to the nurse who steers a wheelchair into the room.

"Hospital policy. I'm sorry."

Donna shrugs apologetically, and I hand River to Gabe as I settle myself into the chair. He hands River back to me and kisses us both again before I'm wheeled into the long hallway that leads to the room where the Moores are waiting for us.

"Everything's taken care of," Donna assures me. "There will be a couple of papers left to sign, but other than that, Walter's done a fine job wrapping up the paperwork. And you and the Moores have been the easiest families to work with."

The closer we get, the more I feel like I'm approaching some kind of a death. I'm far beyond butterflies. If I weren't already sitting, I'm not sure I'd even be able to stand.

"You okay?" Donna asks.

I'm sure I look pale. Or ill. Or both.

"I don't know."

She squeezes my shoulder. "They seem like wonderful people."

I'm sure they are. It's not that. It's the emptiness I already feel. The ache of my arms because soon he won't be in them anymore. The fullness of my breasts because I won't be nursing him again.

Help me, Lord. I don't think I can do this.

I'm right here. You can do all things with my help.

Not this, Lord. I can't do this.

We stop when we reach the door. Donna puts her hand on the handle and pauses. "You ready?"

How do I even answer that? No, I'm not ready. I'll never be ready. Whatever peace I had is dwindling. I know why Sudie was mad at God. I don't want to be an Abraham, either. *Test me some other way, Lord. Can't you test me some other way?*

Donna must sense my apprehension. She lets go of the handle and kneels next to me. Takes my hand. "You will always be his mother. He will always be your child. Nothing will ever change those things."

I nod, and the tears fall hot from my eyes.

"*The kind of love that trusts the Lord with her child,*" Mama said.

With the hand that's not clinging to River, I wipe my eyes, my face. I take a couple of deep breaths. "Okay."

41

Joe and Michelle Moore stand as Donna opens the door, and the only thing that helps is that they look every bit as terrified as I feel. I don't know what I expected . . . Confidence? Noisemakers? Streamers? We shake hands awkwardly as Donna introduces us. I can't help but notice they look just like their pictures on the website.

Of course they do.

Still, somehow this is a relief.

Without even knowing her, I can tell Michelle is trying to hold back her emotions, and I am relieved to see not pity, but mercy in her eyes. If I learned anything from Sudie, it's that someone who knows hurt well is kind to hurt in another.

And no doubt Michelle knows hurt from not being able to bear a child.

Joe is about as sure of himself as Gabe was the day we rescued the hawk on the highway. Scratches his head in just about the same place as Gabe does when he's nervous too.

The giggle that erupts out of my throat comes from I don't know where, and I am mortified, especially because I can't stop it.

Joe and Michelle look at each other, then back at me, and they start giggling too.

We're all sitting there giggling. Even Donna and the nurse get to giggling too. And River sleeps right through it in my arms.

"I'm so sorry," I croak. "I don't mean to laugh . . . it's just . . ." I look at Joe. "You remind me of a friend, is all, who does that same thing . . . with his hand and his hair . . ."

"We're sorry too," the Moores say in broken unison, wiping the tears from their eyes like me.

Donna sobers first. "Okay, you guys. I've never had that happen before." She fiddles with the file and some papers, setting them on the table with a couple of pens.

The giggling stops, but the tears don't. Michelle and I start talking at the same time.

"We meant what we said, in our letter—"

"I knew when I read your letter—"

We almost start giggling all over again. These nerves.

"You go ahead," she says, and Joe nods in agreement.

"Amanda told me about your website. When I read the

part in your letter about giving River a chance—that's when I knew. God picked you a long time ago to be the ones to raise him."

Michelle's chin trembles. "Thank you."

"Michelle's right. We meant everything in that letter," Joe says. "We didn't want . . . we don't want you to feel like . . . we're not taking your baby. We're just carrying on where you're leaving off."

With that, all three of us launch into all our likes and dislikes, our dreams, our hopes. They tell me all about their house and their town, their church and their extended families, and the North Carolina beach. I tell them how River likes to eat at least every two and a half hours, and that once he's decided he's hungry he cries like he's never had a meal. I tell them how he likes to be burped up high on someone's shoulder, how he looks handsome in blue, and about his uncle Jayden, who he never knew.

I stop there and lay him flat on my lap.

It's time.

No one has said anything, but I know.

River's eyes are wide-open, as if he knows he's about to go on a new adventure. I think my limbs are shaking as bad as his as I unwrap him from the blanket, one thing I've decided to keep to remember him.

"You do look handsome in blue, River." Carla brought me the onesie, pale blue with fine white stripes. "So very handsome."

I have to do this. *Help me, Lord.*

The plaque on Sudie's wall comes to mind. Hosea 14:3. "In you alone do the orphans find mercy." *In you alone do any of us find mercy, Lord. I know this now. Please have mercy on my son.*

I press my lips to River's head one last time, breathe him in, feel the rise and fall of his chest, the beating of his heart.

Help me, Lord.

All you have to do is reach, the voice says.

I think about the woman in the Bible who was bleeding, and all she could do was reach for the hem of Jesus' cloak.

And so I reach. As I lay River in Michelle's arms, I reach for Jesus. And somehow, I find him there and am able to let my baby go.

The Moores collapse themselves around him, and somehow I understand this is not to keep me out, but to welcome River in. After a few moments, they look up and thank me again. And again.

Donna shows us all where to sign the pieces of paperwork that have to be done in these last moments, and things begin to feel awkward again. All I want to do is leave the room. To get away.

The nurse seems to pick up on my panic. "I'll walk back with you, if you're ready."

I nod, unexpected blackness closing in on my field of vision.

"Would you rather ride?"

"No . . . I think I'll be okay." I turn toward the door and walk out of the room. The hallway looks even longer than it did when we came here. Impossibly long. My legs feel heavier. My arms ache more. My breasts ache more.

I need to feed him. He's hungry. He needs to eat.

We're halfway back to my room when I turn and run back to them.

"Wait!" I scream. "Please. Wait."

Terror fills the Moores' faces.

Donna Howard turns pale as a sheet. "Jaycee—"

I wave my hands. "It's not what you think. I'm not changing my mind."

I'm not.

"I just . . . I need you to do me a favor."

"What is it?" Joe says.

"Please . . . just . . . please don't tell him I couldn't afford him."

"Of course not," Michelle says.

"Or . . . that he was an accident."

"All right," Joe says.

Michelle steps toward me. "What would you like us to tell him, Jaycee?"

"Tell him . . . Tell him that I couldn't afford not to let you raise him. Tell him I watched and prayed and knew, and that when God formed him inside of me, he had you and Joe in mind too."

"I will," she says. She hesitates, as if carefully choosing her next words. "I will tell him all of that, and that while I taught him to read, you're the one who gave him sight. I'll tell him that while I taught him to ride a bike, you gave him lungs to breathe. I'll tell him that while I taught him to love, you are the one who loved him first."

ℰ

Within an hour, the nurse has discharged me, and Gabe and I are driving home on the same stretch of road that's taken me to the end and the beginning of myself. We pass the schools and the car dealer, the strip malls and liquor stores, the rickety homes with sagging front porches, the trailers and the farmhouses on stripes of newly mown grass, the corn and bean fields. Everything's changed, but it's all the same.

River is mine.

And he is theirs.

Both at once.

There is no explanation for this.

It just is.

Epilogue

SIX MONTHS LATER

The trees have all dropped their leaves, and the branches clack together when the wind blows through them as Gabe and I hike the trails at the state park.

I didn't need the final adoption hearing at the River County courthouse to remind me it's been six months since I placed River in Michelle Moore's arms. I see him. All the time. Everywhere.

Every face of every little boy on the playground, in the grocery, at church, and in cars and front yards. I wonder if he's trying foods yet, if he can sit tall enough to swing, if he's noticed flowers and birds, if he knows it's winter now and Christmas is coming, and spring will come again.

I wonder if he will have freckles in the summertime, if his eyes will stay blue or turn brown like mine, if he still has my dark hair or if it's lighter, like Bryan's. I wonder if he'll get scared at night, if Michelle knows the words to "Jesus Loves Me" and "You Are My Sunshine" and sings those when he's upset or falling asleep. I wonder what kinds of broken he'll have to face with them, because it's a guarantee he'll have some hurts in life. I just pray they're not even close to the broken I had.

Mostly, I just wonder if he'll ever, someday, wonder about me.

There are glimmers of hope around Riverton. The ash tree outside my trailer made it through the summer. In fact, a team of scientists came by and treated it with a new experimental insecticide for free. The governor started a needle exchange program, and new treatment centers are sprouting up across the county for heroin addicts. Shorty's doing a good job mowing and trimming at the cemetery, although he'll need help in the spring planting the right flowers. I see the Blairs at church, but we are all careful to avoid each other. Not everyone sees the good in breaking cycles of pain. But if there's anything I learned from Sudie and taking care of all kinds of creatures, there's room in God's Kingdom for all of us.

Mama's up for parole in the spring. She writes me letters, telling me in every one how much she loves the pictures I sent her of River, how perfect he is, and how sorry she is that she never got a chance to meet him. I've been trying my best to write her back, because I think I've figured out that no one sets out in life wanting to hurt people. We just get broken and cracked, like the roads and the seasons. Water gets in and freezes and thaws and buckles us, is all. Some folks more than others.

"Did I ever tell you about the monarch, Gabe?"

He takes my hand as we head down the path that leads to the highest waterfall. The winter woods hold a beauty that can't be appreciated in the summers, the thin layer of snow like a silver lining on the decaying foliage beneath it.

"I think you have," he says.

"I think I have too. But can I tell you again?"

"Sure." He grins, the early-winter sun catching on his dimples.

"The monarch offspring eat milkweed when they hatch, which turns to poison, which is what makes their wings bright orange."

"You don't say?" He pretends to be in awe.

"Well, I think it's fascinating anyway, that an innocent creature can feast on poison and survive. It's a miracle the monarchs get back here at all, don't you think?"

Gabe stops and grabs me around my waist. "I think you're a miracle."

"I think you're as big a sap as ever." I kiss him square on the lips and wiggle free.

We stop when we get to the top of the waterfall. Farther up the creek, the water that feeds these falls is the same that runs behind Shady Acres. The rapids leading up to the edge bubble and roil before flowing off and dumping into a larger creek that runs into the slow and meandering Ohio River. I don't know, nor do I try any longer to understand, the reason for pain. I only know loss is as much a part of life as gain. The river that moves and waters and baptizes is the same one that floods and dries up and takes.

I put my hand over the place on my belly where they stretched and pulled and lifted River from my womb. Sometimes I wake up at night and think I feel him there, a foot or a hand pressing against me. But then I remember.

To be sure, the Lord heals the brokenhearted, and he binds up wounds. But scars . . . well, they never go away.

"C'mon, Jaycee."

I take Gabe's hand and we start the hike downhill toward home.

A Note from the Author

The Bible contains 31,102 verses, 23,145 of which are in the Old Testament.

Three of those verses are about a woman named Jochebed.

Three brief verses describe how she had a beautiful baby boy, that she tried to hide him from men who wanted to take his life, and that she had to give him up so that he could live.

And live he did.

His name was Moses, and the glimpses we are given of his mother, Jochebed, appear in Exodus 2:1-3.

As with Tamar (2 Samuel 13), who inspired my novel *How Sweet the Sound*, I wanted to imagine what it would be like to be Jochebed in today's world, a birth mother faced with the heart-wrenching decision to entrust the life of her child not only to a new family, but to the Lord. I began to research birth mothers, and the more I learned, the more my heart broke for the silence and stigma surrounding their journeys. I pored over online support groups and stories, read books and memoirs, and realized that while every story is unique, the one thing that unites them is hope: hope that their child can have, as Jaycee says, a chance.

The other commonality I discovered uniting birth mothers is silence. Many birth mothers don't want to be found. Others feel ashamed. Of the countless birth mother scenarios I researched, so many expressed feeling alone and overlooked and unseen.

I hope this story gives readers a unique and intimate perspective into the heart of what a birth mother goes through. And most of all, I hope birth mothers who read this realize the Lord knows their story. He sees the unending love they have for their children. He can take what feels like a small and unnoticed part of their lives and turn it into something epic. And he sees them as heroes, because heroes are people who choose to protect someone else at their own expense, even when it means letting go (John 15:13).

At the same time my heart was burdened for birth mothers, the opiate crisis was reaching epidemic proportions in southern Indiana and across the rust belt, resulting in needle exchange programs and killing dozens at a time. As an RN, I have cared for newborn and premature babies—some who didn't make it—just like Jaycee's little brother, Jayden, withdrawing from heroin or methadone or both. I've cared for the young adults, too, filling our hospital wards and the obituary pages, their babies overwhelming the already-burdened foster system. This heartbreaking epidemic became an easy parallel to the life-threatening decree of Pharaoh that Jochebed faced. Indeed, the lives of young mothers and children are threatened in rapidly growing and devastating ways, and not just in small towns, either. The opioid epidemic knows no boundaries. At the heart of it are people—like Jaycee's mother—who are hurting and grasping at anything that eases their pain.

Finally, I can't write a novel without infusing it with my love for nature. For *Before I Saw You*, I read countless books on raptors and woodland plants and trees. I hiked in state parks and quarries all across my beloved state of Indiana, including those around my alma mater, DePauw University. While there (and thanks to Facebook), I reunited with the beloved woman who was—and still is—a cook at my sorority, Anita Akins. She helped me with hilarious stories and facts about her and her family's work over the years as cemetery caretakers in Greencastle, which became the basis for Sudie's life and work. (And she makes the best cinnamon rolls in the state!)

I especially enjoyed weaving the thread of wildlife rehabilitation into this story as a thread to parallel Jaycee's journey. During my research, I had the privilege of meeting with a local certified wildlife rehabilitator named Holly Carter in my hometown. I was immediately enamored of her work and the process involved in the rescue, rehabilitation, and release of injured animals, and she helped me immensely by checking my facts and the scenarios I imagined for the hawk and the turtle and other animals featured here.

Finally, the plight of the ash trees was something I knew I had to include, the emerald ash borer killing acre upon acre of the beautiful trees in recent years. This served as a perfect, albeit heartbreaking, parallel to the way the opiate epidemic has spread throughout the Midwest region and beyond. In all the great silences around us, whether grief or praise, I believe God reveals himself to us all across nature. As Jesus said in Luke 19:40, even the rocks cry out and testify, whether turtles and their homing instincts, the migration of monarchs, the lifelong monogamy of raptors, the delicate balance between bats and air temperature, or the emergence of life each spring.

More than anything, I hope through Jaycee and her friends that readers appreciate—as I came to more deeply while writing about them—how so many people fighting silent battles among us are overlooked and forgotten. But God doesn't forget anyone. He has a purpose for everyone. And not a sparrow falls without his knowledge.

Suggestions for further reading on birth mothers, the plight of American small towns, the opioid crisis, and wildlife:

Websites:
- The National Institute on Drug Abuse: https://www .drugabuse.gov/drugs-abuse/opioids/opioid-crisis
- National Wildlife Rehabilitators Association: http://www.nwrawildlife.org/
- Life Centers: https://lifecenters.com/

Books:

- *Delivered: My Harrowing Journey as a Birthmother*, by Michelle Thorne
- *Reader's Digest North American Wildlife*, by the editors of *Reader's Digest*
- *Winter World: The Ingenuity of Animal Survival*, by Bernd Heinrich
- *The Bluebird Effect: Uncommon Bonds with Common Birds*, by Julie Zickefoose
- *Shadow People: How Meth-driven Crime is Eating at the Heart of Rural America*, by Scott Thomas Anderson
- *Dreamland: The True Tale of America's Opiate Epidemic*, by Sam Quinones
- *Hillbilly Elegy: A Memoir of a Family and Culture in Crisis*, by J. D. Vance

Kay koule tronpe soley men li pa tronpe lapli.
"A leaking roof may fool sunny weather, but cannot fool the rain."

Chapter 1

ANNISTON

I thought I'd lived through everything by the time I was thirteen.

Hurricane Frederic nearly wiped the southern part of Alabama off the map that fall, and half of our family's pecan orchards along with it. Daddy said we were lucky—that the Miller pecan farm down the road lost everything. The Puss 'n' Boots Cat Food factory supplied our whole town of Bay Spring with ice and water for nearly a week until the power and phones came back on along the coast of Mobile Bay. Anyone who could hold a hammer or start up a chain saw spent weeks cutting up all the uprooted trees and azaleas, pounding down new shingles, and cleaning up all that God, in His infinite fury, blew through our land. Like most folks who lived along the coast, we'd find a way to build back up—if we weren't fooled into thinking the passing calm of the eye meant the storm was over.

If I'd only known this about Hurricane Frederic—that the drudging months leading up to Thanksgiving would be the only peace we'd see for some time. Weren't no weathermen or prophets with megaphones standing on top of the Piggly Wiggly Saturday mornings to shout warnings of storms and second comings to us.

The only warning was the twitch of my grandmother's eye.

"Happy Thanksgiving!" Mama, Daddy, and I said in unison.

Princella pulled the front door open to let us in, kissing us each coolly on the cheek as we passed. Her graying hair was twisted into a tight, smooth bun on top of her head, and a purple suede pantsuit hung on her too-thin frame.

"Thank you. Oralee, Ernestine will help y'all take that food on to the kitchen."

"How are you, Mother?" Daddy had grouched around the house all morning as we readied ourselves to go to the big house.

"Why, I'm fine. Thank you, Rey. Your father is in his den." Princella nodded toward the book-lined room to the left of the foyer.

I followed Daddy. Though I loved peeling potatoes and painting butter on yeast rolls as they came steaming out of the oven, I didn't feel like being around Princella, who preferred I call her by her proper name, saying she felt too young to be called *Grandma*. I couldn't figure her out. Then again, who could? Mama called her an enigma. I called her old and bitter.

The thick, wide shoulders of my granddaddy, Vaughn, filled every inch of the leather chair behind his desk. Wire-rimmed spectacles sat on the tip of his nose, and he rubbed his neatly trimmed mustache as he concentrated on the thick ledger open in front of him. As soon as he saw Daddy, he got up and threw his arms around him hard, patting him on the back. "Good to see you, Rey."

"You too, Daddy."

"And how's Miss Anniston today?"

"Fine, sir." The sun caught on the silver bevels of a sword sitting on Vaughn's big wood desk, sending shards of light dancing across the walls and ceiling.

"Wow, I haven't seen that in a long time." Daddy gently picked up the sword and let his fingers glide along the blade, down to the tip and back again. Carvings of horses and soldiers wrapped around the thick handle.

"My granddaddy gave me that sword. Belonged to his granddaddy, Gabriel Harlan, from before the war." Vaughn picked up the case, the name *Harlan* inscribed deep into the worn, cracked leather. "I intended to wait until later, but I might as well give it to you now."

Surprise spread across Daddy's face, ruddy from all the days working outside in the orchards, but softened by the kindness in his eyes, which were heavy with the love I saw when he read to me each night, even still, before bedtime. "I always thought this belonged to Cole next."

Vaughn stood up and peered out the window overlooking the orchards. "Granddaddy helped Gabriel plant most of these. Helped him plant the trees, babying them until they pulled in a crop. While they waited for the trees to yield enough to live off of, Gabriel oystered and fished and worked for lumber companies, making an honest living and providing for everyone—including the freed slaves—who lived on this land. One of only a few abolitionists back then, he paid his black workers a fair wage, sometimes choosing them over white workers who needed a job, and at the expense of ridicule and putting his family in danger. He retired from the Confederate Army before the war, so he never fought in it. Granddaddy told stories about how Gabriel wouldn't have fought in that war if he'd died refusing, because he hated slavery so." He turned to face Daddy. "He stood up for what was right and for the weak. Raised me to do the same. And that's how I believe I've raised you."

"Daddy—"

Vaughn held his hand up, and to my surprise, a tear rolled down the side of his face as he kept talking. "Been thinking a lot about this family lately, how I done you and your sister, Comfort, a disservice over the years by feeling sorry for Cole. Listening to your mother when she said I was too harsh with him, when harsh was what he needed. I felt sorry for him, I suppose, not having his real daddy around. I never listened to you or your sister, or anyone for that matter, who voiced concern about his choices and actions. And now I see those actions have taken a toll on all of you, and I'm sorry for that.

I brought him in and raised him as my own—and I would do it again—but you and Comfort . . . You're my flesh and blood."

He took the sword from Daddy's hands and slid it into the leather case. "When my daddy gave Gabriel's sword to me, he said it stood for peace, not war. That it should be given to the firstborn son, a son raised to believe in freedom. Someone who will fight injustice with courage and truth."

Quiet fell over the room, except for the ticktock of the grandfather clock in the hallway.

"Take it, Son. Will you?"

"What's going on in here?" Princella's unexpected voice struck us like a whip across our bare backs. "What are you doing, Vaughn? That's Cole's sword."

Vaughn walked right up close to Princella until he stood about an inch from her face. "Something I shoulda done a long time ago."

"Hey, everybody!"

My aunt, Comfort, and her longtime boyfriend, Solly, burst through the study door, giggling like a couple of kids my age. But their faces fell when they saw Princella and Vaughn standing there in obvious disagreement.

"I'm—I'm sorry. Were we interrupting?"

Princella turned sharp and stomped out of the room.

"Sorry, Solly. You're fine," Vaughn said. "Please come in."

"Welcome to the festivities," Daddy simpered.

"Comfort!" I ran and hugged her despite the tension I felt in the air.

"Hey, darlin'," Comfort said in a tempered voice, hugging me back. Despite my affection for T-shirts, boy shorts, and flip-flops, her outfit, as usual, was to die for. Beneath a striped, fringed poncho, she wore flared white trousers, a bright-orange halter top, and orange plastic platform shoes that matched. Her hair was done up in a high bun tied with a matching orange-and-white scarf that trailed down her back.

"What about me? Don't I get a hug from my girl?" Solly, a burly fellow with curly dark hair that fell over his ears and glasses, caught Daddy's eye as he yanked me into a bear hug. He looked handsome as ever, dressed in what appeared to be a brand-new pair of jeans, a plaid button-down Western shirt, a black cowboy hat, and black boots.

Thank goodness they came when they did. If Princella wanted to be in a snit, fine. But with Comfort and Solly there to brighten the mood, maybe she wouldn't ruin the whole of Thanksgiving Day.

Discussion Questions

1. Discuss the significance of Sudie's green soda bottles. Do you have any tangible traditions like this to honor people you have loved who are no longer with you? Would you like to start one?

2. Even though Jaycee's mother is unable to be a mothering presence in her life at the time of this story, Jaycee does have mother figures in Sudie and Carla. How are they able to minister to her in ways her own mother can't? Have there been people in your life who filled a parental role in addition to what your own parents were able to do? Have you been able to fill that role for children or young people you know?

3. Sudie mentors Jaycee in the skills of wildlife rehabilitation. Was there anything about this element of the story that you found especially interesting? In what ways is Sudie's care for wounded animals similar to God's care for wounded people?

4. Heroin use is epidemic in Riverton, as in much of America. What did that element add to the story? Has heroin—or other substance abuse—affected anyone you know?

5. Gabe tells Jaycee, "Everybody's complicated." Why is it helpful to remember this? Why do we tend to think our own challenges are more than others can understand?

6. Gabe proves to be a true friend to Jaycee, but she is cautious about letting him any closer at first. Do you think she is right to keep him at a safe distance for a while? What do you see happening in their relationship in the future?

7. Early in the book, Jaycee's pastor asks, "What is the Lord asking you to give up today?" What are the specific ways in which this impacts Jaycee's life as the story unfolds? Is there something—tangible or intangible—that the Lord is asking you to give up today? What's holding you back?

8. Did you see Bryan as a villain or as a victim of his own difficult circumstances—or some of each? How do you picture his future?

9. How does Jaycee's relationship with her baby brother, and the circumstances of his death, impact her decision about whether to keep her baby?

10. Jaycee hears and thinks about several Bible stories throughout the book, such as the infant Moses being

set afloat in the Nile (Exodus 2:1-10), Daniel in the lions' den (Daniel 6), and the woman at the well (John 4:1-42). How do these biblical examples help her with the struggles she faces? Can you think of a time when the Bible helped you in a practical way like this? What specific passages have been meaningful to you?

11. Were you surprised when Jaycee decided to give up the baby for adoption? What did you expect her to decide?

12. Has adoption touched your life or the life of someone you know? What are the challenges that face everyone involved in an adoption? What are some of the blessings that can come out of it?

About the Author

AMY K. SORRELLS is an award-winning author whose diverse writing has appeared in medical journals, newspapers, and an anthology (*Indy Writes Books*) benefiting literacy in central Indiana. A lifelong Hoosier and registered nurse, Amy makes her home on the outskirts of town with her husband and three sons. *Before I Saw You* is her fourth novel. Connect with Amy at www.amyksorrells.com.

Acknowledgments

Thank you to Karen Watson, Jan Stob, and Kathy Olson, for not giving up on this story when you had every reason to. To Don Pape, the best cheerleader a writer could ever have. To Sarah Freese—someone please give this woman an honorary counseling degree. And to Sharon Leavitt and my dear friends who have prayed for me and this book—you kept me writing when all I wanted to do was curl up and give up.

To Anita Akins for all the help with my research on being a cemetery caretaker (and for the hilarious stories). And to Holly Carter for all your time, amazing stories, and expertise on wildlife rehabilitation.

To Scott, Tucker, Charlie, and Isaac, for putting up with me throughout this process and in general—I could never find enough words to express how much I love you. And above all, to my Lord and Savior. Any good in this story is because he chose to do Ephesians 3:20 things with broken old me.

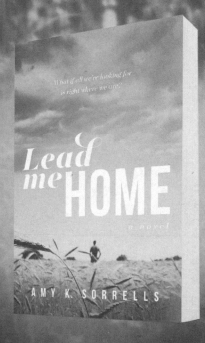

TYNDALE HOUSE PUBLISHERS IS CRAZY4FICTION!

Fiction that entertains and inspires

Get to know us! Become a member of the Crazy4Fiction community. Whether you read our blog, like us on Facebook, follow us on Twitter, or receive our e-newsletter, you're sure to get the latest news on the best in Christian fiction. You might even win something along the way!

JOIN IN THE FUN TODAY.

 www.crazy4fiction.com

 Crazy4Fiction

 @Crazy4Fiction